I0608111

Shuffle Ball Change

A Novel from Ken Coffman's Glen
Wilson Universe

Pat Edwards

Shuffle Ball Change

Other novels in the Glen Wilson Universe

Steel Waters
Alligator Alley (with Mark Bothum)
Twisted Shadow (with Mark Bothum)
Glen Wilson's Bad Medicine
Toxic Shock Syndrome
Immortality, LLC
The King of Alaska (with Mark Bothum)
Glen Wilson's Terminal Velocity
The Sandcastles of Irakkistan

Shuffle Ball Change ©2022 Pat Edwards, All Rights Reserved

Print ISBN 978-1-949267-94-5
ebook ISBN 978-1-949267-95-2

All rights reserved. No part of this book may be reproduced in any form or by any electronic or mechanical means, including information storage and retrieval systems—except in the case of brief quotations embodied in critical articles or reviews—without permission in writing from the author at pat.edwards.author@gmail.com. This is a work of fiction. Names, characters, businesses, events and incidents are the products of the author's imagination. With the exception of public figures, any resemblance to actual persons, living or dead is coincidental and not intended by the author. Certain long-standing institutions, agencies, and public offices are mentioned, but the characters involved are wholly imaginary. The opinions expressed are those of the characters and should not be confused with the author's.

Cover design by Guy D. Corp
www.grafixCORP.com

STAIRWAY≡PRESS

STAIRWAY PRESS—APACHE JUNCTION

www.stairwaypress.com
1000 West Apache Trail, Suite 126
Apache Junction, AZ 85120 USA

Author Alert/Content Warning:

This book contains subject matter that may be challenging to some readers. These topics include, but are not limited to, the following: suicidal ideation, violence, coarse language, cancer, AIDS/HIV, rape, death, war, the N-word, discussions of racism and the Black experience in the United States.

Dedication

To Pamela Von Ulrich, who once told me that so many others wasted so many pencils on so little talent, but felt I was "worthy of the wood." She thus set my feet on a previously unconsidered path and started this whole mess. She always lived life her way.

Just like Roxy.

CHAPTER 1

Steve's Date with Death: T-Minus 57:04:11 and Counting

IN THREE DAYS, Steve Stephens would be dead. Not because some doctor told him so or because he could foretell what the future had in store for him. He wasn't a damned psychic.

Steve was going to die because he planned to.

Sunset tonight. Sunset tomorrow. The sunset after that would be his last.

Thank God. Not that God would have anything to do with it.

It wasn't the first time Steve had anticipated his death. He'd planned to kill himself the minute he retired from the DEA, over a decade ago, but Natalie had needed him to straighten out a clusterfuck that had pulled him halfway around the world to knock some sense into that numbskull son of hers.

So he'd postponed his death and kicked around a while longer. Now his nephew was happily married to two pretty Middle Eastern women and had three kids with another on the way.

And Natalie, Steve's only sister, was dead.

Damned ovarian cancer. Natalie hadn't deserved to die that way, but at least she'd been surrounded by extended family in that weird compound in Sorrento, Italy. Her death could have been even uglier, but his nephew, Curtis, and the sketchy crew of mercenaries who shared the compound with him had access to any drug in the world, legal or illegal. They'd given the best of them to Natalie.

Steve had been there for her last few weeks. He'd tried to get her to come back to the States, to go to a better hospital, but she'd already been through all that. The treatments. The surgeries. Pills. Poisons.

He hadn't known.

She hadn't wanted to worry him. And then she was done fighting the inevitable.

So she'd ended her days higher than Keith Richards on a Saturday night thanks to the drugs from Curtis and his friends, laughing and sleeping and playing with her chubby-cheeked grandchildren. Natalie's had been as good a death as could be managed.

Curtis had scattered his mother's ashes in the blue Mediterranean waters.

Steve planned to die alone, in his ugly-but-decent house in one of the cheaper neighborhoods in West Palm Beach. He didn't give a flying fuck what happened to him after that.

Curtis would get a letter in a few weeks, provided Steve's attorney could locate him. If he still had an actual address or a SAT phone with him. Curtis's off-the-books, the-government-will-deny-all-knowledge-of-your-activities work meant he could be anywhere.

Hell, he could be dead.

Just like Steve planned to be.

Three days from now would be the second anniversary of Natalie's death. Steve figured that this way, Curtis would have only one day a year to remember and grieve both his mother and his uncle.

If he even cared.

If he was even still alive.

"It'll be a good day to die."

Saturday evening. It had rained that day two years ago, and he'd have liked to see rain one more time, but the weather bimbo on TV was cheerily predicting more goddamned sunshine.

Fuck her.

He'd spend the day remembering Nat and Mama and all those who'd gone before him, and then he'd join them.

Maybe. God hadn't been on his side much lately. Probably never. God could be such a dick.

And Natalie would be pissed at him. "You got to keep fightin', Steve," she'd have told him. And then she'd have rattled off a Bible verse about only God knowing the length of his days.

Fuck that.

Natalie had fought and it hadn't mattered. And Steve was sick and goddamned tired of people telling him what to do. Eighty years of taking orders was enough for any man.

His parents. The army. Police chiefs more interested in politics than policing, agency bosses more interested in brass-burnishing busts than saving a kid's life. And every rednecked mouth-breathing asshole who thought his white skin just naturally made him superior to Steve.

Fuck all of them. Steve—not God—was going to decide the date of his death. And it was going to be this Saturday. His way. His time. His choice. Not God's, not some fresh-out-of-officer-school butter-bar lieutenant's, not some ladder-climbing bureaucrat's. *His* choice.

Steve wasn't sure he believed in heaven. Mama had done her best to get them to church on Sundays, but God hadn't done any favors for Mama. Or for Natalie. Same disease claimed them both. Nat's life had been better than Mama's, and his own hadn't completely sucked, but the years were piling up on him, stealing the breath from his lungs, crushing his body and his spirit. The pill bottles and potions had overrun the skimpy medicine cabinet and now occupied an entire drawer in his bedroom dresser that used to house the black socks and neckties that had been part of his daily wardrobe for most of his life.

"Hope they find my body before it rots too much. Between the June heat in Florida and the cockroaches, I ain't gonna be a pretty corpse."

Maybe he'd get lucky and an early hurricane would spin up in the Atlantic and sweep his bland-as-oatmeal house and rotting corpse out to sea.

There was nobody to hear Steve's ramblings. "You're losin' it, old man, talking to yourself. The men in white coats will come to haul your ass away and fuck up all your plans." His voice was dry and rusty from disuse. Sometimes he talked to himself just to make sure his voice still worked. He'd lived in the neighborhood just over a year, but he'd never been the kind to let anyone get too close. He'd worked in this area years ago, but when he'd moved back last year, finally gotten fed up to his eyeballs with the slimy politicians, swampy summers, and sloppy winters of DC, he'd had no inclination to look up old buddies or get to know the folks who shared his street. The open sliding doors leading to his tiny lanai admitted the heat and pesky geckos but had never welcomed any friends. Even Curtis, who'd paid for the house, had only ever visited for a few days to help Steve move in, then had disappeared back to whatever nefarious shit he was into.

Steve hated the heat. It reminded him too much of his hardscrabble upbringing in Mississippi. Of stinking, sweaty southeast Asian jungles. But mornings weren't too bad. He'd be forced to close the doors and run the air conditioner once the relentless heat of the day kicked in.

For now, he needed to blow the stink out of the house. Empty beer bottles piled in the sink overflowed onto the cheap Formica counter, and the chitlins he'd fried up for last night's supper had left a clinging oily stink that oozed into the suffocating miasma that Florida called summer.

Chitlins were usually a holiday food, meant to be shared with friends and loved ones. Though you could buy them already pre-washed these days, he'd found it soothing to stand at the sink, washing and rewashing them, just as his mother had taught him, remembering the sound of aunties in the kitchen gossiping and chattering while he'd longed to join his cousins in the yard, his daddy and his uncles sneaking brown liquor into their cups of Christmas punch. But all his loved ones were gone now or living on the other side of the world. There was no one left to celebrate anything with anymore.

So Steve had declared this his own personal holiday. His getting-ready-to-off-himself day. A couple of days of indulging himself leading to the grand finale. He wished he'd learned to make Auntie Althea's potato salad, but some recipes were tightly held secrets, and she'd taken the secret to the grave with her. But he did know how to make a mean mac and cheese. Maybe he'd celebrate the almost-end-of-his-misery with a big pan of it tonight.

"What in the hell is that now?" he asked when the house shook.

Helicopters flew in low and fast, the thump of the rotors echoing against the stucco walls. The realtor had called the walls ocher; Steve wasn't sure that was even a real color. It wasn't a bad house. A tidy, not-bad bungalow in a tidy, not-bad neighborhood. Except for the semi-regular helicopter flights. And the jets coming in low to land at the Miami airport, or the private ones flying in to West Palm.

Steve turned the TV volume up on the rerun of *Dragnet* he'd recorded early that morning. His days as a cop had ended a lifetime ago, but he'd never gotten over the deep-seated need to see justice done, even if the one-hour Hollywood fakes were pure fantasy and had nothing to do with the blood and stink and unfairness of real life. Now he took immense pleasure in hate-watching old cop shows and tearing apart all the shit they got wrong, while he enjoyed his midmorning snack. Today's snack was pork rinds. His doctor would read him the riot act.

His doctor could go fuck himself too.

Whomp. Whomp. Whomp. The helicopters were probably rushing to the hospital after some stupid accident on 95. Maybe drug dealers running from cops. Maybe they were searching for a hapless boater who'd gotten in trouble out on the Atlantic. They didn't sound like the military from Homestead doing maneuvers, but they were definitely flying a pattern, back and forth. He cocked his head, listening. That was their third pass. Damn. Couldn't a man watch TV and plan his suicide in peace anymore?

Steve had seen a lot of other shit that chilled his blood since his days in combat, but even more than fifty years after Vietnam, the pulsating whir of chopper rotors still made his nerves pop and crackle like bacon in a frying pan. He'd been young then. Twenty years old, fit, strong, and gung-ho army. Helicopters could bring welcome gifts for a soldier—covering fire, rescue, maybe Lola Falana or Joey Heatherton or Sammy Davis Jr. on a USO tour.

Or they could rain down death from the sky. Stinking napalm or the rat-a-tat-tat of machine gun fire aimed at the enemy but which could just as easily hit a US Army soldier hiding in the tall grass and trees.

Steve levered himself up from his recliner, stretched his aching back, and moved to close the doors. It wasn't easy getting two hundred and fifty pounds into motion these days, even if most of it was still muscle. But his bones and brain and heart betrayed him more every day, tired of all the weight he carried. He wore slippers, but he didn't shuffle across the tiled floor. "Keep your head up and walk like a man," his daddy had barked at him from the time he was little up. Where Daddy left off, his drill sergeant had taken over. Getting into motion might take a minute these days, but once Steve got going, his gait still had the military stride he'd perfected over twenty years of army service.

Service. That's what they called it. Same when he was in the highway patrol. "Thank you for your service." Maybe all those oh-so-earnest folks meant well when they said it, a half-assed apology for shitting on him when he got back from Vietnam. For denying him rights because of his skin color. For putting his ass on the line for them so they could stay safe in college and in their nice little suburbs while men like him got slaughtered in godforsaken hellholes halfway around the world.

They could take their mealymouthed little thank-yous and

shove 'em.

Florida in June could give a Vietnamese jungle a run for its money when it came to sweltering humidity. The difference between then and now, aside from the fact that his army-hard body was now eighty years old and rotting from the inside out, was that now he could flip on the air conditioner and pull a cold Miller Lite out of his fridge. Which sounded good since he was up anyway. And as long as he was up, he might as well go take a leak. His big body was failing in a million aggravating ways, but at least he wasn't in diapers. Yet. Every odd new twinge flashed a warning signal that that day might not be far off.

Before Steve could get the door closed, other sounds replaced the racket of the fading helicopters. Sounds that managed to irritate him even more. One of the damned neighbors had wind chimes. They weren't the tinkly little annoying ones, but their deep, sonorous bonging still made him want to sneak over and cut the strings. The musical tones were low and, to his ears, mournful. Like church bells.

Church bells at a funeral. Natalie's funeral.

Grief and anger roiled in a toxic mix in his gut.

He could deal with the helicopters. The wind chimes were more than a man should have to tolerate.

His KA-BAR was in his nightstand drawer, within easy reach if he needed it. The knife was a hand-me-down U.S. Air Force #1262 knife, a semi-valuable collector's piece Steve had carried in military battle. The KA-BAR's compacted-disk leather handle was stained and dark, its powder-coated blade faded by years of redundant sharpening.

Yeah. He'd slice and dice those damned chimes like the throat of a—

He clenched his fist, then unclenched it and rolled his shoulders. If he didn't watch it, he'd give himself a heart attack before he could kill himself.

Another, closer sound intruded before he could slam the lanai door—laughter and shouting and cheers from the country club across the street. What did those morons have to be so

7

happy about? Couldn't they see how fucking hot it was? How shitty the world was? People all over the world starving and killing each other and dying of a stupid fucking disease that could have been cured long ago if only there wasn't so fucking much money to be made on chemicals and false hope?

Damn it, Nat. Why'd you have to die? How could you go off and leave me all alone, with no one but that idiot son of yours to even care if I ever lived at all?

That damned laughter sounded again, one voice rising above the others. Like the stupid wind chimes, it was rolling and melodic and made him want to throat-punch the owner.

He could march over there right now and do something about it. Curtis had insisted on giving him a membership to the club as well. He wouldn't even need his KA-BAR.

"You can't just sit in the house and wait to die, old man," Curtis had said. Steve loved his nephew like a son, but the boy had never learned to be respectful of his elders. Or much else, really. "Mom would have been over there every day, toasting her skin next to that pool or having lunch or drinks with the ladies. She'd be making friends. She'd want you to do that. To not be a lonely old grouch sitting around waiting to die."

"You think all those nice white ladies would have let your mama sit and have drinks with them?" Steve still remembered the bitter taste in his mouth as he'd said it. The nice progressive folks might think they'd made a dent on past grievances with their integration and civil rights, but in the South, at least, their smiles and politeness were only a veneer spread damned thin over a bred-in-the-bones bigotry.

"Times have changed," Curtis said. "It's not a fancy country club, just a little neighborhood one. Not even a golf course. But they have a pool and a couple of restaurants, a gym—" Curtis had stopped and given him a grin. "Not that anybody wants to see that big black ass of yours in gym shorts. But that club over there looks like the United Nations. I know you're too old to be pleasing the ladies anymore, but you could swap war stories with the other old vets. Maybe take a knitting class." Curtis had dodged Steve's swat and walked away laughing.

Not that many years ago, a country club like that wouldn't even hire Black waiters. Now they let folks like him sign up and play on their tennis courts and shuffle ball courts and pickle ball courts. What the fuck was pickle ball? All Steve knew was that the pickle ball courts were straight across the street from his house, and the chain-linked fence and thin line of palm trees did nothing to deaden the god-awful *PLONK thwack PLONK thwack* that often went on late into the evening.

There was that laughter and cheering again. Steve gritted his teeth. He should be feeling as chipper as the idiot mockingbird that sang daily from the scraggly palm tree in his yard since three days from now none of this would be his problem ever again. But his nerves had been jangling and jumping all morning.

Maybe the knot in his gut was just all the fried chitlins he'd wolfed down last night.

The sound of people laughing and having fun grated on him more than the helicopters. More than the wind chimes. More than the moronic mockingbird.

He moved away from the lanai doors and peered through the curtains at his front window, but the pickle ball courts were empty. Who'd want to go out and work up a sweat in air that made breathing feel like inhaling through a wet towel in a Turkish steam bath?

But there *was* color and movement under the shade of the thicker trees off to the right. The shuffle ball courts. Not that he knew what shuffle ball was either. Curtis had insisted on taking him on a tour of the place, so he knew the general layout. And Curtis had been right about that whole United Nations look. Middle-class Jewish folks who'd moved south, middle-class Caribbean islanders and Latin Americans who'd moved north, a few Middle Easterners who'd moved west, and African Americans in every shade from light fawn to his own black-as-midnight-at-the-bottom-of-a-coal-mine skin.

Mixed in were all the nice white folks from God knows

where. A lot of the pale pink or sandy-white women ended up heedlessly lying poolside in the blazing sun, toasting themselves like marshmallows in hopes of turning their pale skin the same color as the naturally brown-skinned folks they'd have snubbed back in their Midwestern hometowns while their husbands did the same out on the fishing boats, coming home lobster-red or russet or looking as much like old tanned leather as their wives did.

Every other Saturday was all-you-could-eat barbecue night at the club, with proceeds going to various local charities. They had probably shit their pants the first time his six-foot, 250-pound body strolled through the door, imagining all their profits disappearing into his gullet, but he'd restrained himself in spite of how damned tender the ribs had been.

Didn't matter that he was eighty years old—he'd stayed alert to all the little glances and maneuvers other club members had made. *Microaggressions* they called them now, the seemingly innocuous paper cuts that added up to soul-deep, seeping wounds that a man like him had endured for a lifetime. One or two of the women might have inched their purses a bit closer. One or two of the men might have looked him over, deciding if they could take him down if he suddenly went berserk. Still, while he hadn't made friends exactly, he'd gained a nodding acquaintance with a few of the folks.

But he'd declined invitations to poker games and karaoke nights, Taco Tuesdays, horseshoes, bingo, and all of the classes they had on offer. The pool, the gym, and the tiny spa held no allure for him. He was too old to be making new friends. He'd lost too many old ones already.

He'd always worked in places where people—good people—died. Where death was just a part of the job. Where the next person he encountered could need his help or want him dead and it was damned hard to tell the difference. The soldier with the gun pointed at him for political reasons neither of them understood. The strung-out meth head who'd slaughtered his girlfriend and was determined Steve would be next. The Russian in the alley who'd dared him to shoot first.

He'd always worked to clean up the world's shit. A lot of times, the shit won. He'd never had a death wish when he was working. But now?

Life was too damned dull and too damned painful to continue on. Time to get the hell out.

Still...there was something about that laughter. It got under his skin. Steve shut off the TV and washed up the dishes, leaving the door cocked open to admit the noise.

One woman's voice rose above the others. "You go, Graciela! Give 'em hell! Smack that sucker right off the court!"

What was it about that voice? Steve couldn't tell if the itch it raised under his skin was annoyance or attraction. The not-knowing was definitely an annoyance, and what use was any attraction when he had only three days to live?

He let his imagination wander while he rinsed out empty beer cans and scrubbed his greasy dishes in warm soapy water. His body might be old, but his brain worked just fine. Mostly. He could still remember the rush and exquisite intimacy of losing himself in the tender flesh of a woman. The heat. The soft moans and loud cries, the lush curves and hollows, the sweat and sweetness and slide of his body against someone else's.

How long had it been since he'd touched another human being? Since anyone other than a cold, impersonal doctor touched his?

It might be nice to add one more event to his self-planned going-away party. He had pills. He had booze. He had a good cigar. Maybe one last fuck before he went home to be with Mama and Natalie?

Although considering the life he'd lived, he was probably headed the other direction.

Steve wasn't sure he believed in hell any more than he believed in heaven. Then again, he'd been to Vietnam. He'd killed people. Shit, he'd grown up a Black boy in Mississippi in the forties. How could any hell devised by a pissed-off God be worse than some of the places he'd already been?

He dried his hands and neatly hung up the dish towel. What business did an eighty-year-old man have for wanting quick piece of ass?

Steve glanced down at his clothes. He hadn't yet gotten to the point of living in a bathrobe all day, and he'd had a shower just that morning. His khakis and polo shirt should be fine for going out, and beer from the tap in the country club's bar might taste better than one in a can from the fridge. All he needed to do was change his shoes.

He could use the exercise.

His doctor would fall over in a dead faint if he heard Steve say that.

He'd investigate the source of the racket. Give them a piece of his mind, not that he had much mind left to give. And check out the woman with the loud voice. Probably one of those lily-white women who'd tanned her skin into leather. A loud New York transplant with a bleached-blond perm, garish red lips, and rhinestone cat-eye sunglasses. And a muumuu. On second thought, he'd always had a soft spot—or rather a hard one—for cherry-red lipstick.

The only thing Steve was right about was the sunglasses.

CHAPTER 2

Sexy Firefighters Calendar Word of the Day:
Foofaraw: [foo-fuh-raw] **Noun**. a great fuss or disturbance about something very insignificant.

"DO IT AGAIN, Graciela! You've got him on the run!"

Roxy Fields danced a jig as she cheered on her friend in the Flamingo Palms Country Club's over-sixty ladies' shuffleboard tournament. She yanked off her straw hat and waved it like a cowboy urging on a stampede.

"Graciela, you got this! One more round! Win or lose, I've got a pink mai tai waiting for you!" Roxy jammed her flamingo-pink hat back on her head and shoved her rhinestone sunglasses back up her slippery nose. Even without playing the game herself, Roxy's enthusiastic support for her friend had worked up a sweat. She could use one of those drinks herself about now.

"Pink mai tai? That some sort of girly tropical drink?"

Roxy twirled to face the owner of the sexy bass voice. "Not the way I make them," she said. She winked at him and added in a conspiratorial whisper, "I double up on the dark rum. Sometimes the light rum too."

Not a lot of tall, decent-looking men on the plus side of seventy wandering free in the world; the man in front of her had a couple of inches on her and looked to be in her own age range. Roxy had given up any hope of being a delicate retiring violet in the sixth grade, when she'd shot up to five feet ten and a half inches and towered over every kid in her class as well as the

13

teacher. The vast majority of that height ran from hip bone to heels. A lot of men had eventually caught up to Roxy's height, but height wasn't everything.

She glanced at his hand and happily noted no ring. Not even the ghost of one on his thick fingers.

Not that she was looking for a relationship. No way. But her friendly nature could be misinterpreted by a possessive woman. She was too old to get caught up in some "*Housewives of West Palm Beach*" melodrama.

The man cocked a grizzled eyebrow at her. Then stuck out his hand. "Robert Stephens. But if folks know what's good for them, they call me—"

"Please don't tell me your middle name is Louis."

"What?"

"Robert Louis Stevens. You know, *Treasure Island? Dr. Jekyll and Mr. Hyde?*"

"That was Stevenson, not Stephens."

He wiped a meaty hand over his face and glared at her. Kind of like those army drill sergeants in the movies. The kind of glare that was supposed to have green recruits shaking in their not-polished-to-his-standards boots.

Roxy had never been in the army and was impervious to pretty much any kind of glare.

"You're gonna be a handful, aren't you?" he said.

"Always have been, always will be. Of course, it all depends on whose hands…" She returned his glare with a cheeky grin. "So, Bob—"

"Steve. Like I started to say, everyone calls me Steve. Last guy who called me Bob is still eating his food through a straw and will be for life. One before that is on a missing-persons poster in post offices."

Oh no, a smartass with a smart mind. Her favorite kind of man. And tall ones. And ones with a sense of humor. And how could she resist her propensity for poking at puffed-up egos? Her brain frantically clanged bells and set off warning flares. *Alarm! Alarm! Intruder! Run for your life!* The rest of her body thrummed with an entirely different response.

Yeah. This guy might be her Waterloo.

"Roxy," she said, taking his hand. "Roxy Fields. That's Roxy, not Rocky," she added, just as he opened his mouth. His raised eyebrows told her she'd read his mind right. Or maybe not. She thought he'd been about to make a joke, but his glower didn't look like one of those jovial mocking ones. More like he was actually mad.

How could anyone be mad on a day like today? The sun was shining, and the weather girl had promised a day without the usual summer rains. She was vertical and on the right side of the grass. Mockingbirds and painted buntings flitted in and out of the trees, and a threadbare breeze was enough to carry the Zen-like sound of her beautiful wind chimes as far as the courts where she'd gathered with her best friends. What an utterly glorious day.

Was this mountain of a man going to try to ruin that for her? He didn't know what he was up against. Her red hair might not be natural, but the color most definitely suited her temperament. Roxy never let grumpy people ruin her day.

Wrinkles radiated out from Steve's eyes under the blue thick-rimmed glasses he wore, but the grooves around his generous mouth told her the lines had come more from stress than laughter. His big hand engulfed her smaller one, but she returned his handshake with equal strength.

At the sound of a *whoosh* followed by a *crack*, Roxy extricated herself from Steve's hand and turned back to the court. "Graciela, you did it!" The woman who'd made the winning shot was instantly engulfed by cheering teammates.

Steve nodded toward the court. "So, your friend won? Exactly how does somebody win this shuffle ball thing?"

"Shuffle*board* not shuffle ball." Roxy pointed to the court. "That's shuffleboard. Basically, you use a stick to push a disk down the court and try to get points, especially if you can knock your opponent's disk out of play without fu—um, messing up your own score."

She pointed to her pink-sequined sneakers. "*This* is a shuffle ball." She executed a quick dance step. "Well, technically a shuffle ball change, and it's not as impressive in sneakers as in tap shoes, but you get the point." To emphasis that point, she repeated the step—soft-shoe version—a couple more times. Then she strode over to the now empty court and repeated the steps. "Now I'm doing a shuffle *ball* change on the shuffle*board*!"

She danced her way back over to Steve. "Think you'll remember now?"

Steve's eyes had widened the smallest fraction, but his mouth was still pinched at the corners. "So," Steve said, "you're some kind of hoofer? Is that the right word?"

"Yeah, and I'm glad you were real careful to say *hoofer* and not *hooker*. Last man who made that mistake is still eating his food through a straw and will be for life. One before that—"

Steve's laugh was more of a snort. It sounded rusty, and judging from the surprise in his eyes, the sound had startled him as much as it had her. She liked the sound of it. She was smiling up at him when Graciela made her way over to them.

"So, where's that mai tai you promised me, chica? And who's your new friend?"

Roxy performed a quick introduction, noting the courteous way Steve bent over to shake her much shorter friend's hand.

Steve stepped back. "I'll just leave you two now—"

"Nonsense, Steve. Come join us in the clubhouse. Have you been there before?"

"Only on rib night."

"Ah," Graciela said. "That would explain why Roxy's never seen you here before. She never comes to rib night."

He turned to her. "You some kind of vegetarian or something? One of those organic-only, new-age, scented candles and potpourri ladies?"

"Not a vegetarian," Roxy said. "Yes to organic food, when it's available, no to scented candles, because my house makes its own good smells, and potpourri is just dead flowers and I won't have them in my house. Bad feng shui. I do eat meat, though not in vast quantities."

"Good to know in case I ever want to invite you over for a steak." Steve's quick blink matched Roxy's own, as if he hadn't expected those words to come out of his mouth.

Roxy hadn't expected them either. She'd long ago grown accustomed to men hitting on her. Despite being seventy, dancing kept her in the kind of shape men seemed to like. Was he suggesting a date? She'd been vaguely aware, of course, of Steve as the reclusive stranger down the street, but to her knowledge, he'd never shown an iota of interest in anyone or anything in the neighborhood before.

Before Roxy could respond, Graciela grabbed the conversational ball and ran in a different direction. "Rib night usually coincides with the night Roxy is a volunteer cuddler."

Steve's eyebrows shot up. "You volunteer to cuddle people? Most women get paid for that. Although, I suppose, given your age—"

Graciela swatted his arm before Roxy had the chance to. "You're a nasty man, Mr. Stephens. Roxy volunteers at the hospital. She rocks babies in the NICU—the intensive care unit for very sick babies—when their families can't be there."

Steve suddenly swayed. Catching himself, he blinked again, slowly this time, as if trying to focus. Graciela hadn't swatted him that hard. What was wrong with the man?

Beads of sweat gathered on his forehead, at least the part Roxy could see under the brim of his straw panama hat, then dripped through his brows and down his face. She didn't think the extreme reaction was solely from the sweltering heat.

"Uh, Steve? You okay?" Roxy pressed her hand against his arm. "You look a little overheated there, buddy." She yanked off her hat and fanned it at him to stir up a little breeze.

He stared at her, focused for a minute, then swatted at the hat. "Get that damned thing outta my—my—" He wobbled again. Took off his glasses and mopped at his eyes before propping his glasses back on his broad nose.

Any sane woman would have stepped back in fear the giant

17

man would fall on her.

Not a soul in the world had ever accused Roxy Fields of being anything close to sane. Not even in the same ballpark as sane.

She glanced at Graciela. The woman's expression matched her own—concern but not real fear. Heat got to everybody sooner or later in this climate, even if you were used to it and had lived with it for years. But people her age and Steve's age—they needed to be careful.

"How did you get here, Steve?" Roxy asked. "Anybody with you? If I help, can you make it to the clubhouse?" She needed to get him out of the sun, into some AC, and get cold water into him. And on him. A nice cold washcloth at the base of his neck. A cool shower. They had those in the gym locker room.

She didn't think they needed a squad. Not yet.

Steve shook his head, but his eyes didn't look so good. For the first time, Roxy noted the pale yellow tint to the whites of his eyes. No, that wasn't good at all. Heat exhaustion maybe. If it was heatstroke, he wouldn't be sweating. But if she didn't get him into the shade and cooled off soon...maybe that ambulance wasn't such a bad idea. She reached for the phone in her pocket, but Graciela had beaten her to it and was speaking in rapid-fire Spanglish on her own phone.

Several of Graciela's teammates had joined them. Their chattering died down. A ripple of curiosity and unease emanated from them.

Steve raised his arm and pointed. "Over there," he said, his voice gone raspy. "The baby-shit-brown house just across the street." He shook his head, like a man hearing bells or trying to clear his vision, and almost lost his footing.

Roxy caught him. Thank God for her daily exercise routines and a lifetime of strength training. Steve might be an old man, but there was nothing small or frail about his big, muscled body.

"My meds—"

Graciela had called for help, but Roxy could get him to his house before they got there. It was closer than the clubhouse and closer to whatever pills he was missing. If he didn't recover fast, she'd call 911 from there.

She spotted the house easily through the tall chain link fence and the palm trees, four doors down from her own. A three-minute walk, maybe four or five. But could Steve make it that far under his own steam?

"Graciela, about that drink…"

"Go," she said. "I know there's no stopping that big heart of yours when you've found something helpless to mother."

"I'm not helpless." Steve's words had a slurred edge.

Two of Graciela's teammates stepped forward. "Let us help—"

Roxy and Steve simultaneously waved them off. Roxy had known men like Steve all her life. Big men. Proud men. This guy might be older than water, but his neatly pressed khakis, the almost military creases, and the tucked-in polo shirt broadcast that this was a man who took pride in appearances. A man who wouldn't want to be seen as weak.

"I'm going to walk him home and get him settled in with a nice cold glass of tea or ice water. This heat can get to anybody."

"No need," Graciela said. "Iggy's on the way with a golf cart."

So she hadn't called an ambulance, she'd called her son. Graciela had barely finished her words when Iggy whipped around the corner and slammed the brakes on one of the carts used by the employees. Iggy's usual job was gatekeeper, but when Mamma said *come*, he hustled.

"Don't need no ride," Steve muttered. "Can walk." His words were becoming more slurred, his weight heavier against Roxy.

"Stuff it," Roxy said. "The rule is, the sick one doesn't get to make the rules. Now get in that cart, and Iggy's gonna give us a quick ride."

Steve balked. Damn. Maybe he was the kind of tough old-fashioned geezer who'd respond to feminine charm? She hooked her arm under his. Her heart beat a thousand miles an hour. What if she was hurting him more than helping him? She should probably lay him down on the court and wait for the EMTs. Steve's shirt was pretty much soaked and heat radiated from his skin.

"Look," Roxy said, "I plan on taking you home, but it's hot, and these old legs of mine are tired. My house is just a couple doors down from yours. See?" She waved at the neat row of houses across the street. "I sure would appreciate it if you'd ride along with me, because I'm not sure I can walk that far." It was a bald-faced lie, but it did the trick. Steve grunted his assent.

He might be a proud man, but he wasn't stupid. One of the other shuffleboard players joined Iggy in helping load Steve into the back seat of the cart.

Roxy offered Graciela and the men a tight smile, if only to ease Steve's prickly ego. *See*, the smile said, *nothing wrong here. Just big ol' you helping little ol' me get home.* The smile was meant to fool her mind into ignoring the prickles of fear slaloming along her nerves. "I'd appreciate it if you folks keep an eye on us until we get there. In case I trip over my sneakers or Iggy loses his way or we get carjacked."

She eased herself into the seat next to Steve and patted his knee. "And just so you know, Steve, if I go missing, you'll be top of the suspect list. If I'm not home by dark, my friends will rat you out in a split second. And I think one or two of them are strong Second Amendment proponents. A couple of others are *well connected*, if you know what I mean."

Not a word she said was true, but what did she know about this large man who was apparently pissed off about something and who'd shown up out of the ether five minutes ago?

In spite of whatever pain he was feeling, Steve managed a grin. "But what if you *want* to go missing? For all you know, this could turn out to be the best night of your life."

Good. Flirting was good. "Let's go find out."

She hissed at Iggy, "Yellow house, across the street. Drive

it like you stole it."

She turned to Steve. "You have your house key? Can you get it, or am I going to have to fish for it?"

She'd known the man five minutes, but he struck her as the kind who'd never let a double entendre go to waste. In spite of his glower. In spite of the strangely angry energy he'd radiated earlier in the same way he was currently radiating heat.

She knew it was bad when Steve reached for his pocket without even making a joke about letting her go in search of his keys herself.

CHAPTER 3

Steve's Date with Death: T-Minus 56:10:13 and Counting

"HERE. DRINK THIS." Roxy appeared at Steve's elbow with a glass of the overly sweet tea he kept in a jug stashed in his fridge, a guilty pleasure from his long-ago childhood. Another forbidden pleasure his doctor would blow a gasket over.

Fuck doctors.

Steve leaned back in his recliner as he waited for the nitro tab under his tongue to take effect. He wasn't certain the heart palpitations were actually the warning of something worse, but dissolving one of the pills couldn't hurt. More likely he'd fucked up his blood sugar again. Or the damned heat had got to him. Or the aggravating woman currently buzzing around like a fly trapped under a glass. "Getting old is not for pussies."

"You need to be thinking less about pussies and more about why you damned near passed out on me over there. Are you sure you don't need Iggy to call a squad?"

The young man in question shuffled from foot to foot, his phone already in his hand. His brown face had a sickly hue to it. "My *titi*—Rosalina—had the same thing happen. But she died." He bowed his head and made the sign of the cross, then stared again at Steve.

"As you can see, Steve's not dead. Just needed to cool off a bit, right?" She gave Steve an encouraging nod.

He looked up at Iggy and matched Roxy's nod. No need to scare the kid any more than he already was.

"I expect it was the deleterious effect of an old man with a heart condition ogling a lady's legs when he shouldn't have been."

What kind of woman used a word like that?

"Deleterious," Roxy said.

Damned woman was scary good at reading his mind.

"Harmful in a subtle or unexpected way."

"And you got that word from where?"

"I'm not stupid, you know," Roxy said. "I didn't have the greatest schooling, but you're never too old to learn something new. That one's from my *Sexy Firefighters With Cute Puppies* word-of-the-day calendar. Every year I get a new calendar and learn interesting stuff. Started when I was nineteen."

"You must know the entire dictionary by now."

"Oh, it's not always a word of the day. Some years it's only one fact a month." Roxy finally stopped flitting around, settled in a chair, and crossed those ridiculously long legs in those ridiculously short shorts. Her face lit up. "One year the calendar was the great castles of the world. Another year it was chemistry stuff, like elements and atoms. I really loved the year every month was different animals of the rain forest. This year it's a word-of-the-day calendar."

"With sexy firefighters holding cute puppies."

"Well, no harm in a little eye candy to go with the education."

"You mean no deleterious effect in having the eye candy."

She threw back her headful of glorious red curls and laughed. Laughed right at him. Not some cackling old-lady laugh either or a stupid airhead giggle, but a genuine, straight-from-the-belly laugh.

He liked that laugh. Liked it in a way he'd forgotten was possible. Damn. Eighty years old and a woman's laugh—and her wild red hair, and mile-long-legs—stirred up feelings down below that he'd been pretty sure weren't going to get stirred

23

ever again. Thank God for little blue pills. Would she be interested in playing a little tube-snake boogie with him?

His own interest was piqued, but would he just embarrass himself? Maybe he'd be better off not getting involved. She'd be better off for sure. He was going to die in three days. A little less than that now. Not a nice thing to do to a nice lady, fuck her and then die on her.

"Iggy, you go tell your mama everything's fine now."

Roxy must have decided he was going to live.

"Tell her I'll stop by tomorrow and buy her that drink."

"Yeah, what she said." Steve had his breath back under control, and his head had stopped buzzing enough that he could marshal his thoughts into coherent order. "And, uh, thanks, kid. Iggy, is it?"

"Ignacio Diaz, sir. But yeah, Iggy."

Steve tried to juggle the glass of sweet tea while reaching for his pocket. "Let me tip you for the ride. And the help."

"No need, sir. You come 'round the club some time and buy me a Coke, okay? We're square." Iggy nodded again and darted out the door as if he'd been shot at. Who knew the engine of a golf cart could be revved that way?

How humiliating. It had taken a scrawny Puerto Rican kid and an old woman to wrangle him in and out of the golf cart and into his house. His life had turned to shit, and God had hit the flush handle. His temper had been up, he'd walked too fast, the sun was too hot, and a redheaded woman had sent his sluggish blood to a place that wasn't used to getting it instead of the places that needed it.

Shoulda known better than to leave the house without his pills. Shouldn't have bothered taking them when he got home. Except he had his own plans, and no stupid heart attack was going to fuck them up. He was going out in his own sweet way on *his* schedule. Not God's.

"Nice kid, that Iggy," Steve said. What he really meant was "Stop fussing and get the hell out of my house," but the command wouldn't come out. Must be loopier than he'd thought.

"Yeah, he is. He's studying to be an architect. That's why he's working as a gate guard, because it's quiet and he can get a lot of studying done. His mom, Graciela, has her own real estate company and wants to help with his college, but he's determined to succeed on his own, just like she did. Got himself a scholarship and a couple of jobs and carries a full load of courses. He turned down your offer because he's a nice kid and he's proud and a natural-born helper, but the next time you're at the club, you better offer him more than a Coke."

Steve took a long swallow of his tea. He knew Roxy's kind. The kind of woman who knew everyone and everything going on in the neighborhood and all the connections between people, seen and unseen. The kind of person he'd cultivated associations with back in the days when he'd been a cop and a drug agent.

But he didn't need anybody like her anymore. He didn't care who was doing what with whoever and when. Not his problem. Not anymore. Three days—

"Here." She handed him one of his own dish towels soaking wet. "Put this on the back of your neck. Right up against the base of your skull."

He tried to figure out how to juggle both the iced tea and the dish towel. Roxy indicated he should continue drinking while she placed the towel herself.

He yelped. "Damn, woman, you trying to kill me?"

"You haven't given me reason to. Yet. I'm waiting to see if the heat exhaustion does you in first and saves me the mess and bother of trying to explain to the cops how I got your blood all over me."

In spite of the pain, in spite of his simmering anger, Steve laughed. "I know some cleaners who could help you. Wipe out every trace of DNA and give you an airtight alibi for why it couldn't have been you that snuffed me. But it'd cost you."

"Do these cleaners of yours offer an installment plan? I could afford that."

The look she gave him was dead serious, which made Steve

laugh again. When was the last time he'd done that? A year? Two? Before Natalie died?

Roxy derailed that train of thought when she said, "You've got the emptiest refrigerator I've ever seen, even for a single old man living alone. A jug of tea, a few pieces of leftover Popeyes chicken, and a plate of something that looks and smells disgusting. And not a single vegetable in sight."

Steve had cleaned out the refrigerator two days ago. He didn't want some poor soul to have to clean rotting food out of his house. Bad enough they'd have to clean up his rotting corpse. He'd have to make arrangements about that too—

"Steve? You still with me?" Roxy had her phone in her hand, her eyebrows beetled together, and her hot pink lipstick half-chewed off. The flush on her pale cheeks looked more like it came from exertion than from makeup.

"Have some respect, woman. Chitlins are God's gift to the south. Cooked 'em myself, just like Mama taught me. My daddy said at least one of the reasons he married Mama was to get her recipe for chitlins. And how do you know I live alone?"

"A woman would have added decoration to the place. At least added a picture or two." She frowned pointedly at his mostly blank gray walls. "A woman would have food in the fridge. And a woman would never have allowed that chair to pass through her front door."

Another pointed look, this time at his monstrously oversized leather recliner with the built-in cup holders, 360-degree swivel, adjustable lumbar support, built-in heat and massage, and pockets to hold his remote controls. Another gift from his loving nephew.

"Plenty of women in my life. None at the moment, though."

"Ex-wife I should call in case you croak? Kids?"

"No and no. My lawyer's number is by the phone. Are you actually concerned or just being nosy?" Yeah, he'd pegged her right. Pretty and chatty and a better interrogator than most of the drug enforcement guys could ever hope to be.

"Just being a concerned neighbor," Roxy said. "If there's going to be an ambulance screaming up the street, I'd rather it be in the middle of the afternoon than when I'm trying to sleep." Roxy settled herself into a corner of his big gray sectional, her legs wrapped under her.

"You must be ex-military," she said.

"Former. You're never really *ex*, not when you've served as long as I did. How'd you guess military?"

"I was looking for a clean dishcloth. Everything in your kitchen drawer was folded in thirds and flush left. My ex-brother-in-law used to insist my sister Natalia do it that way. She bitched about it all the time."

"You have a sister named Natalia? Mine was named Natalie."

"Had a sister, not have. We called her Tally, but yeah. *Was*, not *is*? You too?"

He nodded.

"How?" she asked.

"Ovarian cancer."

"Breast."

"Fuck cancer," they said in unison.

Great. She'd started chatting. Getting to know him. Prying information out of him. Now how was he supposed to get her out of his house? Although he wouldn't mind looking a while longer at those long, long legs the tawny color of lightly toasted Wonder Bread. Redheads weren't supposed to tan like that, were they?

She'd propped her rhinestone-framed sunglasses on top of her head, where they held back the russet curls that hung to the tops of her shoulders. Crow's-feet rayed out from her eyes, and small grooves bracketed her mouth, but for a white woman, her skin looked in remarkably good shape. She could have had work done, maybe a little injection or two of Botox, but even on such short acquaintance, Roxy Fields didn't seem the kind of woman to allow age or vanity to dictate her life. She wore makeup but hadn't troweled it on as so many older women did.

27

She wasn't overflowing in the boob area, but the V-neck tie-dyed T-shirt revealed at least a generous handful, even for a guy with hands his size. Steve shook himself. *What the fuck are you thinking, old man?*

But it was the legs that got him. Taut, tanned, toned legs. Legs plenty long enough to wrap around a man his size and—

"Have you seen enough or should I stand up and let you check out my butt too?" Roxy had caught him mid-ogle.

Steve's eyes met hers. "Well, if you don't mind..."

She uncurled her legs slowly, then leaned back and stretched her arms over her head, drawing the T-shirt tighter. She smiled and blinked slowly at him.

Then she laughed. "Just checking your heart rate," she said. "Looks like you'll survive."

God, what a great woman. Funny, flirty, unpretentious. The kind of woman a man could—

Then it all came crashing back down on him. All the years. The deaths. Natalie.

The phone call he expected any day now from the doctor.

Just as he'd started to enjoy the ray of sunshine Roxy brought into his world, the cave walls closed in on him again.

A walking dead man had no business indulging himself in hopes and dreams.

"I don't need a mother hen. You can go now," he said through gritted teeth, although he wouldn't have minded watching her stand up and sit down a few more times, if only to see those legs in action.

His lizard brain—the part in charge of fight, flight, freezing, feeding, fear, and fornication—had apparently woken up hungry. He thought he'd killed that part of himself already. You had to kill the lizard brain before you could kill the body. But the fornication compartment apparently had a stronger survival instinct, judging from the stirring below his belt. His mouth may have spat out the words demanding her departure, but Big Bob in his trousers suddenly didn't want her to leave.

"Should I call you an Uber or anything?" Steve said. He had

plans. Roxy wasn't going to interrupt them. "Call that Iggy kid to take you back to the club?"

"No need," Roxy said. "I'm only four doors down. The shrimp-pink house."

Oh God. Oh no. "The one that looks like an outlet for the local yard and garden store?" Steve said. "The one that looks like a florist shop puked on the front lawn? The one with the pink flamingos and fat, ugly midgets?"

"Well, yes, I guess I do have a lot of plants. They're so cheerful and they grow so well here. And those are gnomes, not fat, ugly midgets. And I like flamingos. With legs like this, it's a nickname I've been called all my life, so I may as well have fun with it."

"I'm sorry, Ms. Fields," Steve said, "for ogling and stuff. I didn't realize you were the lesbian."

Chapter 4

Sexy Firefighters Calendar Word of the Day:
Badinage: [bad-n-ahzh] **Noun**. humorous or witty conversation, playful repartee. **Verb**. to banter with or tease playfully.

ROXY HAD STEPPED through the looking glass. Or fallen down a rabbit hole. Or been beamed up by aliens.

"I beg your pardon? What the devil did you just say?"

Steve set his iced tea into the cup holder on the arm of his chair. "Not that there's anything wrong with that. I realized my mistake the minute you told me where you lived. All those rainbow doodads in the yard. That flag—"

"It's June, Steve. Pride Month. The rainbow flag display doesn't mean I'm a lesbian. It means I'm an ally who supports my friends in the LGBTQ+ community."

"You know a lot of 'em?" There wasn't any judgment in Steve's eyes, just honest curiosity.

Old, old memories rose unbidden in Roxy's mind. "Not as many as I used to. Living in New York in the seventies and eighties, working in the theater world—" Roxy wished she'd poured herself a glass of tea while she'd been in the kitchen. It would have helped her swallow the sudden lump in her throat. Joey. Giorgio. Madame Duval...

"Sorry," Steve said. "I guess we've all got memories that are better left locked away." He looked genuinely contrite as he cleared his throat. "So you lived in New York?"

"Hard to be a Rockette unless you do. Although it's a part-time job, so I suppose I could have commuted from Jersey, but yeah, I lived there for a while."

Steve leaned forward in his chair. Whatever medication he'd taken was working; he'd stopped sweating and his round brown cheeks had a healthier hue than the previous sickly grayish cast.

"You were a Rockette? For real? One of those ladies on the Christmas shows kicking up their legs together like they're connected at the hips and doing that toy soldier dance where they all fall down?"

Roxy's sad memories of her friends gave way to happier ones. "Yeah," she said. "For real. And I can't tell you how much I love that the dance you remember most is the Parade of Wooden Soldiers. It was my absolute favorite to perform, although it's really super hard to do."

"Do you have pictures? Could I see them?"

Yeah, Steve was a guy like every other guy. And his interest in her, her legs and her past as a dancer revealed he was feeling better.

"Yes, I have pictures. No, I don't carry them around in my butt bag," she said, patting the fuchsia-pink fanny pack at her waist. "Maybe when you're feeling better, and if I'm in the right mood, I'll invite you over to see them one of these days."

What had prompted that? Her former life as a dancer was one she rarely shared, even with close friends. What on earth had made her mention it to this stranger? Roxy also never shared her mementos of those days with anyone. They were locked away in her private sanctum. Too many people asked too many questions and made too many assumptions, even if her dancing days were fifty years in the past.

"So, what do you keep in your butt bag?" Steve asked.

A minute ago Roxy could have sworn he was ready to call the cops if necessary to get her out of his house. Now he was throwing off vibes that begged her to stay.

She surprised herself by not minding that at all.

31

She mentally gave herself a shake. No, she was only doing a good deed and helping a neighbor. Just checking to make sure he was going to be okay. Anything to keep him talking, right? She didn't want to make a quick exit only to have to explain to the cops later why she'd left a sick man alone to die.

Roxy opened her pack and spread the contents of her bag on the sofa next to her floppy-brimmed hat. "Lipstick," she said. "Today's color is Passion Panic Pink." She peeked up at Steve. "Rockettes are all required to wear the exact same shade of red lipstick. It's a hard-and-fast rule. You wear either MAC Red or MAC Russian Red. After I stopped dancing, it took me years before I could bear to wear that color again." She fished through the bag and laid out the rest of the items. "Comb, phone, reading glasses, switchblade." It wasn't her best switchblade, but it was sharp and hidden safely in a plain leather case.

Steve sat up straighter and reached for the last item, but she smacked his fingers away.

"Why a switchblade?"

"Because my favorite sword won't fit."

"Favorite sword? As in you have more than one?"

"Well, yeah," Roxy said. "Although I got rid of most of them when I downsized and moved down here. I kept the half a dozen that I use for my fencing classes."

"You take fencing classes?"

"I *teach* them. Every Friday at the senior center. You want to come next week?"

Steve's expression was suddenly as closed up as if he'd put hurricane shutters over his thoughts. "Nah," he said.

"Would you be more interested in hearing what it's like to be a Rockette?"

The shutters remained locked tight.

Roxy stood and tugged her shorts into place. From the corner of her eye, she watched Steve watching her.

"And in case you still have any doubts, I'm not a lesbian. Not even bi. I'm not sleazy, and I'm definitely not easy. I know my value." She paused for a long moment while she stuffed her possessions back into her pack and adjusted it on her waist. "And I'm worth the effort."

She had no idea why she was interested in this taciturn man or what had prompted her to say that. Maybe Graciela was right, that Roxy was always looking out for someone to mother. Maybe that instinct was because she'd long ago lost her only chance to be a real mother.

Or maybe her interest was because even in his current state, the big man appealed to her in a way she wasn't ready to examine too closely. He stirred up feelings that had been dormant since the last century.

"Happy hour at my house always starts at five. Dinner is at six if you're interested. I have a swimming pool and a hot tub big enough for four, so it ought to have enough room for a man your size. If you're not there tonight, I'll be over to check on you."

She headed toward the door. "Bathing suits are optional."

She didn't look over her shoulder as she dropped the bomb and closed the door behind her.

CHAPTER 5

Steve's Date with Death: T-Minus 48:07:17 and Counting

STEVE STEPHENS HAD no intention of having drinks and dinner with a mouthy redhead, no matter how enticing those mile-long legs were. Playing footsie with some broad was not in his plans for his last few days on Earth.

He kept telling himself that right up until 4:45, when he opened his fridge door and found exactly three beers and a container of cold chitlins.

He didn't have a number to call to tell her where to shove her drinks and dinner and Nurse Nanny act, and it would be rude to leave her hanging. Mama would have tanned his hide for doing that to a lady, even if the lady in question was a nosy, interfering, rainbow-loving liberal.

With mile-long legs.

Fine. So he'd grab a shower and throw on one of those guayabera shirts his nephew had sent him for his last birthday.

"Why'd you send me those?" he had complained when Curtis finally answered his call. "You want me looking like a Cuban pimp? With all those damned pockets, they're the shirt version of cargo shorts."

"Unk, you've worn some kind of uniform all your life. Army. Cop. Consider this your South Florida retirement uniform. Wear 'em with chinos. But whatever you do, old man, don't tuck the shirt in. Try not to look like any more of a *contadino* than you can help."

"What did you just fucking call me?"

"It's Italian, Unk. A peasant. A rustic. A rube." Curtis had laughed and hung up on him.

Steve didn't mind admitting the linen was soft on his skin and cool in the tropical weather. He didn't even mind admitting he particularly liked the dark coral shirt that matched the band on his panama hat. But he really, really hated admitting how much he'd come to enjoy having his shirttails hanging out in the breeze.

Barefoot, wearing denim shorts and a hot pink vintage bowling shirt, Roxy didn't even blink when she swung open her door in answer to his ring.

"Make yourself at home while I finish throwing together some munchies." When she turned away, Steve read the words "Hit 'em hard, hit 'em fast" emblazoned across the back of the bowling shirt. She disappeared into the kitchen, leaving him alone in her living room.

Stupid woman didn't know him from Adam, and she'd invited him in without a second thought and left him alone to rifle through her drawers or pilfer a few pieces of jewelry or sneak up behind her and slit her throat.

Steve huffed, muttered an imprecation under his breath and jammed his hands in his pockets. One nice thing about his flapping shirttails was that they covered the small bulge of the gun he never went anywhere without. He didn't know Roxy any better than she knew him.

She might be full-on batshit cray-cray. In spite of those legs.

Roxy's house was nothing like Steve's own. It wasn't only that she had three bedrooms to his two; Steve hadn't made any alterations to his house since the day he'd moved in. His walls were an innocuous "buyers will love this neutral" gray. At least they weren't pea green like in the army or the government-issue smoke-stained beige that had adorned the walls of his office at the DEA, a color that offended no one by being universally hated by everyone. His furniture was bland, purchased to fill the space. The only piece he cared about was his high-end recliner.

Roxy's house looked more suited to funky, laid-back Key West than upscale West Palm Beach. Nothing cheap or tacky, but she'd definitely embraced Florida kitsch.

While Roxy banged around the kitchen, Steve wandered through her living room, past the plump, overstuffed chairs and a pair of love seats all covered in a print of giant palm leaves to the ceiling-high white bookcases that covered one wall.

Rows of books filled the shelves, the books lined up with almost military precision, as organized as any public library. Books were in order by author and then alphabetical by title, which seemed odd for a woman who struck him as infinitely chaotic. Mysteries and romance dominated, but he couldn't find any familiar horror authors like King or Koontz. A few nonfiction books had a shelf to themselves; books on tropical gardening mingled with books on religion, mostly of the "Jesus was married and Mary's gospel was suppressed by the patriarchy" type.

He pulled a random romance from the shelf, opened it in the middle, and read aloud: "He kissed her, his hands gripping her shoulders. 'Please, Jessa, I want you to touch me. I want to give you relief too. I know what you're feeling. I know how to ease the ache. Right there, between those lovely legs.'"

"Sound interesting to you?"

Steve whirled to find Roxy standing behind him. She wasn't blushing or anything. So why did he feel heat rising in his cheeks, like a kid caught with his hand in the Sunday offering plate? "You read this stuff to get off?" he asked.

"No, but they certainly are something to aspire to." Roxy took the book from his hands and placed it neatly back on the shelf, swapping the book out for a beer in a frosty glass.

"And that armory on display over there?" Steve pointed to the array of swords on the far wall. A katana, rapiers, and something else long and heavy. Pointy things for which he had no name. He could recognize and name dozens of different guns from yards away, but neither the army nor the Florida Highway Patrol nor the DEA had provided training on swords. The only training he'd had on pointy things was to run toward a gun and away from a knife. "Are those inspirational as well?"

"Those are the weapons I trained with and that I train others to use now. Mostly just the fencing foils these days. I took up fencing when I was living in New York as a nonboring way to train on footwork and flexibility and strength during the off-season when the show wasn't running. Eventually I picked up money teaching it." She shrugged and turned away, not finding the topic interesting.

Steve gawked behind her back. He'd run into a few Russian agents over the years who'd trained in sword fighting, but Roxy was the unlikeliest woman he'd ever suspect of keeping an array of weapons on her wall like just another art display. He crossed the room and reached toward the katana.

"Uh-uh," Roxy said. She most definitely was fast and light on her feet, pirouetting in his direction. "They may look pretty, but I keep every one of those in fighting shape, honed to a lethal edge. Good thing I don't have any grandkids and don't let children in the house. I'd have to lock them up like guns. Although you'll notice, each one is latched to the wall with a small lock. Still, you can take a finger off with any one of them." She grinned at him. "I'd hate to see you lose anything important."

Steve grunted, took a sip of his beer, and turned to the paintings. A half dozen brilliantly colored abstracts picked up the emerald green of her walls. "You must like that artist," he said.

She sipped her own drink, something tall and pink. "Dean Lauderdale," she said. "I met him the first time at one of those art shows. Fell in love with his work and made a point to go every time I knew he'd be in town." She guided him closer to the artworks. "He had a unique technique. Airbrushed colors on acrylic, then he'd layer them before carving away the layers to reveal the design. People are kind of like his art. They cover themselves up in these murky layers, but if you work at it, you can coax away the layers and find the beauty hidden under them."

She sighed and took another sip. "He's dead now, but every now and then I'll find one of his pieces for sale and snatch it up." She smiled up at him. "Graciela loves them too, so I've promised she can have them after I'm dead."

Talk of death hit too close to the bone for Steve. Plans for his own death might have absorbed his every waking moment for the last month, but that didn't mean he wanted to talk about it. Yeah, this woman was definitely starting to ping the red zone on the crazy meter.

He turned to examine the other objects in the room. A three-foot-tall pink wooden flamingo stood guard duty at the door. A collection of carved elephants in different materials formed their own herd on a shelf by the kitchen. An enameled ruby red vase had pride of place on the mantel over a real fireplace, a rarity in the overheated south Florida The vase seemed like a safe topic. He pointed at it with his glass. "Another art piece from a starving artist?"

She shook her head. She rubbed a hand lovingly over the smooth surface. "No, this is my funeral urn. Someday I'm going to be cremated and my ashes will go in there. At least for a little while."

Steve choked on his beer. "Good God, woman, how much more morbid can you be? You some kind of weirdo or something?" What the hell had he gotten himself into?

Roxy laughed. "Well, you're not the first one to think I'm a bit...um...odd, but it's not as gruesome as you think. I try hard not to lie to myself and I like to be prepared." She stroked the urn again. "I've had three dogs in my life that I loved as if they were my children. All of them lived to ripe old ages. And when they died—because everyone and everything does, Steve—I had them cremated. I bought this urn and put all their ashes in there. When the time comes, I've made arrangements for us all to be scattered together."

She cocked her head. "Besides," she said, "why should I let somebody else pick out some butt-ugly urn I'd hate? The person scattering my ashes is going to have a fine time carting this through airport security and explaining to anyone who asks that he's taking a Rockette to her final resting place." She laughed again. "Poor Iggy."

"Iggy? That kid who drove that golf cart like he was in the Indy 500? What's he got to do with it?"

In trying to ignore death, Steve had walked right into this. Maybe God was just being a dick again. So-fucking-what? He'd made up his mind. A handful of hours more and it wouldn't matter what the hell God thought.

"Iggy's going to be the one scattering my ashes. He's a great young man. His dad died when Iggy was a baby. He had a meeting at the World Trade Center on 9/11. Graciela's done well for herself selling high-end real estate, but they had it rough for a long time. Not a lot put away for college, which is why Iggy's working his way through school doing all kinds of odd jobs and picking up shifts at the country club. Since he's studying to be an architect, when I die, my will asks that my ashes be scattered in a number of places around the world—places I've never seen but that have some of the world's finest architecture. There's money for Iggy to travel to those places, throw some ashes around, and see those buildings firsthand."

"So you're leaving all your money to some Puerto Rican kid that isn't even yours?"

Steve took another drink of beer, his throat oddly parched. He hadn't bothered making a will or any plans for what happened after his death. There'd be a note on the door to contact one of his old buddies on the local police force and a note inside to contact his nephew Curtis, if they could find the little dickhead, but beyond that? They could send him to the local landfill for all he cared.

"No, I'm not leaving everything to Iggy. There's a bunch of charities that get the rest. One that gives books to kids, another that feeds people in disaster areas. And, of course, Sheldrick."

"Old boyfriend? A current boyfriend I should know about?" The last thing Steve needed in his final days was for a jealous boyfriend to shoot him before he could kill himself.

Roxy shook her head. "No boyfriends. Sheldrick Wildlife Trust. They rescue orphan elephants, raise them, and return them to the wild. They're good people doing good work."

"Why would you work your whole life just to save a bunch of big dumb animals?"

"You should be grateful I have a soft spot for creatures like that."

"Are you calling me dumb?"

"No, Steve, I'm calling you big." Roxy wandered over to one of her cushy chairs, tucked one leg under her slim body, and sank down gracefully.

Yep, she'd been a dancer, and her training showed. Steve plopped more than sank into the opposite chair, managing not to spill his beer in the process.

"Still think it's morbid to have a funeral urn on your mantel like it's a vase of posies or something."

"Steve, there's nothing wrong with talking about death. You have your own plans for yours, right?"

The beer Steve was in the middle of swallowing went down the wrong pipe when he gasped, setting off a coughing jag. Roxy instantly leapt from her chair and pounded his back—harder than he'd expected from such a slender woman. Must be all that fencing and stuff that gave her such strong arms. Even in the midst of choking to death on a beer—a fitting and ironic end as far as he was concerned—Steve wondered how it would feel to have those arms wrapped around him.

He'd once heard the term "skin hunger." All kinds of bad things could happen if a person didn't get enough touch from other humans. It reminded him again how long it had been since anyone hugged him or he'd hugged another person. Hell, when was the last time he so much as shook hands with somebody? Maybe that's all this was, these weird feelings Roxy aroused in him. The feeling of being one-foot-out-the-door and rooted to his chair at the same time. It made him squirmy inside, craving contact while also desperate to retreat back to the safety of his self-imposed solitude.

Time for a subject change. He'd known this woman for only a few hours and they were already talking about death and sex.

Maybe it was just a matter of being old and knowing there weren't that many sands left in either of their hourglasses.

"I guess I could use another beer, Roxy. And are you planning on getting me drunk on an empty stomach and then taking advantage of me in my weakened state?"

"Would it work?" Roxy winked at him as she rose from her chair. "A lady never takes advantage of a man without feeding him first."

Chapter 6

Sexy Firefighters Calendar Word of the Day:
Pangloss [ˈpaNGglôs] **Noun.** *a person who is optimistic regardless of the circumstances.*

STEVE FOLLOWED ROXY into the kitchen.

"Grab that tray of crudités out of the fridge and grab yourself another beer while you're at it. It's cooling down now, and we can have our appetizers on the lanai."

"What the hell are crudités?"

"That tray of veggies."

"Well, why didn't you just say that?" Steve set the tray on the counter and pulled another beer from the fridge. He eyed the colorful array dubiously. "Don't you have any pork rinds?"

Roxy opened the pantry door and surveyed the contents. "Graciela likes hummus, so I always keep a container of that in the fridge. You can dip the crud—I mean veggies—in that, or I have ranch or blue cheese dressing as a dip."

"Can I choose none of the above?"

"Let's see what else." A bag rattled as she pulled it off the shelf. "Iggy likes these super-spicy chips, and Jane, the woman on the corner in the white house with orange trim, likes these organic rice and flaxseed crackers." Roxy shrugged and pulled her phone out of her pocket, tapping the screen.

"Who are you calling?"

"No one," Roxy said. "Just making a note to add pork rinds to the grocery list."

Steve gave a quick wash to his empty glass, put it in the freezer, and pulled out a new frosted glass. "No need to get anything special just for me."

Roxy had a hard time reading his face. Somewhere between embarrassment and anger. She mentally reviewed her words but couldn't see what she'd said that would have caused either emotion. He'd seemed fine a second ago. Such a prickly man, but then again, maybe he still wasn't feeling a hundred percent after his sudden illness earlier.

She opted to ignore the look. "It's no problem. I like to keep snacks on hand that people like, for when they drop by. You may have noticed the stash of Peppermint Patties in the back of the freezer. Ms. Freeman is fond of those, especially on days her kids are driving her nuts and she needs a break. If it's really bad, she gets peppermint schnapps instead."

Steve picked up the tray and went through the French doors onto the lanai, setting the tray on her wrought-iron table.

Roxy followed with a bowl of cheese dip and a fresh mai tai.

"You stock up on random food for everybody?" Steve asked. "Why would you do that?"

Steve's puzzled look made Roxy smile. She leaned back and sipped her drink, the mai tai tart and sweet and cool on her tongue. "Steve, there have been times in my life when I've been so hungry I could feel my belly button touching my backbone. Times I've been so scared I didn't think I could last another second. Times I've felt like a ghost, like no one could see me or how I hurt. When I didn't have two cents to rub together. I was all closed off, sure no one could, or would, understand how bad I felt. I was too stubborn to let anyone in and too proud to let anyone help. And yet, somehow, there always seemed to be someone there. Just the right person came along at just the right moment and helped me, whether I wanted them to or not. And most of the time, that help started with feeding me. Sometimes something as simple as a soft drink and a bag of chips or a candy bar was enough to break through my misery."

Steve snorted. "That sugarcoated Coke-and-a-smile philosophy, right? The cure for everything if you listen to the hippies."

"It wasn't what they gave me. It's that in that moment, they were present. They were listening. They were trying, even if they might not have much themselves. I promised myself, way back then, that when I had the chance, when I had a real home of my own, that I'd try to be as welcoming as those folks."

Roxy looked around her spacious lanai and rambling gardens and sighed in satisfaction. "I've worked hard for all this," she said. "And I like sharing it." She smiled innocently at Steve. "Even with borderline curmudgeons."

Steve shifted his big body in the chair, grimacing. "I'm sorry to be such a grouch." He appeared on the verge of saying more but lifted his beer instead, covering his expression as he swallowed.

"Everyone has crappy days," Roxy said. "But I don't allow them here. Just look at all those flowers and listen to the birds and breathe for a few minutes."

Silence sat between them for long minutes. It didn't bother Roxy. She couldn't put her finger on why, but she liked Steve. Her sister had once accused her of being a soft touch, of taking in every stray cat and orphan and broken-winged bird. Maybe Tally was right. Sure, she'd been burned a few times, but mostly good things had come from keeping an open mind and an open heart.

Steve appeared less comfortable with the silence. He stared into the distance, his eyes roving through the garden as if he sought ninjas waiting to spring from the hibiscus and sprawling bougainvillea.

Finally, he spoke. "You're good at manipulating people into doing what you want, aren't you?"

Was she? She always tried to help where she could, but could her helpfulness be perceived as manipulation? Roxy shook her head.

"I prefer to think I'm good at giving people suggestions and giving them the opportunity to decide for themselves what they might be missing." She plucked a piece of broccoli from the tray and chewed it thoughtfully. Steve, she noticed, hadn't touched the bite-sized vegetables.

"But you always get them to do what you want in the end, don't you?"

"People always have free will to decide which path they're going to choose," she said. "They can, and do, ignore me just fine. I simply like to make sure folks know they don't have to stay on the road they're on if the going gets too hard. They can always choose a new direction. There were people in my past that did the same thing for me. I was a lost kid in a lot of trouble. Folks helped me out of that trouble. They mopped up the blood and tears but didn't let me wallow. They explained that I had options, gave me the space and safety to get my head straight, and gave me the tools to get me pointed in a different direction."

She stood. "Hold on, I'll be right back." She dug around in the kitchen and returned with a bowl of pretzels and another of potato chips. She set them beside the barely touched veggies. She'd also grabbed an orange, a banana, and the strawberries she'd planned on serving with shortcake for dessert. For good measure, she'd tucked in a couple of peanut butter cup candies.

In her opinion, Steve could use some healthy options, but he'd probably ignore the fruit the same way he'd ignored the veggies. His dusky skin had an unhealthy undertone and she worried about the yellow tinge in his eyes, but she barely knew the man. Getting him to eat anything at all, no matter how unhealthy, was better than nothing.

She hoped he liked fish, because that was what he was getting for supper, like it or not.

"You may think your past was troubled, but did you ever come close to dying, Roxy?"

The question caught her by surprise.

"Ever lie in dank, rotting grass, hoping it was high enough to hide you from the bullets? And praying the grass wasn't also hiding poisonous snakes or disease-carrying bugs that would end up killing you anyway? Ever pull over a speeding car on a moonless night on an empty highway and had some strung-out teenager spitting and screaming at you and hope to God he didn't have AIDS? Or worse, pull over some roided-up asshole with a gun and your closest help is still three miles away and you don't know if he's gonna get there in time to save your ass?"

Steve leaned forward in his chair, one fist clenched on top of his beefy thigh, the other threatening to crush the heavy glass beer stein. "You don't really know what trouble is. You don't even know what death is. It ain't pretty urns on a mantel."

Roxy leaned forward and cautiously laid her hand on top of Steve's fist. She'd misjudged men before, but she didn't think she'd been wrong about this one. Something inside him was bound up tighter than a drag queen's dick. It had honed his emotions into lethally sharp razor blades and was slicing and dicing his insides to bloody ribbons. She couldn't fix that.

But she could, if he'd let her, give him a few hours of respite from the fight, even if only so he could take up arms again tomorrow and launch himself into whatever battle he fought. For tonight, she could provide a moment of peace.

If he'd let her. Sometimes getting a person to talk about their troubles helped. But Roxy didn't think that was going to work with Steve. He came from the macho shut-up-and-stuff-it-down-the-memory-hole generation.

She had too, but she'd gotten over it. So she'd do what she'd learned to do best. Tap dance. At least metaphorically. Distract him with noise and music. Give his body something to chew on besides his own stomach acid, and his mind something to dwell on besides the murky swamp of his own dark thoughts.

"I've never been in a war, Steve, and won't even pretend to know what you've dealt with in your career. You were a police officer?"

"Florida Highway Patrol," he said tersely. "Then DEA. Drug enforcement. Field agent for a while, then a desk job." He raised his beer and took a long swig. "Reams of paperwork will suck the life out of you too, just a lot slower than a bullet between the eyes."

"I haven't come close to death like you have."

This man had demons indeed. She needed to pull him away from whatever precipice he stood on. She drew a deep breath, inhaling the fragrance from her lush garden.

"I've had a close shave a time or two in New York." She settled back in her chair, popped a baby carrot into in her mouth, and hoped Steve would follow her action.

A long moment later, he reached for a pretzel, then leaned back as well.

Good. His eyes had started to lose that glazed look, the tension that twisted his features into a fierce scowl easing.

"You gonna tell me about it?"

Curiosity about something beyond his own troubles—that was a start. She sipped her drink before saying, "Mom always said God watches over fools and drunks, and back then I didn't drink, but Mom must have been right. If God hadn't been watching over my sorry, foolish self, I'd have died over a bucket of Colonel Sanders chicken and biscuits."

The tension around Steve's mouth melted a little more as the beginnings of a grin made an attempt to shift his lips. "Choke on a chicken bone, did you?"

She shook her head. "I was brand-new to New York. Greener than any fresh-out-of-rural-Ohio newbie ever had a right to be, even though I'd already been there four or five months. I spent the first few months staying with a friend who mostly kept me out of trouble and gave me a jab in the ribs whenever she caught me gawking too hard at the rainbow of humanity and weirdos and taught me how to use the subway and buses. Three of us sharing a tiny apartment—a sixth floor walk-up in the Village—but at least it had its own minuscule bathroom and a two-burner stove. But I'd finally gotten a little money together..." Roxy paused, dragged a piece of cauliflower through the dip, popped it into her mouth, and chewed. Lot of old memories there, and not all of them good.

"That's another story by itself," she said. "But anyway, I'd come into some money. Enough to let me enroll at Marymount Manhattan College. Have you heard of it?"

Steve shook his head.

"Dance major, of course. But I minored in mathematics. I liked the juxtaposition of creative and linear." Now there was a happy memory. "I really liked the bookkeeping part. It's what got me the gig later on with Madoff."

Steve sputtered. "Madoff? As in Bernie? The crook who swindled a bunch of little old ladies out of money and ended up in prison? That Madoff?"

"Yeah, well, I had nothing to do with that part, and he mostly swindled rich old people, not that that's any better. I didn't know about his back room."

"What did you do for him?"

"I ran numbers for him."

Steve's eye got bigger than an owl's on a moonless night. "Jeezus, Roxy! That's mob stuff. I didn't know he was into that shit."

Roxy couldn't hold in her laughter. "God, how did you ever make it as a cop being so gullible? I answered phones and plugged in numbers on one of those calculators with the big rolls of white paper and recorded those numbers in ledgers and when those numbers didn't add up, my boss said he'd deal with it. But I wasn't the dumb blonde from Ohio they thought I was. I could read and write and everything. Even without the swindle, there was money being made, and I took a flier on a few investments myself."

"And how'd that work out for you?"

"I did okay. Not buy-a-yacht okay, but every little bit helped. Anyway, with the money I'd come into, I enrolled at Marymount and got myself a room at the Barbizon Hotel. I don't suppose you've ever heard of that either?"

Steve shoved a handful of chips into his mouth and said nothing.

"It's all condos now, but back then it was a hotel

exclusively for women. When young ladies came out of the cornfields to the great and dangerous metropolis of New York City, if they had the money, they stayed at the Barbizon. That way, all the fretful mamas back in Abilene and Albuquerque and Cut and Shoot, Texas, didn't have to worry so much about their precious little virgins mixing with druggies and hippies and subversives. There were other women-only hotels at the time, but the Barbizon was considered the best, the most upscale, most professional—the most expensive. One of those places meant to protect young women, give them what today they'd call a safe space. No men allowed past the first floor, a matron who kept a fierce watch over the ladies, that kind of thing."

Roxy cocked an eyebrow. "Not that we didn't manage to get up to no good now and then anyway. The hotel was starting to get somewhat rundown by that time, and liberated young ladies were starting to chafe at the idea of chaperones and had taken to shouting in the streets about the patriarchy and declaring their independence. I was there in the last of the Barbizon's heyday. A couple of the elite modeling agencies kept rooms reserved there for their girls. I remember one who nice to me; she was one of those willowy giraffes that looked like Twiggy, a very popular style at that time. Pamela something or other. People thought I might be a model, because of the height, of course, but I didn't have the look. A dancer's body is nothing like a model's, at least back then."

Steve relaxed enough to give her a once-over. "I like a woman with a little meat on her."

Roxy chortled. "Glad to hear that. Kinda like a man the same way."

Steve wasn't fat, but there was nothing small about his body. She caught herself mid-ogle and took up her story again, pressing her drink to her cheeks to cool the unexpected flush of heat.

"Anyway," she said, "it was all very heady. I'd turned eighteen, moved from the Village on the West Side of Lower Manhattan to the Barbizon on the Upper East Side, and gotten myself into what I considered a prestigious school. I split my study time between statistics and shuffle ball change steps, taught a dance class twice a week, and had my little Barbizon apartment all to my own self. For the first time in my life, no one was the boss of me other than the woman at the front desk who made sure no testosterone so much as wafted up the stairs. I thought I had the world by the tail. But I was just a small-town guppy in a town full of sharks. The Barbizon lasted six months before I decided I wanted even more independence."

"Got yourself into trouble, did you? Tired of not being allowed to have boyfriends in your room?"

"Boyfriends were the last thing on my mind. And I'd already been in trouble and gotten out of it and had the scars. But having survived that gave me a weird feeling of being bulletproof and a longing to be all by myself. To show I could do it, I guess. I moved into a postage-stamp walk-up on Sixty-Sixth Street, between First and Second Avenues on the Upper East Side. No roommates to advise me. No matron watching to make sure I was safe. Just me and the half dozen door locks I installed the day I moved in."

"At least you were smart enough to do that."

"Yeah, well, trying to get them all open would have been a major disaster in an emergency, but they let me sleep better. So, on the night I'm talking about, what I wanted more than anything in the world was biscuits from Kentucky Fried Chicken."

"Wait. You're in what is arguably one of the culinary capitals of the world, and you wanted KFC?"

"Small-town Ohio girl, Steve. I wouldn't even have known what the word culinary meant. And yeah, there were dozens of places close by that sold fried chicken and biscuits, some of them probably a lot better than KFC, but that's what I wanted. Not the chicken so much but the biscuits. Soft, fat, hot biscuits."

Even now, Roxy could smell those biscuits dripping with butter and a drizzle of honey. The kind of soul-deep craving you can't ignore.

"Good lord, Rox. Couldn't you just make some? Girls in Mississippi pretty much slide out of the womb knowing how to make biscuits."

Roxy shook her head. "I'd never really cooked for myself much. I'm better now but still run screaming if the recipe calls for kneading. My apartment had a hot plate but no oven. I didn't even have a toaster oven. And I was going to throw myself in front of a bus if I didn't get biscuits, so I checked the phone book—this was years and years before Google, of course—and found the closest KFC. It was in Harlem."

Steve's shout of laughter filled the lanai as he slapped his thigh. The sound sent a happy shiver down Roxy's spine. Man, she really liked that laugh.

She liked it even better that she'd pushed back against whatever was eating at him.

"Oh God, woman," Steve said when he finally got his laughter under control. "I haven't spent much time in New York, but I've been to Harlem. It was 1956. My buddy and I stayed with relatives of his there. Not a nice place even for someone like me, a big Black guy from Mississippi, but for a scrawny little white girl like you? Please tell me that Pamela girl or somebody talked you out of it."

"Couldn't have if they'd tried, the hankering was that bad. Probably hormones, but I was going to get KFC biscuits or die trying."

"You clearly didn't die. What happened?"

"Well, that was the second time in my life I was pretty sure I wasn't going to survive the stupid situation I'd gotten myself into." Roxy saw the question lurking on the tip of Steve's tongue and rushed ahead.

"I mapped out exactly what I had to do. I took the bus straight up First Avenue, then walked a block over to Kentucky Fried Chicken, at that time on Second Avenue at 103rd Street. But it was a lot later than I'd planned when I finally got there; I hadn't really calculated how far the place was. It was getting dark, but I wanted those biscuits. I walked in and—you remember those old E. F. Hutton commercials? Somebody at a crowded party says 'E. F. Hutton says...' and the whole place falls deadly silent? It was like that. You could hear all the air being sucked out of the room in one massive, collective gasp."

"Not used to seeing a girl so melanin-deprived, were they?"

"Maybe," Roxy said. "It might have had more to do with the miniskirt and sweater and knee-high boots."

"So they thought you were a hooker? Plenty of those in Harlem in those days, but probably not too many of them with pasty-white skin."

Roxy pretended to be huffy about his words, then laughed along with Steve. "It didn't matter. I'd come this far and I wasn't leaving without my damned biscuits. I started to make my way to the counter, when three young punks stood up and blocked my way. They got close, right up in my face, making all the expected kissy-face noises and catcalling me. I'd only just started a self-defense class two weeks earlier and didn't know how to throw them over my shoulder or anything fancy. The only advantages I had were youth, naiveté, and hunger. You ever try to get between a girl and her food when she has PMS?"

"Only been that stupid once. Damn near lost a finger."

"These boys hadn't learned that lesson yet. Or that it didn't matter to me that there were three of them and one of me, because they were standing between me and my biscuits. I opened my mouth to say something that probably would have ended with my body being found behind a dumpster in an alley, when this bass voice booms out behind me. 'You fellas step out of the way and leave this woman the hell alone. She just want some chicken and 'taters and biscuits, same as all the rest of us.' Except it wasn't fellas, it was the N-word and that was the kind of word even I knew better than to use. I figured whoever he was, he was going to end up with his body beside mine in that alley. I turned around to wish the poor guy goodbye, and that's how I met one of my best friends in New York."

"Your new best friend was a man who lived in Harlem?"

"Well, she preferred to be addressed as a woman. I'll never

forget that first moment. She was built a lot like you. Over six feet tall, and that was without the five-inch gold peep-toe pumps. Two hundred fifty pounds of solid muscle and skin the color of a Yoruba goddess. Red patent leather miniskirt, matching jacket, blond bouffant with a jeweled tiara, and earrings the size of a chandelier in Versailles. Madame Jubilation Duval, born and bred in New Orleans, one day to become one of the finest drag queens in New York City. Those skinny boys backed right the hell up in the face of Jubil Duval."

Roxy ignored Steve's gaping mouth and plunged ahead with her story. "Jubil said 'Ain't nothing wrong with a scrawny little white girl wanting some chicken, even if she is apparently the most foolish creature God ever created. You know what the good Lord says, boys. God looks after fools and drunks, and I don't think this little chickie is drunk. That means she's got God himself watchin' over her. God and Jubilation Duval.' And then she walked me right up to the counter, added her order to mine, paid for the whole tab, and walked me to the bus stop. She rode with me until she thought I was in a safer part of town. Safer for me, not her. And she gave me a number to call when I got home so she wouldn't be, as she put it, up worrying her pretty head off all night about letting one of God's fools get hurt."

Roxy finished the last of her drink. "Jubil had quoted my mother without even knowing it, and I figured right then that she was sent to be somebody special in my life."

Roxy stood and picked up the tray. "Less than a year later, I had a bigger apartment, a couple of new roommates, an audition for the Rockettes, and Madame Duval and her partner living next door. More important was the fact that Jubil knew how to make biscuits better than KFC ever served. We had them every Saturday morning along with mimosas."

"So a Black man saved your life?"

Roxy headed toward the kitchen. "She did. I only wish I could have saved hers."

Chapter 7

Steve's Date with Death: T-Minus 47:11:08 and Counting

FOR THE FIRST time, Steve saw Roxy's relentlessly annoyingly sunny smile falter. "Should I ask what happened?"

Roxy shook her head. "A story for another day. We were talking about my near brushes with and narrow escapes from death."

Steve picked up his empty glass and followed Roxy into the kitchen. Her house, like his, was older, but somebody had gutted and updated the kitchen. Judging from the shiny white countertops with turquoise glass speckles and the turquoise and yellow mosaic backsplash, that somebody had probably been Roxy.

"Anything I can do to help?" he asked.

She pasted a smile on her face and made a shooing motion at him. "Just sit there at the bar while I get everything together for dinner."

Steve heaved himself into one of the tall chairs and leaned his elbow on the counter between him and the working area of the kitchen. Roxy flitted from cabinet to drawer to sink to stove in a sort of ballet, humming along to the music she'd turned on as a low background sound. He liked watching her move, especially when she bent over to get something out of the crisper in the bottom of the fridge, exposing those long creamy legs and a surprisingly taut butt for a woman her age.

"So," he said, more to distract himself from the unexpected twitch in his nether region than because of a real interest.

That was a lie.

The woman was a chatterbox, and half of what she said probably wasn't true, but her stories kept him from thinking about the way his own story was soon to end. "You take a gamble on death by wandering into Harlem more than once?"

"Only when Jubil was doing her thing in one of the clubs there and only in the company of her or one of our husky male friends." She paused, spatula in hand, as the mouth-watering scent of the sausage cooking on the stove filled the room. "Of course, as luck would have it, not a one of them was with me on the subway the day a couple of teenage gangbanger wannabes decided a car full of innocent citizens would be easy pickings."

"Got yourself mugged, did you? I hear it happens sooner or later to everyone in New York."

"I got warned early on not to wear jewelry or a purse of any kind in public. But yeah, I had my wallet snatched once. After that I carried a mugger's wallet. It had an expired credit card and fifty bucks in pretty good-looking counterfeit bills. I kept my real cash in one of those plastic tampon cases, an extra twenty in my shoe, and my real credit card, metro card, and keys in my bra. But this time on the subway..." Roxy paused and grabbed a jar from the fridge.

Steve could have sworn she deliberately went after items on the bottom shelf just to have the chance to wiggle her ass at him.

"I had an audition that day," Roxy said. "A cattle call for a Broadway show, but I hadn't had that naive Midwest shine knocked off me yet and had high hopes. I'd gotten up early and spent forever getting my hair and makeup just right. I pulled on a brand-new pair of stockings and dithered forever over what to wear. And of course, as a result, I was running late. I hadn't even noticed the weather until I was halfway to the subway station. The sky was overcast, but I thought I could make it."

Steve smiled wryly. "I assume you didn't? Raincoat? Umbrella?"

"Neither. And yeah, the skies opened and damned near drowned me. Which really didn't matter, because a damned taxi drove by half a block later and soaked me in filthy gutter water."

Roxy blew out a breath and shook her head. "And then I broke the heel on my shoe and toppled headlong down the steps to the station. By the time I got on the train, I was the sorriest, most beat-up woman in a ten-mile radius. Looked like I'd gone a couple of rounds with Ali. Or ticked off my pimp. And I was pissed off. I mean steaming, raging, red-hot pissed off. That hulking green superhero level of pissed off. Lasers-shooting-out-my-eyes pissed off."

Steve's wide grin actually made his cheeks hurt. "Whooee! Never fuck with a pissed-off redhead!"

"At that time I was blond. Sort of. Anyway, there I was, my hair hanging in dank strings around my face and my mascara making black inroads on my cheap foundation. One eye was beginning to puff up and turn purple, and I'd split my lip open. I had one broken shoe, and I'd ripped the shit out of my brand-new expensive stockings and had blood running down my leg from cutting my knee open. The palms of my hands weren't in much better shape."

She drew in another deep breath and blew it out between pursed lips. "And that's when the dudes with the guns showed up."

Steve drew back and let out a whistle. "Dudes? Plural? Roxy, you aren't going to tell me—"

"I was having a really fucking-bad day, Steve. That audition was going to be my ticket to the big time. Then these assholes hopped on at one of the stations and started waving their guns around, ordering all the passengers to the back of the car and yelling at everybody to empty their pockets and dump out their purses."

Roxy glanced over at him. "I had exactly enough in my pocket to get a bus ticket home after the audition. My metro card was expired, and I'd hopped the turnstile to get on. Not even enough extra change to buy a Coke or candy bar. Did I mention I'd skipped breakfast so I wouldn't look too fat?"

Steve studied her for a long moment, incensed on her behalf. "Did you let any of them live? How long did they spend in the hospital? How much time did you have to do?"

"Fair enough questions, and if I'd been on my way to fencing lessons, the answer would be zero survivors. Even a just-out-of-school-wet-behind-the-ears public defense lawyer would have gotten me off with no time. I was young and stupid, and once again the good Lord was watching out for me. Or maybe he'd given up on me and decided I was mean enough to manage a couple of dickwads all on my own."

She heaved a sigh. "Anyway, I was done. Just done with the day and done with being pissed on and done with putting up with all of it. All the rest of those poor folks were crowding into the back of the car. I stood up and shouted, 'I have had more than enough of this bullshit, and the last fucking thing I need today is another motherfucking asshole trying to fuck up my fucking day!' Right then the train came to a stop. So I stalked right between them and shoved one of them into the door, which happened to open at just that second. He fell out onto the platform, and wouldn't you know it, I fell over the son of a bitch on my way out! On my good knee, the one I hadn't already scraped the shit out of! Both of us were struggling to stand up, although to any observant person, it might have looked like that time Mike Tyson took out Frazier in thirty seconds. Did I mention I was really, really pissed off?"

Steve was slapping the counter and breathless with the kind of silent laughter that made a guy's abs hurt.

Roxy emptied the contents of a pan into a bowl, then said, "The train took off with his buddy still on board. The last I saw of the guy was him standing open-mouthed and gawking at us through the window as a horde of irate passengers lunged at him."

Steve released his laughter in a whooshing gust, clutching

his chest until he could get himself under control. He grabbed a huge white handkerchief from his pocket, pulled off his glasses, and mopped up the tears streaming down his face. "Did the dude you flattened run off? Get arrested?"

"Well, I was trying to get myself untangled at the same time I was trying to figure out how to kill him, when somebody grabbed me from behind and yanked me off him."

"Somebody with a death wish?"

"Close"—Roxy shrugged—"but no, it was one of the Guardian Angels."

Steve frowned, then tapped the side of his head when recognition dawned. "Not the kind with wings," he said. "I remember reading about those guys."

"Right. The Guardian Angels were—and still are—a self-appointed citizen crime prevention group that patrols the subways. They wear red jackets and red berets. So one of them got hold of me and another got hold of the other guy. The mugger was a pudgy, pockmarked teenager who kept shouting about me being crazy and begging the Guardians to arrest him and protect him and then crying for his mama and swearing they were just joking around and the gun wasn't loaded."

"How much time did he get?"

"Not a clue. There were enough other witnesses on the train. I didn't stick around."

"Did you get that Broadway role?"

Roxy snorted. "Hell no. They wouldn't even let me sign up for the audition looking the way I did."

"Did you learn to carry an umbrella after that?"

"No, but I learned to carry a switchblade."

"A gun would be better."

Roxy shook her head. "Guns can get you killed, Steve. Give me something sharp and pointy every time."

"Ever had to use it?"

Roxy looked him over from head to foot and winked. "Not yet."

Chapter 8

Steve's Date with Death: T-Minus 46:51:38 and Counting

ROXY'S GRIN FADED. "Then again, the world is getting scarier. Young people thinking they have no future and nothing left to lose. These days they'd just go ahead and shoot me. Or maybe it's just me getting older."

"Smarter," Steve said. He shook his head. "Damn fool kids. I dealt with them more than enough times in every job I had. Being a drill sergeant gave me the chance to knock some sense into a few of them. At least enough so they didn't get their asses shot off ten seconds after they got off the plane in some hellhole. Tough, macho kids who thought they were hot snot on a silver platter and had to be taught they were nothing but cold boogers on a paper plate. Some learned. Too damned many didn't."

He sighed. "Early on, while Vietnam was still going on, you either learned fast or your mama got a visit from a bereavement officer and your body in a box." He picked up his glass but found it empty. He shook his head when Roxy offered another. His tongue was already getting ahead of his brain, but the story poured out of him like a runaway train he had no power to stop.

Maybe it was the booze. Maybe it was knowing that in three days—almost two now—every story locked in his head would stay locked away and unheard forever.

Damn. Roxy had made him laugh more than he had in

years, and all he had to offer in exchange was stories of punk kids coming to bad ends. But they were his stories. Maybe it was time to tell them to somebody.

A stranger, like this woman who'd wandered into his life just that morning, might be the perfect person. No baggage, no entanglements. Next week or the week after, maybe she'd tell Curtis these stories.

Maybe she wouldn't.

Maybe he should get up right now and take his sorry ass home and leave this nice lady to her rainbows and flowers and safe little life.

She turned off the stove, put something in the oven, then propped her elbow on the counter, chin resting in her hand. Ready to listen to whatever he had to say.

Stupid woman. His stories weren't for folks like her. What could a nice white lady in her nice white world possibly know about the ugly side of life?

The side he'd been mired in for most of his life.

But something about Roxy kept his ass right where it was. Maybe it was the graceful way she moved from sink to stove to fridge that mesmerized him. Maybe it was the lights and color and music in the cheerful world she'd created, so unlike his own.

He looked at the world through a telescope, focused on what was right in front of him, peering into the empty black void of space.

Roxy, apparently, viewed the world through a kaleidoscope, like a child constantly delighted by the world's shifting shapes and colors.

When was the last time he'd laughed like he had tonight?

But all the *maybes* and *might haves* and *could have beens* in the world weren't going to change a damned thing. Even this pretty redhead couldn't save him from the dark path he'd already chosen.

Tonight, the path had led to Roxy's door. Which was where he should be headed right now if he had one iota of compassion left in him.

"I'll bet you saved a lot of lives in your career, Steve."

How did she manage to survive with so much shiny optimism in such a shitty world? He shook his head. "I'm no fucking hero. Twenty years in the army smacking the crap out of pissant knuckleheads. More time working highway patrol. There would be days I'd pull over a carful of kids for a busted taillight and get a face full of Mary Jane when they rolled down the windows, and they'd be laughing their heads off while I called their mamas to come get 'em off the road. That was a good day. An easy day.

"On an average day," he said, "the kid would be mouthy, disrespectful, downright belligerent, and after they got a bad case of road rash from being face-planted on the highway shoulder, I'd call their daddies to come bail 'em out of jail."

Steve swiped a meaty hand over his face and wished he'd taken Roxy up on that offer of another beer.

"And on bad days? Were there a lot of them?"

"Too many, Rox. On bad days I'd call the squads and the tow trucks and kick the empty forty-ouncers that rolled out of the cars into the ditches. Then I'd call the guys with the hazmat suits to get the blood off the roads. And then I'd call their families—I usually tried to get the dad first, because when I got their mamas first, it would take weeks to get that soul-deep wounded animal howling out of my head."

Steve clamped his jaws tight, then deliberately lowered his shoulders and twisted his head from side to side to ease the muscles that threatened to lock up on him.

He changed his mind and held out his empty glass, which Roxy promptly filled with another beer. Steve took a long swallow, then reached into the darkest memory hole and opened the door to the howling creature locked inside.

"Cops don't come home with amusing little anecdotes from work," he said. "If they do, they're lying to you. At least the cops that still have souls. Some are power-hungry psychopaths from the get-go. Some start out actually wanting to do good, but it doesn't take long to smash those rose-colored glasses into dust. Some get out in time. Some eat their gun."

Kinda like what he was planning on doing three days from now.

"You don't look like a psychopath to me. Prickly, yeah, but not whacko. At least I hope that's true."

Roxy, bless her heart, trying to lighten up the mood, but the creature inside was determined to have its say.

"Twenty years in the army knocked the Pollyanna right outta me," Steve said. "But I wasn't psycho. I needed a job and I'd made a promise of sorts. I didn't have a God complex, but I was still young enough to think I might be able to make a difference. To save one or two folks from shitting their life away."

Steve shook his head. The howling was louder now, the old memory refusing to go back into its cage. "It was one punk kid that got me to quit the force," he said.

Roxy moved around the kitchen, gathering ingredients while he talked, then she settled across the counter from him, stirring and mixing. She must have been planning on feeding an army.

Or one very large, very hungry man. When was the last time he'd actually sat at a table and eaten a real meal?

He wrapped his hands around his glass, cold against the palms that had grown hot.

"I'd had a good job offer from the DEA. I'd worked with them on a couple of drug trafficking cases, cartels bringing their crap into Florida and driving the shit up the coast to DC and New York. I was thinking about taking the offer when I got called to help at an accident scene. A seventeen-year-old hotshot in a stolen Mustang had cut off a semi hauling a load of grapefruit. The truck jackknifed and hit one of those little Volkswagen Beetles, throwing it into the compact sedan of a nice little family—Mom, Dad, two kids, and another on the way."

Roxy stopped her mixing and reached out to him. "Steve,

stop. It's in the past. You don't have to go back there."

But the past had gripped Steve by the throat. He'd never talked to anybody about this before, blowing off the shrink his commander had threatened to force him into seeing. He'd quit the patrol instead.

"The ambulances hadn't gotten there yet. One officer, on the force for all of maybe three months, was in the middle of the road trying to halt traffic like an ant trying to stop a tsunami. His partner was on his knees on the shoulder, throwing up everything he'd eaten for the last three days. I was the senior man there. My recruit—my rookie trainee—was with me, a guy named Tommy Jackson. Good guy. Levelheaded. About to get the worst introduction to the patrol a man could ever have."

Steve bit his tongue, but now that the memory had surfaced after all these years, it bubbled up in his throat and knocked on the back of his teeth, determined to be told. Roxy didn't deserve this, but she was the one who'd insisted, demanded, he come for dinner. He'd accept her dinner and pay her back with his nightmares.

If he was capable of feeling anything other than rage and despair at what the doctor was probably going to tell him at his next appointment, he'd feel guilt for dumping this shit on such a nice lady. But he no longer had the time or capacity for guilt.

"The truck was laying on its side, the engine still running. I climbed up and leaned in to get to the key and turn it off so we didn't add a firebomb to the mess we already had, although at that point, a fire might have actually made the situation better. There was only the lower half of him in the cab."

Roxy tightened her lips, moved to the stove, and pulled whatever she was baking out of the oven, but she didn't say a word. She didn't try to stop him either.

"I realized that what I'd thought were chunks of meat I'd stepped through as I got to the truck were not from whatever he was hauling. But that wasn't the worst. At least he was dead. I turned off the engine. I wish I hadn't. The noise had drowned out the screaming."

"Steve—"

"The woman in the Beetle was a goner. The engine's in the back of those, you know? Twenty-two-year-old college student on her way to pick up her graduation gown. They literally had to pick parts of her out of the Beetle's engine. But like the trucker, she wasn't going to suffer, even if her family was in for hell."

Steve held out the glass he'd emptied. Roxy handed him another beer without saying a word.

"The family in the sedan wasn't so lucky. The dad had broken both hands and a leg and bent the steering wheel in half. His wife—the car had seat belts but no airbags back then, and because she was so pregnant, the belt had been too uncomfortable for her to fasten. That's what her husband told us later. She went through the windshield. She survived, and miraculously, so did the baby, but her face was never gonna be the same and she had traumatic brain injury. I heard later she learned to talk a little and mostly feed herself, but whoever she was before was wiped out in eight seconds that day."

"And their kids? The two you said were in that car?" Roxy's fingers tightened on the counter. Her face had grown paler under her tan, but she stood tall. Strong. A woman who'd listen to the worst, then help carry that burden.

"They had seat belts and car seats, but they don't help in a crash like that. So there was this dad, half a dozen broken bones, his pretty young wife permanently disfigured and brain damaged, his two kids dead, and a few hours later, a newborn son."

Who was this woman and where had she come from at just that particular time? Had God sent some kind of final confessor to him?

Nah. Steve had never been much on God's good side.

Steve raised his beer glass, then set it down again without drinking. He'd already had too much. No amount of booze would wipe away the memory. "Some of the guys on the force still check in on him. He and Tommy got pretty close. The wife died eventually and the man remarried. The son's in college now. He wanted to be a cop, but the guys on the force talked him out of it. He's going into forensics instead."

"And the kid that caused all that? The one in the Mustang?"

"Not a scratch on the motherfucker. Cuban kid, no license, tripping balls on angel dust. Every person there from the rookie patrol officer to the commanding fire chief wanted to gut the guy, rip off his testicles, and open his asshole with the jaws of life, but I wouldn't let them. I seen some shit, but never anything like that. So I cuffed him and walked him all over that scene. Made him climb up in that cab and look at that trucker with his top half missing. Made him watch them picking that college girl's intestines out of that engine. Made him stand there and listen to that nice couple who couldn't stop screaming. And then he made a mistake." He held up a couple of fingers. "Two mistakes."

Roxy loosened her grip on the counter and squeezed Steve's arm.

"He said, 'Stupid assholes shoulda got outta my way.' Then he tried to run."

The taut muscles in Steve's body suddenly relaxed their iron grip. "He spent two weeks in traction and not even his mama would've been able to pick him out of a lineup. They don't do much in the way of plastic surgery when a guy gets multiple life sentences, but I heard tell his cellmate didn't mind at all that the boy didn't have many teeth anymore."

Roxy tightened her grip. She didn't let go. Didn't run screaming from his nightmares. Just held him.

The demons still bit hard, but now he had a shield between him and them. An unexpected anchor that for the first time in eons kept him from being swept away by the roaring tidal wave of his memories. Rock-solid Roxy. How the hell had he ended up in just this place with just this woman on just this night?

"Kids, Roxy. A couple of little ones who never had a chance. One hovering on the edge of being an adult with her whole glorious life ahead of her. And one drugged-up kid who thought he owned the road."

Steve leaned back in the tall chair. He rolled his neck again. He hated that story. Hadn't thought of it in years, but something in him loosened, as if spilling the poison out had eased the pressure on a deeply hidden, rusted-shut valve.

"One good thing came out of it all, and I try to hang on to that. That sometimes buried under the deepest pile of shit is a nugget of gold. Tommy Jackson, that rookie of mine? He met his future wife that night. Danni's a pediatrician and was working the ER when they brought in the kids. Couldn't save them, but a year later, I stood by Tommy when Danni walked down the aisle. Couple of grown kids of their own now."

At least something had gone right for somebody on one of the worst days of his life. Not for him, but if not for that accident, maybe Tommy would have ended up as fucked up as he was instead of a happy family man.

But the gold nuggets in the piles of shit were few and far between. Mostly the hard nuggets were just more shit.

He set his glass on the counter and patted Roxy's hand. "Sorry about that. Shouldn't have been telling such a gross story while you're cooking something that smells so delicious. Hope I haven't put you off dinner."

She squeezed his hand, then stood up. "Lots of others have sat right where you are and told me some pretty hair-raising tales. Jubil used to say that God gave me broad shoulders because he knew I was going to need them. You just keep right on talking if that's what you want to do."

Whether she wanted the role or not, Roxy was apparently going to become the final receptacle for all his untold stories.

He could only hope she didn't buckle under the weight of them. That she didn't someday find herself planning her own death just to finally silence the goddamned demons.

CHAPTER 9
Steve's Date with Death: T-Minus 46:29:36 and Counting

"I TRY NOT to blame parents when kids turn out fucked up," Roxy said. "I mean, Jeffrey Dahmer's mother was a compassionate woman who worked with folks who had HIV and AIDS, and had no idea she'd raised a murdering monster. Then again, Ted Bundy's whole family was pretty messed up. That kid you were talking about? Who knows why some kids rise above really horrible pasts and other kids who have everything break in the slightest breeze? You see a bunch of cute little kids playing in the park and you never know which one is going to be the next Bill Gates or Oprah and which one is just a few years away from shooting up their school."

"Maybe more kids would benefit from getting The Talk like Black kids do." Steve shrugged. "I dunno. Maybe Hispanic kids are like white kids; they don't get those lessons. No matter where I worked, the world was full of dumbass kids who'd apparently never gotten The Talk."

"I've heard about 'the talk,'" Roxy said, putting the words in air quotes, "but have no clue what that really means."

"That's because nice white girls like you don't need it. It's not right and it's not fair, but the world is the way it is. One way for white folks and a whole 'nother way for us folks with an abundance of melanin. That's what The Talk's about."

Steve rolled his shoulders and sighed deeply. "The need to understand that difference starts out when you're a little kid. Smart, careful parents and aunties and uncles start stripping the innocence out of children before they've even had a chance to lose all their baby teeth. Mama started giving me The Talk when I was getting ready to go off to school. 'Stand up straight and look folks in the eye when you speak to 'em. Don't daydream. Pay attention and always, always say yes ma'am and no, sir. Most especially if it's a white person speaking to you.'"

"Lots of white parents teach their kids that too," Roxy said. "Basic respect. Although up north, not the ma'am and sir stuff so much."

"Kids in the South are all raised to use *ma'am* and *sir*," Steve said, "but a Black kid not saying that could have a whole other set of consequences than if a white kid forgot to say it. The difference between bein' disrespectful and bein' uppity."

Steve drummed his fingers on the counter. When he talked about Mississippi, about his childhood, his accent tended to drift back into the drawl he'd worked damned hard to erase. He pressed his lips together as he grappled with the onslaught of memories. Finally he released his breath in a long sigh.

Roxy, apparently guessing that whatever fever had built up in Steve had broken, patted his arm and turned back to rattling dishes and pans for whatever it was she was putting together for dinner, a pleasant, homey sound that went a long way toward drowning out his monsters. But she kept one eye on him, listening.

It had been a long time since he'd talked to anyone like this. Too long. Who knew he'd spend his last days spilling his guts to a white chick from the middle of Ohio?

"So, when I got to be what they call a *preteen* these days," Steve said, "that's when Daddy sat me down for the real talk. He reminded me I was growing and looking to take after his side of the family. Which meant I was going to get pretty big. And out there, beyond the borders of our own front yard, there were going to be plenty of people who equated tall young Black man with potentially violent thug."

Roxy flinched at the words, but kept working, never talking her eyes off him.

"Daddy pressed on me hard, making damned sure I understood that even the tiniest mistake—an eyebrow quirked wrong, a laugh at the wrong time, a single second of looking like I might lose my temper—and my mama would be getting a police officer and the pastor knocking on the door in the middle of the night to make funeral arrangements."

His words tumbled out faster now, his daddy's voice in his ear as if it were yesterday instead of nearly seventy years ago. "Or I'd end up on the wrong side of a cell door and not even God himself would be able to get me out. If I was ever pulled over by a cop, I had to smile, be honest and friendly, and above all keep both hands in view every single second. He reminded me that I *would* be pulled over, even if I never went a single mile over the speed limit and obeyed every rule to the letter. That it's called DWB—Driving While Black—and that how I acted during those moments could determine my whole life."

Roxy shook her head, her lips drawn tight. "I've heard of that. Had it happen to friends of mine, even while I was with them. It's not right, Steve. It's not fair."

"Spoken from a place of privilege. Everyone knows it's not right, but nothing ever happens to change it. Not really. Folks marched. Lobbied. Protested. Fought like hell to get representation voted into office. Fucking died for it. But you're never gonna change some people's hearts. I'm a grizzled old man now, but if I'm shopping at the local Target, you can bet a clerk's going to be following me around. SWB—Shopping While Black. It's just a fact of life. World looks a whole lot different to man named John than it does to one named DeShawn."

Steve couldn't help the fringe of bitterness that decorated the edge of his chuckle. "At least nowadays I'm not likely to be hauled out and strung up for having dinner with a pretty white woman. Not around here, at least. Back home in Mississippi?

Yeah, that might still happen. Especially if we were both fifty years younger." He waggled an eyebrow at her, but for the moment, his heart wasn't in it. Even his dick, which always had a mind of its own, didn't believe him.

"Back in Darby Glen," Roxy said, "even today there'd probably be raised eyebrows and nasty comments if I invited you to my house for dinner. I'll never really know what it's like to walk in your shoes, Steve, but being a female isn't much easier. The only talk I ever got from my mother was 'nice girls don't'. I didn't even know enough to know what *it* was they didn't do, and Mother sure as hell wasn't going to tell me. For girls of my era, *the talk* was a grainy movie in the fifth grade and an extremely embarrassed school nurse waving around thick cotton pads and sanitary belts and trying to explain to us about 'blossoming into womanhood.' I came out as mystified as I went in, but with an added layer of vague humiliation and fear. It was girls only, although the boys had had the same class a week earlier and had spent a week snickering and whispering and pointing and swaggering and we didn't even know why. When we came back into the classroom and the boys knew that we now knew, the snickers turned into outright hoots."

Roxy slammed a drawer harder than was necessary. "That little movie, ancient by the time I saw it, never taught me how to walk through the world as a confident, self-possessed woman. It taught me to be ashamed and fearful. I was out of high school and living in New York before the pill was legalized for single women. Before that, all we were taught about birth control was a running joke that the only pill a girl needed while on a date was an aspirin kept clasped firmly between her knees. But we got taught some of the same bullcrap you did. Smile at boys so they don't get angry with you. Soothe them so they don't get mean. Be respectful and subservient so they don't get their egos injured. Gloria Steinem was out there shouting about women's liberation, but back in Darby Glen, Ohio, the names she got called are not repeatable in polite society."

Roxy stared out the kitchen window a long moment before

turning back to Steve. "So yeah, Steve, my skin gives me some privilege in this world that you might not have. But my chromosomes mean I don't have as much as you think. Your sister had the worst of both worlds."

Natalie. Speaking of her reminded Steve of his plans. Three days until the anniversary of her death. Three days until he'd join her.

"So much shit in this world," he said, shaking his head. "Been going on forever. Feels like it always will be. Sometimes I don't see the point of fighting anymore."

Even in this colorful kitchen, in the company of a beautiful woman, shadows lurked, waiting for him. They wouldn't have to wait much longer.

"We're all just fumbling our way through life, doing our crummy best," Roxy said. "I'll bet you helped a lot more people than you think. I have no doubt that somewhere out there, every night some mother or father gets down on their knees and sends prayers of thanks in your direction for getting their wayward rapscallion home safe to them."

"I tried to save them, Roxy, but it was never enough. Hell, even my own nephew refuses to listen to his wise old unk. Gonna get his head blown off in some foreign sandbox someday 'cause Curtis never listened to The Talk and never learned respect. It's a wonder his drill sergeant let him get through boot camp alive much less sent him on deployment. But hey, a body is a body as far as the army's concerned. And there's not a damn thing me or my sister could say to even slow him down."

Steve stood and stretched, then sank back into his chair. "I've spent most of my life dragging some idiot's ass out of a fire. I used to wonder if it was all worth it. Now I know it wasn't. Folks are going to go right on getting into trouble and killing each other and not listening. They're not worth my time or energy. Most never were. So I retired and do independent consulting now and then, but only for the money. Not because I care. I don't. You should know that upfront. I'm not anybody's keeper, Roxy. In any sense of the word."

He looked up to find her gaze on him. Not judging him so much as weighing his words. Actually listening and considering them. He needed to keep her at arm's length. It would do no good for this long-legged beauty to get too close. His balance sheet in heaven was already too full of black marks. No need to add one more hurt person on his way out the door.

But he was pretty sure he couldn't help himself.

"What about you, Roxy? I know we just met, but you seem like a natural-born bleeding-heart caretaker."

He held up a hand to stave off her words. "Not saying you're a pushover. Not with that many swords hanging on the wall. And yeah, you've been in a scrape or two, but as far as I can tell, getting knocked down a time or two hasn't knocked the glitter off your rainbow-colored glasses."

Roxy fixed her blue-eyed gaze on him.

"I've always believed that life is a choose-your-own adventure book, Steve. It's not the same for everyone, but every single day we're on the right side of the grass, we get to choose. Too many folks don't think they have a choice, but they do. Maybe they lack enough education or they didn't have anybody in their crappy childhoods to show them what the world has to offer. They never learned to dream big enough because they didn't know dreaming big was even possible. Or maybe they're dealing with terrible diseases or horrible families clawing them down into the muck. Something's holding them back."

She resumed her stirring. "So occasionally, when I see a chance, I try to lend a hand if I can, but I'm more cynical than you might believe. I'm not a sucker. And I don't risk my life for anyone."

"And yet here you are with a total stranger in your kitchen, a grouchy, bitter old man, and you're fixing him supper. A man you have no reason to like or trust."

Roxy took a moment to push her hair back off her forehead, her blue eyes leveled on his brown ones, like she could see into his soul.

Steve wasn't sure he liked the feeling.

"Yes," Roxy said. "There are plenty of times people have disappointed me. But now and then I find someone with that spark—that *what-if* glimmer in their eyes. A look that says 'I may be trapped right now and lost as hell, but as soon as I figure out what's what, then look out world!' All I do is encourage them to consider a road they may not have thought of taking. Dust them off a little and get them pointed in a new direction."

Roxy giggled then, a real giggle. "I guess that makes me like Glinda the Good Witch setting Dorothy on the Yellow Brick Road and off on her grand adventure."

"Glinda sent Dorothy—a child—off to the local mob boss, a swindler who blackmailed that poor little girl into being his hired assassin to take out the Wicked Witch, a woman who only wanted her family heirloom shoes back from the bitch who murdered her sister. Could probably get Glinda on charges of child endangerment, animal cruelty, trafficking—"

Roxy laughed outright at that, crossed her arms and leaned back against the counter.

Steve's trouser mouse woke up and noticed the way the movement lifted her breasts under the V-neck of her top.

"You're a real hard case, aren't you, Steve?"

"I've had all the adventure I can stand, Roxy. I've seen and done crap nobody should see or do. I've spent my whole life dealing with the worst scum on earth, shoveling up shit, dishing shit out, and watching the aftermath of ruined lives. And it just keeps coming and it never gets better. I don't want any more adventures. I just want peace now."

Roxy straightened. "I can't give you peace, but I can give you another beer and a decent dinner, some good music, and time sitting in a hot tub listening to the sounds of a hot tropical night."

She held up a hand, forestalling his objection. "I promise it won't be remotely like those jungle nights in Vietnam." She moved around the counter toward him.

"I can't guarantee there won't be shooting," she said, "because there are assholes everywhere who think a big gun

73

makes up for a small dick. But this is a pretty quiet neighborhood, even though the favorite game on the local neighborhood chat board is 'was that fireworks or gunshots?' because it being a Wednesday is plenty enough reason to shoot off fireworks or a couple of rounds into the palm trees."

She offered another smile. "And who knows what unexpected adventure can happen next?" She crooked her arm companionably around Steve's. "Come on. I need you to help me open the jar of sauerkraut."

He resisted her tug.

"Steve, when kids are young, they resist doing what they're asked because they're thinking you're not the boss of me—you can't make me. Most folks eventually grow out of that If they don't, they become crotchety old folks and make everyone around them miserable. Instead of thinking like a grumpy, overgrown teenager, change the dialogue. Instead of thinking nobody's going to *make* me drink beer, eat a delicious dinner, and sit in a hot tub with a naked woman, think I *get* to do all that fun stuff."

She waggled her eyebrows at him, much more successfully than his own waggle had been minutes before.

Steve drew in a deep breath, then blew it out. "Woman, it doesn't matter how old I am, no one can make me eat sauerkraut."

"Betcha I can."

CHAPTER 10

Sexy Firefighters Calendar Word of the Day:
Cogitation: [koj-i-tey-shuhn] **Noun**. the action of thinking deeply about something; contemplation. A thought; design or plan.

THEIR DINNER FINISHED, Roxy left Steve sitting alone on the lanai. She'd turned on the hot tub and laid out fluffy towels. "It's your choice, Steve," she said, "whether or not you're in the mood for some nice warm bubbles. I'm going to go do a quick cleanup in the kitchen, and no, I don't need any help," she said, waving him back into his chair when he moved to rise.

She stood at the sink in her favorite thinking stance, left foot propped against her right knee, a pose that had long ago earned her the flamingo nickname from Jubil.

Would Steve take her up on her earlier flip comment about clothing being optional in her hot tub? Getting naked with a stranger—or even semi-clothed—was hard enough at the best of times. At their ages? Well, some things were better left to the blessed covering of darkness. If he was going to take her up on her invitation, he probably wouldn't want to stand there and strip down in front of her.

Then again, maybe he would.

Years of quick costume changes backstage in front of hordes of strangers had left Roxy with an utter nonchalance about nudity. But getting naked in front of a man she might sort of like?

That was a bad idea. A very bad idea. She should go tell Steve that right now.

But what if she caught him midstrip? God, how embarrassing for both of them.

She invited friends to enjoy the hot tub all the time. Some had bathing suits, some swam in their skivvies, some went commando. It never bothered her what they chose.

Just friends. Just like Steve was just a friend, albeit a very, very new one. No worries, right?

Wrong. It had never been like this. Not like this *at all*. Not with all these freaky undercurrents swirling around and electricity zapping between them and her heart doing that weird zinging thing every time she touched him.

He hadn't carried anything with him tonight, but maybe he had swim trunks on under those neatly pressed khakis.

Roxy shook her head. If the man had ever even owned swim trunks, she'd eat her pretty straw hat. Boxers or briefs? And would he climb into her hot tub in either one?

Probably not. Then he'd have to go home in wet undies. No, if she went back out on the lanai and found him in the hot tub, she would bet the house that every inch of him was as naked as the day he'd come into the world.

Maybe she'd go back out and find him still fully clothed, sipping his beer and contemplating the meaning of life.

Yeah, right.

What the hell was I thinking?

She'd left the choice to him. Maybe so she could avoid making any choices herself. The pan in the sink remained half-washed, the soapy water cooling around her wrists while she stared into the past and into her heart.

She'd spent a lifetime being the fool who rushed in where angels feared to tread. She was older now, but had she gotten any wiser? She'd started the day with nothing more planned than cheering on her best friend at a shuffleboard contest. Now she was contemplating jumping naked into a hot tub with a man she hadn't even known a few hours ago.

And not just any man. A man whose life experiences were a world away from her own. An attractive man, yes. She wasn't stupid enough to deny that he appealed to her. She might be a fool, but she'd tried hard to never lie to herself.

Hadn't she?

She liked his voice. She liked his big body and his laugh when she'd been able to coax it from him.

But he was sick. That much had been evident this morning.

And the man had demons.

Hadn't she paid enough penance yet? Hadn't she seen enough of illness and death?

Why did God always send the most broken ones to her doorstep?

"*Because I trust you to know what to do. How many times were you picked up when you were broken? Karma. Payback. Whatever.*"

That voice. Roxy's heart skipped a beat.

How long had it been since the voice had spoken to her?

"*I talk to you all the time, Roxy. You just don't always listen.*"

Roxy called the voice he or him, but she'd never been sure if it was God or a ghost or a guardian angel, or if it was simply a conjuring of her own misfiring neurons and synapses, but it had always seemed a thing apart from her, something outside herself. She called the voice God for simplicity's sake and because she'd rather not think she'd gone crazy.

She'd first heard the voice clearly when she was fifteen years old. She'd been struggling through the bible study classes that were a big part of teenage social life in Darby Glen. Every night she dutifully sat down in her bedroom and read verses from the battered copy of *Good News for Modern Man* that a friend had loaned her. It contained only the New Testament, because Jesus was all that mattered.

All her friends were joyfully proclaiming the wonders of their newfound faith, their teen years playing out on the cusp of the era of rainbow suspenders and Jesus folk music and hippies and hormones and a generation looking for answers to questions they didn't even know how to ask.

But Roxy just didn't get it. She'd tried. She'd prayed. But she'd never felt whatever Holy Spirit or whatever it was that her friends claimed had zoomed into their lives and possessed their souls and gave them a weird joy that Roxy found off-putting somehow. Then one night, alone in her room, trying once again to unravel the mystical magic of the words—to find the alchemy that would transmogrify a gawky, lost teenager into a saved soul—she'd said, "God, I just don't think this is going to work for me."

And she'd heard hands clapping and a happy voice booming, "*YES! That's right! Not for you, not in this lifetime*," as clear as if the speaker had been sitting right next to her, as joyous as a teacher thrilled that a particularly slow student had *finally* understood the lesson. And she had never felt so much at peace as she did in that moment.

She'd dropped out of bible study, lost a number of friends, and explored alternate religions for a couple of years. She'd never abandoned her own style of belief in God, but she'd given up on Jesus and traditional beliefs thanks to the voice and a particularly corrupt preacher. These days she believed in a power greater than herself, but one that expected her to help herself too.

The voice had spoken to her again off and on through the years, but not often. Usually only in times of great stress or danger. The voice had once warned her seconds before a traffic accident. It hadn't stopped the other car slamming into her, but it had been enough of a warning that she'd taken the hit in her headlights instead of broadside to the driver's seat, where she might have been badly injured or killed.

She owed a debt to life. She'd tried to help. She thought she'd done enough.

And yet there was Steve, sitting on her lanai, another broken, sick person who'd appeared out of nowhere, and the damned voice was once again demanding she do something about it.

Well, not demanding. The voice didn't do that. But it gave suggestions and nudges and outright pushes that were damned hard to ignore.

She just couldn't do this. Not again. No matter how appealing the man was. Could she even begin to fix whatever was broken in him?

"You're good with the broken ones because of your own broken places. Kintsugi. Remember."

Haven't I already dealt with enough broken people?

"It means you have the experience to take on this one too."

But what about my own broken places? Tomorrow is—

"Kintsugi."

She'd taken a pottery class as an elective in college with no idea what it entailed. Just an easy class so she could get the credit. She'd been stunned when presented with a pile of potsherds and told the goal was to reassemble them but in a very special way.

Kintsugi, Roxy learned, is the Japanese art of using gold to make broken things beautiful again, to return the object to usefulness. It was about not hiding the broken places, but using the gold to embellish them, celebrating the cracks and holes as scars of something overcome. It was about using the broken places to make the item stronger than it had been before.

The art represented healing. Resilience. It was meant to be done with an attitude of love and care, of doing no further harm, of honoring and protecting and cherishing the broken one.

"It's also about recognizing that no one and nothing is perfect, Roxy. It's about—"

But Roxy had heard enough.

She had a choice. Life was all about choices. And taking chances. And leaping before looking and treading paths others might not have dared. And her life was once again spinning out of control and it had been a long time since that happened and maybe she was overdue for a good shaking up.

Maybe Steve was sitting on her lanai fully clothed, ready to go home. And if that was what he chose, fine. She'd invite him back for dinner again in a few days and see what happened.

And if he was naked in her hot tub, that was fine too.

It wouldn't be the first time she let fate decide what would happen next.

But she knew what choice she was hoping Steve had made.

She finished washing the pan, dried her hands, picked up the tray filled with after-dinner delights, then headed out to the lanai to see if Steve had made the same choice she had.

CHAPTER 11

Steve's Date with Death: T-Minus 44:09:12 and Counting

STEVE LEANED BACK in the steaming, bubbling water and sighed. Jets of water blasted against muscles he hadn't known were hurting until the pain had eased away. Beneath the water, lights shifted in a slow, mesmerizing loop: pink to purple to blue to green. Pink to purple to blue to green. The effect was hypnotic.

Well, the lights, the heat, the bubbles, the satisfyingly full stomach, the relaxed muscles, the way Roxy's naked boobs floated tantalizingly just under the bubbles, the way her long, flexible foot rubbed against the outside of his thigh—

"Ready for another limoncello?" she said.

Steve's glass—his second—sat empty on the edge of the hot tub. He shook his head. "You make this yourself?"

Roxy nodded, then gestured to a tree out in the darkness beyond the screened lanai, lit by little solar-powered lights that wove in and out among shrubbery and overflowing flower beds and along a path that led to a long, narrow building toward the back of her property. "I grow my own Meyer lemons."

"It's a great garden, Roxy." Steve reached beneath the water and rubbed Roxy's searching foot. Was he up to accepting what she appeared to be offering? He had a couple of condoms and two of those little blue pills in the pocket of his trousers, now neatly folded on one of her patio chairs.

He hadn't planned to accept her dinner invitation. Hadn't meant to do anything more than knock on her door and tell her he wouldn't stay for dinner.

And yet some part of his lizard brain had put condoms in his wallet and a blue pill in his pocket.

Should he take one? When? Damn, when had fucking a woman gotten so complicated?

Sounds of Bill Evans playing jazz piano drifted from decent-quality speakers on the lanai. After he'd gotten that stinky jar of sauerkraut open for her, she'd prepared the rest of the dinner to the pounding rhythms of Jethro Tull. She'd switched to jazz when they sat down to eat. The light evening breeze mixed the sonorous sound of finely tuned wind chimes in with the music.

Of course the wind chimes that had been driving him crazy belonged to Roxy. Three sets. She'd pointed them out, each precisely tuned to a specific key or chord, on the earlier tour of her garden.

"Did you know wind chimes are used as memorials to those we loved who passed away?" she'd asked. "The sound encourages us to pause and remember and know that they're always near. One set is for my dogs, one for old friends, and one for someone I loved."

And just like that, Roxy was talking death again.

I get it, God. I'm dying. But I'm going out my own way on my own schedule, so fuck right off.

Steve sank further into the bubbles, letting the roar of the tub's jets drown out the chimes. "Thanks for dinner, Roxy. You're a good cook. But I never want to hear about my *stinky chitlins* again. I'm pretty sure sauerkraut is white people's revenge for chitlins."

Roxy laughed. The laugh that reawakened long-forgotten feelings, sending messages along nerve endings he'd thought had been short-circuited years ago and arousing long-dormant body parts. Was her foot roaming his thigh close enough to discover the effect she was having on him?

"Sauerkraut sausage balls are a great appetizer," she said. "Not good for you, but I think the grilled tilapia and salad made up for it."

"I don't suppose you know how to make mac and cheese." Steve had a powerful craving for it just one more time before he died. If heaven were real, St. Peter would greet him at the pearly gates with a gigantic bowl of Auntie Althea's potato salad and a pan of his mama's mac and cheese.

"Sure I do," Roxy said. "You open a one of those blue boxes—"

Steve snorted and Roxy laughed.

"Actually," she said, "you start with a nice roux on the stove and end with a steamy pan of dark yellow creamy goodness coming out of the oven. It has to be baked or it's not real macaroni and cheese."

Steve blew out a long, satisfied sigh. "And when you dish it up, there's all those long strands of cheese—"

"Of course, I put fried Spam in mine. It's how I grew up eating it."

"Woman, you are speaking sacrilege. Outright blasphemy. Must be a white people thing."

"I think it's a Midwestern thing. Or maybe just my family. Mom learned to cook during World War II, when meat was rationed. Spam wasn't, so it substituted for ham or bacon in a lot of stuff we ate. Heck, I grew up thinking a fancy hors d'oeuvre was a saltine cracker with mayo, a little square of cheese, and a piece of Spam right out of the can."

"Ew! That's gross."

"You eat hog intestines, so don't talk to me about gross food."

"I'll make you a deal. You don't put Spam in my mac and cheese and I won't make you eat chitlins."

He held out his hand. Roxy didn't hesitate to shake it.

The connection lasted a moment longer than necessary. Deep inside, something shifted in Steve, the way the movement of a tiny pebble precipitates an avalanche.

When she released his hand, he resisted the urge to look at it, as if the electrical spark of her touch had left a mark he could see. A residue that he could wipe away before it became permanent.

He had questions. Lots of them. But here, tonight, in the bubbly water and with a pleasant little buzz going, he didn't feel like asking them. What did it matter if he was going to be dead in three days anyway? Or was it two days now? Was it after midnight?

Steve inhaled deeply, oddly calm. What was happening to him? Was it something about Roxy? About the night? Or was this the calm so often mentioned when a person had fully made up their mind to end it all? The peace that happens when a man stops fighting the current and lets the waters flow freely and carry him inexorably toward the inevitable?

"What smells so good?" he asked. "It's a nice change from that sauerkraut. Which, by the way, I have to admit was better than I expected."

Roxy leaned back and inhaled, her breasts rising for a moment above the turbulent water. Marshmallows, Steve thought. Big marshmallows. Pale white, pillowy, a decent-sized handful, even for a guy with hands the size of his.

"That would be my midnight garden," Roxy said, answering the question he'd already forgotten he'd asked. "Everything in it is the color of moonlight or night, and most of the flowers smell their best after dark. Night-blooming jasmine, moonflowers, gardenias, stuff like that."

Gardenias. They always reminded Steve of Billie Holiday. Lady Day. The woman who'd altered his life's path. The path that had led him here, in the end, to moonlight and limoncello and a naked white woman in a hot tub.

"So all the flowers are black or white?" Steve asked.

"Yes."

"Like us."

He hadn't meant to bring up race. Maybe he did. Men like him needed to be cautious around NWLs—Nice White Ladies.

Graveyards were full of men who'd made the mistake of thinking times had changed. NWLs might have a nasty Mandingo fetish. They might accuse him of rape. He was old and he was going to die, but he didn't want the story of his life to end with ugly smears against him. The lessons and The Talk from his mama and his aunties had never left his mind in all his long years.

Besides, in these fraught "me too" times, it paid to be careful. *Consent* was the word young folks used these days. He needed consent. A good thing, Steve supposed, but awkward as hell for a man his age to figure out.

"Would it be a problem for you if maybe someday I might respond to what you seem to be offering?" he asked.

Someday? Hell, it was going to have to be tonight. Tomorrow night at the latest. Maybe it would be better not to get Roxy tangled up in his plans. She was sexy and funny and nice. She didn't deserve to be the one to find his rotting corpse.

Roxy sipped her limoncello, taking her time answering him.

He'd never had limoncello before, and he liked it. Like Roxy, the drink was sweet and tart and probably not good for him.

"I like that you asked, Steve, even if having my foot damn near wrapped around your balls wasn't enough to let you know what I'm thinking. Too many men have assumed that because I was a dancer—no matter how many years ago that was—that it must mean I'm a thirsty floozy. Like having flexible legs means I also have flexible morals. I've been around a time or three, but not as often as you'd think. I'm choosy. I'm old enough to know what I want, too old to play games, but not too old to still want to do more than just play footsie with the right man. I think that might be you. Not for anything long-term," she hastened to add. "But it's nice to have someone to fall asleep with now and then. So since you asked so nice, Steve, yes, I'm interested if you're offering the same thing I am."

"Any STDs I need to worry about? HIV positive or AIDS?"

Roxy shook her head. "I've been lucky. New York in the eighties taught me caution." She waved a hand, maybe to wave off the past. Then she grinned. "Bad case of crabs once in Las Vegas, but I got that cleared up. You?"

"Gonorrhea back in my army days. Antibiotics took care of it and keeping my dick out of strange places prevented any recurrence. I'm a firm believer in keeping Big Bob protected. Nowadays, well, it's been a long time, Rox, and the vampires at the medical lab have taken so much blood over the last few months, I'm pretty sure they'd have mentioned it if there were any little strangers swimming around in there."

Well, other than those test results the doc was still confirming. The ones they'd be talking about tomorrow.

"Have you ever slept with a Black man, Roxy?" Steve had to be sure. Two days from now he was going to be dead, but he didn't want his last act on Earth to be a meaningless checkmark on somebody's bucket list.

"I find you appealing," Roxy said. "It's always been hard to find a man tall enough to suit me. You're a prickly curmudgeon, and I know shit-all about you, but sometimes you just know, you know? Who knows why one person attracts us instantly and another doesn't?"

"But have you ever slept with a Black man?"

"No," she said. "Came close once, though." A dreamy smile lifted her lips. She closed her eyes for a long moment, then opened them and trained her bright blue gaze on him.

"Forty years ago. New York. Tall, muscular, with shoulders to die for. His name was Barry. He wanted to be an actor. Isn't that why most everyone from places like Dubuque or Amarillo or Darby Glen goes to New York? He went to every audition he heard about. He was a stagehand at Radio City. An audacious flirt. I was too young and flattered to realize he was only trying to make someone else jealous. But ooh, he was a very good kisser. But we never did more than that."

"Did it last very long?"

"A few weeks. Then his lover showed up outside the stage

door one night. A widowed, wealthy, hot-headed Italian named Paola. She threatened to have her family connections demolish my knees and slice my Achilles if I didn't give up Barry."

Roxy chuckled. "Between the two of them, I think Paola would have done better on the stage than Barry. Very menacing, right up until she melted down in an all-out hissy fit and tears."

"You gave up Barry?"

"The heart wants what it wants. Paola wanted Barry. Barry wanted a lover with a penthouse, a personal driver, and an account at Tiffany's. That wasn't a chorine who danced a few months out of the year and did bookkeeping and fencing lessons to make ends meet."

"But Barry was Black. Did that matter to you?"

"He was a sexy man with a beautiful voice and he treated me kindly and made me laugh."

"And had shoulders to die for."

"Yes, well, there was that."

"But are you serious? You never got funky with a Black boy before? Played on the dark side of the street? You know what they say, Roxy. Once you go black—"

"You never go back. Yeah, I heard that." The steam from the hot tub had turned her curls into damp red waves. She lifted her hair off her neck and let it fall again. "It's just, it never really came up before. The opportunity, I mean."

"Are you trying to tell me there were no other brothers in New York City besides some boy-toy stagehand?"

Roxy laughed as she set her drink down on the colorful mosaic tabletop at her elbow. "Plenty of 'brothers,' but not many eligible or available in the circles I ran in. The theater really is a small insular world. And Rockettes didn't draw devoted fanboys or groupies the way Broadway actresses do. Part of the appeal of a Rockette is their uniformity. From the audience, we all look alike. Not much chance for a fan to form an individual attraction. When we got off stage and took off our identical makeup and our identical costumes and unpinned our hair from their identical styles, nobody would recognize us."

She shrugged. "The men in the theater were dancers or actors or crew and if they weren't gay, they were mostly already married or in serious relationships. That was true no matter their race. Slim pickings for a girl from Ohio who was trying to find her own way, working a couple of jobs, keeping up with classes, and just trying to survive."

"What about before New York? Or after you stopped dancing?" Steve didn't know why he was picking on this like a dog with a bone. The particulars of a woman's life had never mattered to him before. He usually took whatever came his way and enjoyed it. But even on short acquaintance, a niggling in his head said Roxy was different.

Special.

Dangerous.

Distant alarms twisted his gut. That same instinct had brought him home from Vietnam without any extra holes in his hide. Had warned him when a straightforward drug bust was about to go pear-shaped.

Or maybe he was lying to himself. Grasping at something—anything—that would allay the ugly thoughts racing through his brain. Maybe he was trying to not die as a dickhead. Roxy seemed like a nice lady. He should just get up and leave now so she wouldn't feel too bad when word of his death got passed through the neighborhood grapevine.

Roxy, of course, couldn't hear his thoughts.

"There certainly wasn't the chance to date men of color in the town I grew up in," she said. "That tight little town was as pristine white as a Christian lady's gloves on Easter Sunday morning."

Roxy scrounged through the towels stacked on the side of the hot tub and came up with a scrunchie, white with bright blue sparkly polka dots. "I never met a Black person until I went to New York. When I was a kid, we'd drive up to Columbus and go downtown to the big Lazarus department store, and we'd see Black ladies all dressed up shopping, but even there, the area was pretty white. At least the places we went." She did that thing that all women somehow know how to do, gathered up her hair without looking in a mirror and pulled it into a ponytail.

"And you, Steve? Ever tangled up the sheets with a white woman?"

"The town I grew up in," Steve said, "all us Black folks stayed in the same neighborhood. And if I'd even so much as glanced at a woman like you, a beating would have been the least that happened to me. There were still laws back then, and boys like me best always remember that and not get on the wrong side of them."

"So you never 'got funky' with a white woman before?"

"Ah, hell, woman. I'm retired army. I've been all over this world. You name a color in the rainbow, and I've probably had sex with it. As long as she has the right equipment, a decent smile, and her husband's not home, I'm up for it."

"Good," Roxy said. "I'm getting too old to be anybody's first time at anything."

The flip answer was on the tip of Steve's tongue and then came tumbling out. "For me all a woman needs is tits, ass, and someplace to put my dick."

He regretted the words instantly. "Sorry about that. I shouldn't have been so crass."

"I wouldn't have expected anything less from you." Roxy surprised him with a chuckle, taking no offense at all.

"Let me try again," he said. Maybe it was the booze talking. Maybe it was the heat and citronella candlelight and Roxy. "The short answer is yes, I've spent time wrapped around white women. But not until I was a grown-ass man. In the town where I grew up, Picketsville, Mississippi, it didn't pay for a young buck to hanker after white pussy. Population less than eight hundred. White folks lived on their side of the tracks and we stayed on ours. It wasn't until 1967, when I was twenty-seven-years-old, that *Loving v. Virginia* passed, allowing black and white folks to marry. In Picketsville, what little's left of the town today, it's still 1950. Anybody find me in a hot tub with you and I'd likely still today end up as 'strange fruit.'"

"Billie Holiday," Roxy said. "I have that on vinyl somewhere around here."

Maybe God was a dick after all. Here Steve was, with his perfect plans to die all set in stone, and God had sent Roxy Fields to dredge up old memories. Why else would he randomly end up in a hot tub with a beautiful woman who had Billie Holiday on vinyl?

Because God was dicking around with him.

Maybe he was already dead. Maybe this was some sort of afterlife review. Steve refused the bait.

"Remind me to tell you about Billie someday," Steve said.

That day would never come. He'd told a few guys about Billie over the years. Back in the army for sure, chewing the fat late at night with that asshole Glen Wilson. Had he ever told Curtis? In two and a half days, there'd be nobody to remember or care about his stupid old stories. Nobody to remember or care that a troubled Black angel had changed the life of a lost dickhead kid.

Roxy would never know. He was running out of time to tell anybody anything.

"Anyway," Steve said, "back then, a smart boy didn't go dipping his wick anywhere, Black or white, unless he planned to marry. Birth control was hardly a thing, and I had plans to get the hell out of Picketsville as soon as I could manage. I wasn't the captain of the football team, but I played. There was always a girl or two around. But I made sure to stick to all the pretty dark-skinned girls and never went near the white stuff. In Vietnam, I just swore off women altogether."

"I noticed the photo in your house—taken in Vietnam? Want to talk about it?"

Steve shook his head. "Nothing to talk about. Plenty of pretty Vietnamese women, but I kept Big Bob in my trousers. If birth control depended on a cheap condom back in Mississippi, it was a fantasy dream in 'Nam. Some of those women were just scrawny, starving little girls selling the only thing they had left—themselves. Some of them were hoping an American GI was their ticket out of hell. Some fell in love, deeply. Some made it out. Most didn't, left behind for the wives and girlfriends back in the World. I'd seen too many men leave behind shattered lives and mixed-race babies who'd be rejected by their families like vermin. I wasn't going to be one of them."

Steve glanced up at Roxy. There was no pity in her eyes. No sick, avid curiosity. Only quiet.

"Sounds like your parents raised a good man."

"I'm like you, I guess. Choosy. I like keeping things light and easy and no hard feelings after. Everybody gets an itch. No harm scratching it."

He settled a little further down in the tub. "So why me, Roxy? We've known each other less than twelve hours. I've been sick and grouchy." Steve had no idea why her answer was important to him, but suddenly it was.

"I have a flower in my midnight garden called a Black Star calla lily," she said.

Well, her response was certainly oblique.

"It reminds me of you. Inky black with cool plum undertones and smooth, tightly curled petals. That flower has hidden depths. And it's not the easiest plant to grow—true high maintenance. But it's worth it." She shook her head. "Who knows why one thing attracts us and another doesn't? Deer don't like the taste of my calla lily. Butterflies and hummingbirds can't help being attracted to it."

"Are you a hummingbird?"

"More a butterfly, I think. I've spent my whole life flitting here and there, never landing any place too long."

"Anyone ever caught you?"

"If you're asking if I've ever been married, yes, once. Worst week of my life. Las Vegas wedding, Las Vegas divorce. The devilishly handsome ones aren't to be trusted. Thank God I was smart enough, even then, to get a prenup."

"He was after your fortune?"

"He thought the rhinestones on my cocktail waitress costume were real diamonds. He was oh-so-pretty but not

91

bright. Two days after the wedding he lost a bundle at the poker table and thought I'd bail him out. Instead, I bailed out of the marriage. Still not the stupidest thing I've ever done, but it's up there.

"And you," she said. "Been married?"

Steve shook his head. "Not even close. Plenty of women, but not the sticking-around kind. My line of work was not conducive to being a family man. I knew that. So I never asked anyone to take that on."

"Besides the highway patrol, what line of work was that?"

"Boring, crappy shit that has to be done to keep the world from going completely down the toilet." The conversation was getting too close to the bone; time for a subject change. "You said you'd tell me about being a Rockette."

Roxy wrinkled her nose in distaste and blew a raspberry at him, then gulped the last of her limoncello. "Four years of my life. It was only four years, and yet that's the part everyone is curious about. Isn't there anything else you'd like to know?"

"Sure. What's in that oversized shed back there?"

Roxy had left that out of the earlier tour of her house and garden. The building ran almost the full width of her property, curtains drawn tight over closed windows, an electronic keypad lock on the door.

He wondered if it had anything to do with the ridiculously large marijuana plants thinly disguised by other plants in her semi-jungle of a garden. He couldn't deal with dopers; he'd spent too many years putting them in jail. It would be one of God's last little kicks in the balls if the last woman in Steve's life was a junkie.

"So...being a Rockette," she said, neatly ignoring his question about the shed as if he'd never asked it.

What was she hiding? But no internal alarms went off. Either his cop instincts didn't think there was anything worth getting his shorts in a twist about, or were too dulled by booze and boobs. Maybe those instincts had already died and were just waiting for his body to catch up.

"It all began because I was the klutziest four-year-old in Darby Glen, Ohio." She paused to check the cell phone lying on the deck surrounding the hot tub. "It's getting late, and I'm not in the mood for a stroll down memory lane right now. How about I walk you home? Maybe I'll tell you all about the not-so-glamorous life of a Rockette over breakfast."

She leaned forward and placed her hand squarely in the center of his chest, running her palm over the sparse curls there that used to be black but which were now a uniform gray. She pressed her lips against his as he raised his own hands to pull her closer.

She carried the scent of chlorine and jasmine and something distinctly her own. He licked his lips as she pulled away, tasting the sweet lemon she'd left behind.

Roxy stood up, her body golden in the candlelight, flashing naked tits and ass as she climbed out of the water and reached for a towel, a woman pushing toward seventy, still fit and trim, whatever wrinkles she had smoothed out by moonlight, a couple of beers, and a cordial glass or two of sticky sweet limoncello. She stretched her arms over her head and unclipped her hair, unleashing a river of red that flowed to her shoulders. The steam had taken the curl out of it, but it was still beautiful, with tiny water droplets glistening in the candlelight. Her nipples puckered in the cool night air.

She waved a towel in his direction. "I hope it's big enough," she said with a provocative arch of her eyebrows.

Maybe God wasn't such a dick after all.

Chapter 12

Steve's Date with Death: T-Minus 35:43:27 and Counting

STEVE WOKE UP to the sounds of the morning news and traffic reports, bright sunshine streaming through his window, and the smell of bacon. He'd have preferred to wake up the same way he'd fallen asleep, with an armful of Roxy.

They'd made it to his front door, and then in a tangle of arms and legs they'd made it to his bedroom. Their tussle in the sheets hadn't been like when he was in his twenties or even in his fifties, but it hadn't been a disaster either. Little blue pills could do only so much, but so much had been enough.

He'd hoped Roxy would be gone in the morning. This was his last full day to live. Tomorrow, probably before sunset, he planned on checking out of life.

He didn't want to spend his last day apologizing or pretending to a redheaded Rockette he'd just met. He needed to double-check his suicide plans and make any final notes. Or maybe he'd spend the day staring out the window, waiting for sundown.

Like he did every other day. If it weren't for tomorrow being the anniversary of his sister's death, there was nothing to stop him from checking out today. But his whole life had been chaos, waiting for other people's whims to tell him where to go and what to do and when. This time, the plan was his and his alone. And he was going to stick to his plan. No disruptions this time. No last-minute rescues of boneheaded nephews. No surprise regrets over a woman who'd exploded into his life at the last possible second.

Roxy had never gotten around to telling him about being a Rockette. He hated not knowing how stories turned out. He heaved himself out of bed and into the shower, then followed the noise of plates and pans being banged around in the kitchen.

Roxy stood there barefoot, elbows propped on the counter, wearing an eye-watering pink floral shirt open over running shorts and sports bra. Steve's laptop was propped open on the counter. Dramatic music and the sounds of a woman sobbing reached a crescendo, then died away to a commercial.

"What in the world are you watching? And is that toast I smell burning?"

"And now, *The Guiding Light*," a voice announced from the laptop.

"Good morning to you too, sunshine." Roxy adroitly turned and popped toast out of the toaster and put in two more bread slices. "How do you like your eggs?"

Steve did not remember having eggs, bread, or bacon in his sparse refrigerator.

"Yesterday on *The Guiding Light*, Bertha Bauer discovered that Bill…"

"Scrambled," Steve said. "And what's that crap?"

Roxy stopped the video and started cracking eggs into a bowl.

"It's a soap opera. *The Guiding Light*. There's fifty-seven years' worth of them, and I've decided to live long enough to watch every single episode." She winked at him. "You're welcome to join me."

"Why would you want to do that?" Steve could think of a lot of better things to do with his time. Like have breakfast and go back to bed.

"Babushka—my Grandma Jablonski—spoke almost no English when she first came to America. She learned to speak it

95

by watching *The Guiding Light.*"

"Jablonski? Your grandma was a Polack?"

"Pole, not Polack. And no, she was Russian. Her husband—my grandfather—was Polish. That's on my dad's side. Mom's side was Republic of Northern Ireland and damned proud of it."

Steve thought for a minute while Roxy poured eggs in the pan, the scent of browning butter mingling with the bacon. "So was Fields your married name?"

Roxy didn't answer while she filled plates and poured the orange juice Steve was also positive had not been in the refrigerator last night. She put the heaping plate in front of him and sat down across from him, taking her time putting a paper towel across her lap. The food fairy must have forgotten to bring proper napkins.

"Please allow me to introduce myself," Roxy said at last. "Rita Jablonski from Darby Glen, Ohio. Population under a thousand, almost all white folks, far enough south of Columbus that you'll only find the place if you get lost looking for a real town."

"So you gave me a fake name?" Steve stuffed in a mouthful of light, fluffy eggs. Yeah, God was a dick, sending a grifter to him on his last day alive. But damn, she knew how to cook.

"No," Roxy said. "That's my real name. I had it legally changed the day after I turned twenty-one. Rita Ann Jablonski became Roxy Fields. Mother named me after Rita Hayworth and Ann Miller."

Steve slapped the table. "That's who you remind me of. I've been trying to put my finger on it. Rita Hayworth. The red curls, the long legs—"

"Yeah, I get that a lot." Roxy sighed. "I hated it when I was young. I named myself after Samuel 'Roxy' Rothafel, who long ago was a director at Radio City Music Hall and creator of the long-gone Roxy Theater. The *Fields* is because I was an uneducated hick from Ohio and thought the name of the Ziegfeld girls—you know, those chorus girls from the early

1900s? Anyway, I thought it was Zieg*field*, not *feld*, so I picked Fields as a last name. By the time I figured it out I didn't feel like changing my name again. If I had it to do over again, I'd have embraced my original namesake and would been Roxy Hayworth." She fluffed her shoulder-length hair. Last night it had been in curls, but this morning she'd shoved it out of the way with a glittery headband. "That's why I dye my hair red," she said.

Steve's long, slow gaze ran from the top of her head to her pink polished toes, pausing in all the usual places a man pauses. "I didn't think I'd ever like a redheaded woman, but on you the color looks perfect."

Roxy popped a piece of bacon into her mouth, chewed and swallowed before responding. "Still, I suppose, I had it easier than my sister, Natalia. She was named after Leon Trotsky's wife."

Steve choked on the juice he'd just swallowed and coughed. "She what?"

"Yeah," Roxy said before forking eggs into her mouth. She chewed, swallowed, and finally said, "Babushka escaped from Russia during their civil war. She was a massive Trotsky fangirl. Until the day she died, she kept a shrine to him in her bedroom, hidden inside her closet. She spent her whole life thinking Stalin or the GPU—the Soviet police—was going to break in one night and murder her for supporting Trotsky." She sipped her orange juice.

"I mean, seriously, it's not like she'd been hiding spies or breaking codes," Roxy said. "She was a teenager who handed out a leaflet or two once. But to her, Trotsky was her tragic, fallen hero and the Soviets would be storming our little rattletrap house in Darby Glen any second. We never could convince her Stalin was as dead as Trotsky. More coffee? Juice?"

Steve shook his head and reached for another piece of bacon. Honestly, listening to Roxy's bonkers stories was better than watching anything on television.

"Anyway, Babushka spoke nothing but Russian but

somehow managed to snag herself a Polish husband and get to America. He died before I was born, and since my dad—their son—died when I was only two, I know nothing about him. Babushka lived with us and took care of me and Natalia—we called her Tally—while Mom worked to support us. We learned both Russian and English, though I'd be hard-pressed to do more than order a meal, find a hotel, or cuss somebody out in Russian these days."

Roxy glanced at her oversized, bright yellow watch, then stood and started gathering dishes. "Hate to eat and run, but I've got a class in half an hour. Tuesdays are bridge, Wednesdays is the ballet for seniors class I teach, and today it's fencing. I'm teaching foil techniques."

Steve sucked down the last of his juice and carried his dishes to the sink. "Oh yeah, you mentioned you teach that. Why would a bunch of little old people want to spend their time playing at being the next D'Artagnan?" He remembered the array of swords on her living room wall, and she'd mentioned fencing before, but he'd had other things on his mind.

Like planning to get into Roxy's very short shorts and then killing himself.

"It's supposed to be for fun and fitness," Roxy said. "Mostly it's a matter of making sure the old biddies don't take revenge on each other over the neighbor's cat pissing in the garden or mixing recyclables in the trash or some other petty grievance."

She paused in her dishwashing. "Well, and making sure Mrs. Koffman never gets good enough to actually off her husband." Roxy stared at the ceiling. "Although, I met the man one night at the club. I suppose if Mrs. Koffman ever needed an alibi, I could supply one for her. And there's lots of room in my garden." She shrugged and went back to rinsing dishes. Steve eyed the butter knife in her hand and kept his mouth closed.

"You're welcome to come along if you want. I've got a couple of men in the class." Roxy wiped off the counter and hung up the dishcloth. "Though most of them aren't really interested in learning to fence. They're just looking for a nurse with a purse."

"A what?"

"You know. An older woman with an independent income who'll mop up their drool and wipe their butts when they get old and sick, but who'll pay her own way —and maybe theirs— and won't take any of their money."

"Can't," Steve said. "I've got other stuff going on today." A doctor's appointment was what he had. Though he'd probably skip it. Didn't need no damned bloodsucker to tell him what he already knew. And he didn't plan on needing a nurse with or without a purse.

As far as Steve was concerned, there was still an elephant standing in the middle of his kitchen. Had he satisfied Roxy? No man enjoyed the reviews that inevitably came after a performance. Especially when he was eighty years old and hadn't performed in way too many years.

"We don't have to do that again, if you don't want to. You know. Last night."

Roxy plopped down in the chair opposite his and inched close enough to bump her shapely tanned knees against his pudgy ink-black ones. She pulled his hand into hers. Made sure he was looking straight at her.

Then she grinned.

"It was amazing. Just the way I wanted it to be. Just the way I needed it. Slow and tender and satisfying. I'm sixty-five years old, Steve. I may seem like a wild woman to you, and I may talk a good game, but I really haven't been around all that much. Not like you'd think. And a woman my age, well, it takes time to get the engine started, you know?"

He did know. It took a little blue pill and thirty minutes to warm up his own engines. Well, thirty minutes and a pair of long legs, bigger-than-expected tits, and a sweet, warm mouth. Her kisses had tasted like fresh, sweet lemonade.

He did a quick mental check, but Big Bob was apparently all petered out for a while.

Didn't stop a man from thinking thoughts, though.

He exhaled, blowing his breath out in a long stream. The tightness in his chest loosened, and his head stopped buzzing like a hive of disturbed bees. "I liked it too, Roxy." After another sip of juice, he found himself grinning like an idiot at her.

Roxy stood and gathered up her purse. "As much fun as last night was, I've got a jam-packed schedule today. But there's a fish fry tonight at the K of C if you're interested."

"Colonel Sanders has a fish fry?"

Roxy laughed that great laugh of hers. Damn. Why did he have to find something so nice the day before he killed himself?

"Not KFC," she said. "K *of* C. Knights of Columbus. Fish fry on Fridays for their charity. It's a great deal. Fish either fried or grilled, with all the sides. Hush puppies, coleslaw, greens with ham—even though they frown on their Catholic members eating that on Fridays, of course, but no one pays much attention to who has what on their plate. And the ladies usually make a nice ambrosia salad. And the best banana pudding you've ever had in your life."

Damn. Banana pudding.

"They run on old-people time, which means they start serving at four, but they serve until seven. I can stop and pick you up if you want. It's only two blocks, so we can walk. Or I can drive."

Steve shook his head. "I've got a doctor's appointment. I'm pretty sure I won't feel like going out tonight."

"Doctor's suck," Roxy said. "Best thing in the world after seeing one is to get out and blow their nonsense out of your brain. I'll just stop by on my way and see if you're in the mood."

She headed toward the door.

"By the way," Steve said. "Where'd all the food come from this morning?"

"Picked it up on my way back from my morning run." Roxy did a little jig. "Something I do four mornings a week."

"Making sure you can get away from the bad guys?"

"Well, it's come in handy for that a time or two, but mostly because I've been doing it since I was a kid and love it. I did track and field in high school; I wanted to go to the Olympics. But training like that costs money. A lot of it. More money than a single working mom with two kids and a batty Russian mother-in-law could afford. Besides, Coach said I'd never be fast enough. Mom got me dance lessons for free instead, in exchange for cleaning the studio two nights a week."

Before Steve could say ask another question, Roxy was out the door.

Good. And good riddance.

It wasn't until he was halfway to the doctor's office that he realized she'd never told him about being a Rockette. And now he'd never know the end of the story.

Unless he was in the mood for fried fish and greens for supper. And banana pudding.

He hated not knowing the end of stories.

Chapter 13

Sexy Firefighters Calendar Word of the Day:
Cacoethes: [kakoēthēs] **Noun.** an irresistible urge to do something inadvisable.

WHY ON EARTH had she mentioned nurses with purses right when Steve had a doctor's appointment? Was he going to think she was warning him off?

Was she?

And why did she even care what a tall, dark, delicious stranger thought of her?

Well, not so much a stranger. Not after last night.

Roxy sleepwalked through the fencing class. Between the lack of sleep, sharing a strange bed with a strange man, and the wholly unexpected attraction to him, she had a hard time focusing on her students. What the devil had gotten into her?

She'd have to keep a closer eye on Mrs. Koffman. The woman was getting dangerously good at parrying and thrusting. Maybe Roxy needed to catch the woman's husband the next time she ran into him at the club and mention it. If the old fool didn't listen—and he probably wouldn't—at least she'd have a clear conscience.

Class ran late, with Mrs. Schaumburger having a rousing argument in the middle of pairs fencing practice with Ms. Buckley over something in the news that Roxy neither heard nor cared about. She knew what they were really fighting about: Lev Abrams, the pudgy retired optometrist, who at one time or another had invited every woman in the class to go out on his sailboat. Mrs. Schaumburger and Mrs. Buckley had both been on the boat and each was determined to be the optometrist's only first mate.

Then Bev Louis wanted to chat about her son's upcoming wedding and what a bridezilla her prospective daughter-in-law was being. Roxy had met the prospective daughter-in-law and had a pretty good idea who the actual monster was in that relationship. The girl was a sweetheart; even better, she was a sweetheart with a backbone. The woman everyone secretly called Battle-axe Bev had met her match.

Roxy then fended off Joe Martinez's request for "private lessons" on her way to use the shower in the gym where she held her classes. Nice enough guy, but at five feet five inches and hirsute enough to be mistaken for one of those shaggy Highland cattle, he was decidedly not her type.

Roxy stood for too long in the shower, letting the steaming water run over her body. What had Steve really thought of their horizontal hokey-pokey last night? Of her no-longer-young body? All the wrinkles and pale, faded scars, the skin that was looser than it had been fifty years ago. Even twenty years ago. Had he really enjoyed their bedsheet bossa nova, or was he just being polite this morning?

She was an old broad, she'd had a full life, and she wasn't in bad shape for being sixty five. The skin might shift differently over her bones now, but the fencing had staved off the dreaded batwing grandma arms and dancing kept her butt in decent shape.

So she'd needed the K-Y Jelly she'd surreptitiously stuck in her pocket before walking Steve home, and he'd needed a not-so-discreetly swallowed blue pill, but still...

The sex hadn't been all thundering stallions and wild screaming mares, but everybody'd gotten where they were going, and it had been nice curling up around his big, ursine body before falling asleep. She'd heard him up once or twice in the bathroom, not odd for an old man, but she could've sworn she'd heard him being sick.

Had the fish disagreed with him? Did it have anything to do with his doctor's appointment today?

And again, why did she care?

But she did. Everything about Steve Stephens surprised her, especially how much she'd come to like him in only twenty-four hours. She'd always been a romantic. Her tenderhearted tendency to jump in before checking the depth of the waters had gotten her into trouble more than once. But it had never stopped her from going out and being foolish all over again.

She owed it to all her friends—those beautiful, fabulous, loving friends—who'd never made it out of the eighties, to live life to the fullest. Madame Duval—sweet Jubil—had made her promise, even as what they'd called the sickness had ravaged her body.

"It was worth it, my brave little fool." Jubil had called her that—brave little fool—ever since that night at Colonel Sanders. "It was worth every second of loving and living and being my true, authentic self. I mean, the ending of my story sucks, but you promise me yours won't. You promise me you'll get out there and live the fucking hell outta life for me. You promise, Roxy? Keep your guard up against the takers, but never let your heart get so locked up and shriveled that there's no room in it to love somebody. Or for them to love you back."

"So how did it go with Steve last night?" Graciela asked.

"Oh, you know. I fed him dinner. Walked him home."

Graciela raised one dark, perfectly arched eyebrow. "I saw you doing the walk of shame at five this morning."

Graciela was the kind of friend who could say stuff like that to Roxy without it coming out offensive or judgmental. They'd connected from their first meeting at the country club, a pair of women who didn't quite fit in with the solidly middle-class members in spite of the melting pot represented there.

Graciela had joined the club because it was a good way to pick up new real estate clients. Roxy had joined when she'd seen a call for volunteers to help out with their fun-run charity drive. The Puerto Rican single mother and the dancer from Ohio had bonded over a shared admiration of old movie musicals and Tom Hiddleston.

"What were you doing out at five in the morning?" Roxy asked.

"Mr. Wiggles needed to tinkle. I saw you strolling down the sidewalk from Steve's house."

Mr. Wiggles was the ancient, asthmatic pug that had claimed Graciela's heart. Even Iggy had wondered aloud on more than one occasion about his place in his mother's pecking order.

"It was fine," Roxy said.

Graciela didn't say a word, but that eyebrow moved a fraction of an inch higher.

Roxy had called Graciela and invited her to the beach for an afternoon of wandering the shops, ogling men in Speedos, and lunch in a sandy beachside café. After last night, she needed salt air and a good friend to help her clear her head.

She enjoyed Graciela's company, but her head wasn't any clearer.

What had she been thinking, jumping into bed with a stranger? Especially one with such volatile undercurrents?

It wasn't as if she didn't have enough on her mind already.

Graciela sipped her drink, her gaze focused on Roxy, and didn't say a word.

"Okay," Roxy said. "He came over for happy hour. We...um...spent a little time in the hot tub. Then he needed some medicine that he'd forgotten at his house. I just wanted to make sure he was okay. I think the heat from the hot tub raised his blood pressure or something."

"Or maybe the heat from a redhead in a bikini raised

something else?"

Heat flared in Roxy's cheeks.

"Oh, Roxy. You wore your birthday suit, didn't you?"

"He hadn't brought a suit with him. It seemed like the polite thing to do."

"*Polite* is a friendly handshake at the front door as he's leaving at a decent hour. Polite is *not* inviting a naked man into your hot tub, especially when you've known him for no more than eight hours." Graciela clucked her tongue and shook her head.

Roxy closed her eyes and drew in a deep breath. Then she leaned on her elbow, propped her chin in her hand, and looked directly into Graciela's eyes. "Do you believe in love at first sight, Graciela?"

"Oh, Roxy—"

"But do you?"

"At our age—"

"But—"

"Yes, okay? I knew the second I laid eyes on my dear Joseph that I would marry him. And I did. And then I lost him and never thought I'd find love again. But you, chica? In all the time I've known you, you've been friendly to everyone but guarded your own heart. You let no man too close. Then out of the blue you jump out of a hot tub and into bed with a man you just met?"

Her friend knew her too well. "Maybe if you took more interest in your own love life you wouldn't be so interested in mine," Roxy said.

"My love life is fine, thank you. I'm having dinner with Faustin tonight. No hot tubs, just a nice respectable dinner."

Faustin was the owner of the jewelry store in the same strip mall as Graciela's real estate office. Roxy was glad to see her friend taking an interest in dating again.

"Will you be seeing Steve again?" Graciela asked.

Roxy sighed. "I asked him to the fish fry tonight, but I'm not sure. He didn't seem excited about it. I know he's ill, but I don't know him well enough to ask about it."

"You know him well enough to make whoopee with him, but not to ask about his health?"

"Some things are personal," Roxy said. "And I'm not sure I want to know. I don't want to get tangled up with anybody who's going to die in my arms again. I've done that too many times already."

"At our age, that's a risk we take every day. It doesn't mean we should stop taking the chance at finding love. You've always been the bravest person I know, the first to leap into new adventures and experiences. But never have I seen you show an interest in a man until now. Have you really seen so much death, Roxy, that it's made you so wary?"

Maybe it was because those past deaths had already been on her mind that morning that Graciela's question opened the Pandora's box locked in Roxy's memory.

Or maybe those memories burst out because today was the anniversary of Lisa Michelle's birthday and her daughter was so tied up with those memories.

"Jubil and Joey and Giorgio," Roxy said. A long swallow of her iced caramel macchiato eased her tightening throat. She leaned forward in her chair. Even today, forty fucking years later, this was not a topic that was usually chatted about over lunch in the company of tipsy, sunburned vacationers.

The thought rankled that people were still squeamish, too often choosing to look the other way.

"Boyfriends?"

Roxy shook her head. "Dear friends. Joey and Giorgio were my roommates. Jubil was one of the dearest people in my world. I loved all of them. And I lost them all."

Graciela's eyes widened. "Oh, I'm so sorry, Rox. An accident?"

"A plague. A scourge. They died of ignorance and fear."

Graciela hissed a breath between her teeth. "AIDS," she said.

"It tiptoed in on us, stealthy, whispered, until it couldn't

107

be ignored anymore. So many in my world, just gone. You have to remember that even though I only danced a few months out of the year, most of my friends were connected to the theater world, which reaches further than most people think about. It wasn't only the actors and people you see on stage. The costumers connected us to the fashion world. The set designers connected us to the art world. Hairdressers and makeup artists. Photographers. The sound techs and musicians and librettists, the publicists and producers—it all spiraled out into the greater world, but at the core was theater and fashion."

"And gay men," Graciela said.

Roxy nodded. "It was only later—so much later—that the rest of the world realized how AIDS was impacting others. Not just drug users and folks they considered perverted or somehow *less than*. It impacted straight people too. Kids with hemophilia. The nice suburban housewives of men who frequented sex workers. A pregnant woman hemorrhaging and getting a blood transfusion. But in those early days, it was mostly gay men."

Graciela nodded vigorously. "We never learn. Whenever something bad happens, strange and terrifying deaths, it's always blamed on the *others*. The poor, the foreigners, the sinful, wicked, perverted ones. Never anything that could happen to nice, middle-class, churchgoing folks. Until it does."

Roxy nodded. "And all the time it was mostly just guys out there living their lives, with no idea they were killing each other and themselves. The world—and the government—was too slow to notice. Why should they care about a bunch of pervs? And all the while good Christian pastors screamed damnation at them."

"Not all of them, Roxy. It didn't make the news as much, but folks tried to help. Maybe not enough. Maybe not soon enough. But they tried."

"Where I was, mostly we just tried to help each other. Took the sick ones to doctors' appointments. Studied every article or scrap of information we could find. Seized on every little thing we could to try to help. We—the friends of all the sick ones—fed and cared for them even in the hospitals because so many health providers were scared to death of those guys." Roxy swirled a chip through the salsa, popped it into her mouth, but it tasted like ashes to her and felt like a lump of clay when she swallowed.

"I don't blame them," Roxy said. "The nurses and doctors. They saw these folks dying and didn't know why. Nobody knew if a breath or a touch could kill you. I was scared too, Graciela. Terrified. But at that time, I owed so much to Joey. He'd kept me sane and kept me from dying when I thought I couldn't bear to live another second. I owed him my life."

Graciela cocked her head. "Joey?"

Roxy smiled then, glad to share a good memory, even if it came wrapped with a whole lot of ugly ones. "Joey Legend," she said. "One of my first friends in New York." She sighed. "It's a complicated story, Graciela."

Graciela glanced at her delicate jeweled watch, deliberately unstrapped it from her wrist, and shoved it into her purse. "I got time, chica. Iggy's working and has a date later. Nothing's hanging fire right now, and my secretary's taking messages. Dinner with Faustin isn't until nine. We've been friends for a while now, Rox. So tell Mama Graciela about Joey Legend."

"I was pregnant when I got to New York." The statement was blunt. And a stupid place to start the story, but she wasn't ready to go into everything that happened before that.

"Not the first girl that's happened to," Graciela said. "Goes all the way back to Eve."

"Yeah, well, I was seventeen. It was 1971. In Darby Glen, Ohio, abortion wasn't an option and neither was hanging around a small town with everybody ogling my belly. My mother was furious and no help at all. She had a new boyfriend then and was enraged that I'd gotten myself 'knocked up.' She never even asked who the baby daddy was. I think she was afraid of the answer."

"Her new boyfriend?"

Roxy shook her head. "No, but still a pillar of our little

community. I…it's not important. But I needed to get out of Darby Glen. My best friend, Meg, had an older sister who'd run away to New York a few years earlier. So I gathered up what little money I had and got on a bus, and at the other end, Meg's sister, Kitty, and her neighbor Joey Legend met me at the station. Joey had come along, Kitty said, to carry my suitcase and keep her company while they waited for me."

"Sounds like a good guy."

"He was. He'd studied at the CIA—"

"He was a spy?"

Roxy did laugh then. "Not the Central Intelligence Agency—the Culinary Institute of America. He ended up the pastry chef at a popular restaurant, the kind where reservations are hard to come by and you need to be a celebrity to get a good table. But when I first met him, he was still working his way up, at a not-so-famous restaurant. But right from the beginning, we hit it off."

"But if this story ends the way I think it does, it was not a romance for you?"

"Right," Roxy said. "Joey was gay. He'd come to New York from Elyria, Ohio, a town outside Cleveland. Small-town guy, like me and Kitty and half of everybody living in New York. A tall, funny, redheaded Irish Catholic. Like Kitty. They'd met at church. Kitty once said it was like they'd instantly recognized one another for the frauds they were. Kitty was a chain-and-jeans-wearing lesbian all week, but on Sundays she put on a dress and heels and went to church. Joey was always a guy's guy, and few guessed he was gay, except for that whole 'loves to bake pretty cakes and French tarts' thing, but he and Kitty gravitated to each other anyway. And Joey knew a doctor. Somebody who could take care of the *situation* if that's what I wanted."

Roxy glanced up at Graciela, a staunch Catholic, but there was no judgment in her eyes.

"You know where I stand," Graciela said. "My beliefs are my beliefs, but God didn't put me here to be his judge."

"Well, Roxy said, "it didn't come to that. I don't know what I was thinking. Well, actually, I wasn't thinking at all. Just a terrified teenager, sleeping on the floor in Kitty's studio apartment. But Joey had an actual bedroom in his, and a decent sofa, and he invited me to stay with him instead. He went to doctors' appointments with me when Kitty couldn't. Took me for walks in the park and made sure I ate. Helped me find a waitressing job. And when I went into labor at only five months along, Joey's the one who got me to the hospital and lied that he was the father so he could stay with me while I lost my little girl."

Roxy drew a shuddering breath while Graciela dug in her oversized purse for a tissue and offered it to her.

"Joey always knew somebody somewhere who could help with whatever came up. He showed up at the hospital the next day with a tiny pink doll's dress and a little glitter-pink urn for Lisa Michelle's ashes."

"Lisa Michelle. That was your little girl's name?"

Roxy nodded. Almost fifty years and the low-level ache in her heart would never go completely away, but it didn't hurt to talk about Lisa Michelle anymore. At least not like it had for those first few years.

"I'd always thought my sister and I had stupid names for stupid reasons," Roxy said. "Natalia, the Russian name my grandmother insisted on for my sister, and me, Rita, named for a flashy actress. I wanted my baby to have a simple name, utterly American, and as common as mud. So that's where Lisa came from. Plucked from thin air just because I thought it sounded pretty. Michelle was because Joey's middle name was Michael and I'd planned on him being her godfather."

"That was good of your friend Joey to bring the little dress and urn," Graciela said.

"Yeah. I carried that little urn with me for a long time. I couldn't let her go. Couldn't seem to let the past be in the past, even though Joey and Jubil and Kitty and all the rest did everything in their power to help me create a new life. But

111

finally I did let Lisa go. Five years, six months, one week, and three days later, I tucked that little pink urn inside a beautiful purple casket alongside her Uncle Joey. I figured he'd take care of her in heaven, just like he'd taken care of me. And just like all of us had helped take care of him when the sickness came upon him. He was one of the early ones. The first in our little circle, before anyone had ever even heard of HIV or AIDS, but by no means the last. He was a canary in the coal mine, a warning of the dark times ahead for us."

Roxy straightened her shoulders and breathed deeply of the salt air flowing through the café's wide-open windows. So long ago. How had forty years flown past so quickly?

Roxy stabbed her salad with her fork, but her appetite had slipped away. She considered ordering a tall cold mojito, but signaled the waiter to bring another macchiato.

She nodded at the waiter and said to Graciela, "Back in the eighties, no matter how generous and open-minded you might be, if you even remotely suspected someone like that waiter were gay, you'd be hesitant to let him get anywhere near your food. You'd never allow him to even bring you a glass of water. No one knew what was causing the sickness. A constellation of symptoms was killing our friends and there was no name for it. A plague. And worse, so much worse, the shame that came with it."

Roxy swiped at the tear trembling on the corner of her eyelash and offered a smile to the young man who set down her coffee along with a fresh bowl of salsa for their tortilla chips. "So much shame. So much silence," she said after he walked away.

"It wasn't that way only in New York," Graciela said. "Miami in the seventies and eighties was nothing like you see today. Run down, shabby, full of drug dealers and mobsters and waves of people coming off boats from Cuba and Haiti. The Mariel boatlift was in 1980, but even before then, people risked their lives to get here. And some of them brought that scourge with them."

Now it was Graciela's turn to reach for the little package of tissues. "Reactions to AIDS and HIV were the same in my own family," she said. "My grandmother insisted to her dying day that my cousin died of a drug overdose or cancer. Even lying that he was shooting up drugs was far less humiliating than admitting the truth. It was okay to die of drugs. But if one even whispered *AIDS*, everybody immediately assumed he was gay and that kind of sin was going to send a good Catholic boy straight to hell forever."

"Yeah, cancer appeared in a lot of obits of young men in those days. Or pneumonia. Anything but AIDS. Joey's family did that back in the local paper in Elyria. They called it an aggressive cancer. And not a single one of them came to New York to see him while he was sick or for his funeral."

So many funerals. I can't stand any more. If Steve is really sick—

"Kint—"

Yeah. Whatever.

Roxy gathered up her purse and her shopping bags and signaled for the bill. "We were all so young then. Imagine it. In your twenties. Life is just beginning and the world is full of possibilities. Vietnam is over and no longer casts a shadow over the future. People are getting married and starting families. The pill gave us freedom. And there we were, in the creative heart of the world. Life was exciting and joyous, and we were utterly fearless. And then everyone around you starts dying. One day Joey's in the kitchen experimenting with new ingredients and feeding us the most amazing desserts. The next, he can't even lift a spatula."

The bill paid, Roxy and Graciela strolled down to the water's edge, found a bench, and sat, staring out quietly as the noisy families around them gathered their belongings at the end of another day, while cranky, sunburned children argued for one last swim and tired parents herded them toward cars and baths and dinner and bedtimes.

"People thought, 'Oh, we're young. We're healthy. We do all the right things to keep our beautiful bodies beautiful. And while we may snort coke and smoke a little pot, we aren't doing IV drugs. We aren't having sex with all that many people.' "

Roxy pulled in a deep breath of the fresh salt air. "We all felt so invincible."

She drew her knees up to her chest. "St. Vincent's hospital was where so many of them went. The medical staff were run ragged. People were dying in the halls. We all talked and decided we couldn't leave Joey in a place like that. So we took him home and took turns nursing him. There were early drugs, but they were all experimental." Roxy pulled the wadded-up tissue from her pocket and blew her nose. "Worst time of my life, holding vigil, holding a friend's hand while he died. Someone my own age. Someone who should be dancing, not dying."

Graciela patted Roxy's shoulder. "It's never easy," she said. "But you did it, and I'm sure it mattered. I wish I could have done the same for my cousin, but I was afraid. My family swore they'd disown me. That I'd be barred from the house if I visited him. If I touched him."

"Being scared is not a sin. Being young is not a sin," Roxy said. "This wasn't a punishment for the perverted, like so many said. And afterward, in the coming years, so many reached out, started organizing, started fundraising. Sponsored research. It's so much better now. Still...

"Back then, so many people died alone or close to it. The one thing a lot of gay folks had in common was that their families had thrown them out when they came out. So they were dying and people they loved shunned them. No comforting mother's touch. No one who remembered them when they were sweet little kids. All they had was us. Their friends, the families they created for themselves. We always tried to notify families when those dear, sweet men got sick, but a lot of them just didn't want to hear. So it was up to us, their friends, to feed and house them and pay their bills when they couldn't work anymore. And when it was over, it was up to us to pack up whatever possessions they had left and clean out their apartments when they died. We'd mostly give stuff to places like Goodwill, but we didn't dare mention the previous owner died of AIDS. People were scared and fear bred ignorance."

The waves flowed in and out. Soothing. Eternal. Not caring one whit about the cares of the world.

"Jubil went next," Roxy said. "Big, brash, bold, beautiful Jubil. During the day he dressed like any other man and worked at a brokerage firm, I think. Something to do with money. But at night she became Madame Duval. She was an early part of the vogue ball scene at the Elks Lodge in Harlem."

Graciela cocked her head. "A what ball?"

"Vogue. Drag queens competing for trophies and bragging rights. They formed into what were called houses, each with its own mother or father. Jubil was only on the fringes, never really a part of any house, but she loved to dress up and compete and just be in the scene. That's where she was heading the night we met."

Roxy shook her head. For the millionth time, she reminded herself of Jubil's frequent admonishment toward the end. To hold fast to the good memories and let the bad ones wash away like debris tossed in the ocean. Roxy sat unmoving, casting the bad memories into the waves in front of her.

"Jubil's death was the one that broke me. Joey was gone. Other friends were dead or sick or trying to hide their symptoms. Radio City, where the Rockettes danced, had gone through tough times, but it was making a comeback. But I just couldn't be there anymore. The stage and the walls were full of ghosts. Jubil had given up her apartment after her partner got too scared of New York and moved back west. Jubil moved in with me and Giorgio after Joey died. We had a few years, but looking back, it seems like only minutes passed. Then Jubil died too."

"Giorgio was Joey's partner, right? Did he get sick too?"

Roxy hadn't thought of Giorgio in years. They'd never been that close, only connected by their mutual love for Joey. "Giorgio de la Fontaine." Now there was a memory that made her smile. "He was a big outdoorsy type who waterskied and snow skied and ran marathons. He was an army brat who'd grown up all over the world. During the day he wrote copy for an ad agency, and at night he taught himself computer coding when not many did and dreamed of living in a garret in Paris and writing the great American novel."

"And did he get to live his dream?"

"I don't know," Roxy said. "After Jubil's death, he thought he'd try his hand at screenwriting. He moved to California. Not that Hollywood was escaping AIDS either. I heard he went back to using his real name—Rupert Kapinski. But we lost track of each other. I left New York about the same time he did. My friend Kitty had rediscovered her religious roots and decided she wanted to be a nun, the strict, cloistered kind, even as the rest of the nuns were giving up their habits and rebelling. I was tired of constantly scrambling for auditions and jobs. A few weeks here, a month or two in some road company, and once a full year in a chorus line, and always filling in with teaching dance or fencing or taking more classes. The dancing was taking a toll on my body and the deaths had taken a toll on my soul. I needed something different. I needed to not be responsible for anyone or anything for a while. Back in 1980 Giorgio had talked all of us into pooling our money and investing in an IPO for a company called Apple."

Graciela gaped at her. "Are you telling me you got in on the ground floor of that?"

"Close enough. And since we'd pooled our money to buy in, we all had wills leaving it to each other. We didn't know it would turn into a tontine, with me as the last survivor. That's how I knew Giorgio —Rupert—had died. I got a letter from his attorney saying I'd inherited his Apple stock. I'd only heard from Giorgio once in all those years, the day he called from California and told me a company called Amazon was going public and I should buy in since he knew I liked books and reading a lot."

"So you're the one I should designate to take me in when

I'm old and sick and poor?" Graciela said, laughing and throwing her arm around Roxy's shoulder.

"Yeah, 'cause that kid of yours, the brilliant architecture student with the straight-A report card is never going to amount to anything, I'm sure."

Like a message from the past, Roxy heard Jubil's voice in her head. *The most healing medicine isn't just laughter, it's sharing laughter with a good friend.*

Roxy sighed. Whatever was going on in Steve Stephen's life right now, he could probably use a friend too. *If* the stubborn man would only let her in for more than just a quick sheet-tangling shuffle ball followed by a "here's your hat, what's your hurry" exit.

"*Kintsugi.*"

Yeah, I know. But this is the last time.

Chapter 14

Sexy Firefighters Calendar Word of the Day:
Sciamachy: [sahy-am-uh-kee] **Noun.** an act or instance of fighting a shadow or an imaginary enemy, 1. sham fighting for exercise or practice.

ROXY PULLED HERSELF away from the old memories that had followed her home after the lunch with Graciela. She'd been a nurse without much of a purse back then. Now she had the purse, but did she really want to be a nurse again? She really hadn't liked the way Steve looked. But he reminded her of Jubilation Duval. Big. Gruff. Proud.

Probably too proud for his own good.

She'd moved too fast, but it wasn't too late.

Roxy laughed at herself. Yeah, it was. She already felt the quicksand of attraction sucking around her red-polished tootsies. Maybe she could keep whatever it was between them light and breezy. Get in and out and no hurt feelings. She damned sure wasn't going to stick around and watch anyone die ever again.

She'd taken her time re-doing her makeup when she'd gotten home from the beach. She didn't want to show up at Steve's house all red-eyed and streaky. The breezy polka-dotted dress she'd thrown on had helped bolster her mood.

She glanced at her watch as she hurried up Steve's walkway. A quarter after. She hated being late. The door opened just as she raised her hand to knock.

"Sorry, Roxy, I'm not in the mood. Thanks anyway."

Roxy shoved her sandaled foot in the door before Steve had a chance to shut it on her. "Can I at least get a drink of water? I'm sweating like a pig at an all-you-can-eat bacon festival."

Steve hesitated for a second too long. Roxy had spent a lot of years shoving her way past New York City doormen; Steve didn't stand a chance.

"Just a glass of water," she said, heading toward the kitchen.

Steve trailed after her, propping himself in the doorway as she grabbed a glass out the cupboard. Florida tap water was notoriously bad or warm. She pressed her glass against the automatic ice dispenser, then opened the fridge door and grabbed the pitcher of water she'd put there this morning, not trusting that Steve had ever known about or remembered to change the filter on the water dispenser.

She leaned back against the kitchen counter and watched Steve watching her as she gulped down half the glass.

"So," she said. "I spent my half my day keeping a bunch of geezers from slashing each other to death and teaching them how to politely stab each other instead. How did your day go?"

Steve hadn't smiled since he'd opened the door, but she swore he fought valiantly against the ghost of one that rippled the corner of his lips. "Roxy," he said, sighing deeply. "This just isn't going to work out." He shoved out his hand, stopping the flow of words that bubbled at the edge of Roxy's tongue.

"We've known each other twenty-four hours. You've fed me twice, stocked my refrigerator, and gave me a great night in bed. That's pushing it for people who come from totally different worlds and don't know jack-all about each other. I'm sorry. You're a great gal, I'm sure, but I don't want this to go any further. I don't know what you want, Roxy, but it ain't me, and it ain't now."

He straightened up, stepped away from the doorway, and pointed toward his front door.

Roxy gulped the water, draining the glass. She took her time washing it, drying it, then returning it to the cupboard.

"Steve," she said.

He pointed to the door again.

Roxy had never been one to give up on anything. Why did she feel so compelled to reach out to him? What attracted her to him, made her nerves pop like iron filings leaping to an oversized magnet?

"I'm going," she said. As she sidled past him, the smell of his cologne triggered an ancient scent memory. She recoiled.

Three hours ago she'd sat with Graciela, wallowing in memories of New York and the memory of the reason she'd gone to New York in the first place. And now those ancient ghosts reached out to her again.

Was God dicking around with her today?

"Something wrong?" Steve asked.

"Old Spice. I loathe Old Spice."

Steve cocked his head, his brow furrowed, a hint of concern in his velvety-brown eyes.

"A long time ago," Roxy said. "Nothing to do with you. You know what? You're right. I'm leaving. You're a nice guy, Steve, and I don't want my thoughts of you to get tangled up with nasty old memories."

She turned her head, inhaling deeply, hoping to fill her nostrils with the scent of dead air-conditioned air. Dust. Body odor. Anything to wipe out that memory. Where were stale beer bottles and chitlins when a woman needed them?

Damn. Almost fifty years ago and the cloying scent took her right back.

Steve reached for her, but she pulled away from him.

"It's been nice, Steve, but you're right. I'm being too pushy. I just——" No, she didn't owe anyone her story. Everybody involved was dead and buried anyway.

Everyone but her.

She strode to the door and opened it, then turned to Steve. "Life is made up of moments, Steve, moments that add up to days and years and decades. Some of those moments suck. I mean totally suck—limp, sweaty, donkey balls suck. But I'm at an age where I recognize I'm running out of moments. And I promised myself years ago that I'd do everything in my power to limit the suckiness of any moments I have left and to not let the good ones pass me by."

She straightened her shoulders. "Do you remember me telling you about the moonflowers in my garden? Each one blooms, spreads its sweetness, and then dies. The blossom only lasts a single night, but oh, what joy it gives in that moment!"

Roxy drew in a slow breath and smiled wanly. "Meeting you was one of those good moments. Really great, actually. I wanted to see if I could squeeze a few more good moments into my life. And I did. I hope you did too. So thanks. And if it turns out that we last no longer than a moonflower, well, so be it. I don't regret a second of it. If I run into you at the club, I'll just nod and smile. No worries that I'll be clingy or talk behind your back or anything. No one needs to know."

The distance from the kitchen to the front door wasn't long. Steve's long legs crossed it in two strides. His big hand wrapped around her arm.

And the memory, buried so deep for so long, swamped her.

Big hands trapping her arms. Her body. The heat. The scent of Old Spice wrapping around her like a miasma, cutting off her breath. She knew what came next.

Pain. Helplessness, trapped on a dingy sofa under a body bigger and stronger than her own seventeen-year-old one.

She'd fought back then, but hadn't been able to stop it. He'd laughed at her measly efforts. He'd laughed while he hurt her, over and over, whispering threats and promises in equal measure.

She knew better now. She'd taken every self-defense course she could afford. It wasn't going to happen again.

The shadow she swung at grunted when she landed the first punch in what she hoped was his solar plexus.

Unlike the man in Roxy's memory, this one stepped back, his hands in the air in the universal sign of surrender.

Not enough. Not enough by a long shot. *Switchblade*. Instinct kicked in. The blade was out of her purse in an instant. She swung toward her assailant.

"Roxy, stop! Damn it woman, stop!"

Roxy's breath sawed in and out of her chest. She blinked sweat away from her eyes, shaking her head like a wet dog.

"I don't know who hurt you, woman, but I'm gonna hunt that motherfucker down and wipe him off the planet for you. I know some people. They'll be using him for target practice in a godforsaken sandbox on the other side of the world. Hell, don't even have to take him that far. I still got friends on the force, and the alligators don't mind rotten meat for lunch. Just say the word, Rox. Put down the knife and tell me where to find the son-of-a-motherfucking-bitch that hurt you."

The words came from far away, echoing down the dark tunnel of her memory. "Meg said almost the same thing. So did Kitty." Roxy sucked in a breath. The blade suddenly weighed a thousand pounds in her hand. She snapped it shut. Shoved it into her pocket. Her shoulders slumped.

"It's already been taken care of. I heard they found him one night down by the creek. After I'd already run away to New York. It wasn't me. One of his, uh…parts was…uh…mangled." Roxy turned back to Steve.

"Play stupid games, win stupid prizes." Steve's words, meant to ease her, still sounded strangled.

"Shit, I'm sorry. I have no idea where that came from." She lied. She knew exactly where that frenzy had come from. A jumble of old grief and old memories and old fears had coalesced and exploded in a perfect storm.

The anniversary of Lisa Michelle's birthday. The baby she'd mourned even though she'd been created in hate.

Old wounds opened at lunch with Graciela.

A long-ago assault she'd thought was firmly in her past.

And Steve, utterly innocent, had gotten caught in it.

"Are you okay? Did I hurt you?" Roxy reached for him, but he backed up a step.

"Just catching my breath," he said. "You throw a hell of a punch."

Roxy waivered in the half-open door. She should go. Just walk out and leave the man alone.

But she'd hit him. He hadn't been looking too good when she'd walked in. He'd had some sort of episode yesterday. He'd been pissed when she met him, and she'd probably triggered whatever happened then too.

"Honest to God, Steve, I don't usually bring this much misery with me. Let me get you some water and then I'll get out of here." She headed toward the kitchen on shaking legs. She could use a glass of ice water too.

Actually, she could use something stronger.

She let the tepid water from the tap run over her wrists, slapping more water on her exposed chest and the back of her neck. She didn't care if the water left spots down the front of her dress. The thought of the fish fry now left her stomach churning.

Steve's bedroom was on the other side of the kitchen. She heard the shower come on. She hadn't gotten a good look at him. Had she bloodied him?

She should go. As soon as her legs stopped shaking. Right now, adrenaline coursed through her. That temporary hormonal rush would be enough to get her out the door, down the sidewalk, and safely into her own house. She'd get a shower of her own, even though she'd had one an hour ago.

She needed to wash off the river of sweat that drenched her skin. Wash off the stink of ancient cologne that had permeated the thin cotton of her dress. Take the dress out to the garage and burn it.

She needed to get out of there while she could. Before the adrenaline wore off and left her weak and exhausted.

Vulnerable.

No. Not vulnerable.

That was then.

This was now.

The shower shut off. Moments later she heard Steve moving from his bedroom to his living room.

Deep breaths. Deep breaths. Say goodbye, apologize, get the hell out of here.

Roxy filled a glass with ice water and carried it to the living room. Steve stood with his back to her, staring out his front window.

"I'll just put this on your end table here, okay?" Roxy set it down and backed up. "Do you need any pills or anything? Should I call somebody?"

Steve swung to face her. His jaw worked, as if he ground his teeth together, while the fingers on his big hands flexed as if looking for a throat to throttle.

Roxy had no fear of him. It wasn't her he was mad at. She didn't know how she knew that, but she did.

"We're going to sit down for a minute and catch our breaths," Steve said. "We'll be dead silent if that's what you want, or we'll talk our heads off if that's what you need. We'll talk about that damned soap opera of yours or I'll recite the FM 38-5 Logistics Maintenance Management Manual, Section III, 'Controlled Cannibalization and Local Procurement of Parts.' Or we can talk about what happened to make you stupid enough to punch a man twice your size in the chest. It's all up to you. And then I'm going to walk you home, Roxy," he said. "Not because I don't want you here. But because I don't want you to be alone right now and I think you'd feel safer in a familiar place. And because I know what the fuck it feels like when some goddamned demon from the past comes slithering out of the memory hole you thought you had the fucker locked in."

He stepped cautiously toward her. "I washed off the damned cologne and put on all clean clothes. I rarely wear it and it's going in the trash. But the bedroom probably still stinks like it and I need to get it aired out. I'm going to walk you home while it does. I'm going to order a pizza and fix you a drink. But first, you need to sit down and breathe."

He took another step.

Roxy stood her ground, not backing up. "It's okay, Steve. I...it just caught me off guard, that's all. It was a long time ago. I'm okay. I'm sorry. I know what to do. I'll be fine."

"I know you will. You're a tough cookie and tough cookies don't crumble. Yada yada and all that bullshit. I'm still walking you home. After you have a glass of water and prove to me you won't fall down. I know how adrenaline works."

She turned toward the door.

"Didn't you call me a hard case just yesterday?" Steve said. "All but accuse me of shutting people out and not accepting help? You're such an altruist, all that concern for other people, but when was the last time you let somebody help you? You think I'm stubborn? Have you looked in the mirror lately?"

Steve's words stung her like pellets of hail. What did he know anyway? He had no right—Roxy reached for the doorknob.

"I don't want—"

"You don't want help? You don't want anybody to see you in a weak moment? Tough shit. Consider this payback. You caught me in a stupidly weak moment yesterday when the sun got to be too much for me and I had no choice but to let you help. Now it's my turn to return the favor."

"I don't need—"

"Yeah, I know. You don't need anybody taking care of you. You flit all over sprinkling your little random acts of kindness, but when someone tries to do one for you, you turn as prickly as a saguaro cactus. Were you just faking it last night? Playing Princess Bountiful to the lonesome neighbor and puffing yourself up with pride at the good deed you were doing?"

Roxy spun toward him. How dare he? How *dare* he?

"I let people help me in the past. They gave me so much and I owe them—"

"Nobody owes anybody jack shit. Random acts of kindness aren't actually random. People do stuff intentionally because there's something in it for them, even if it's just to feel good for a few minutes. Maybe it's because they actually care about somebody. So are you going to let me try to do something nice, or are you going to throw my good intentions in my face and go racing off like a felon on the run?"

"*Kintsugi, Roxy.*"

"Oh, shut up!" She gasped and pressed her fist against her lips, holding back all the words and memories and bile that threatened to pour out.

"No, I won't shut up," Steve said. "The best way to wipe out sucky moments is to replace them with good ones, right, Roxy? Isn't that what you just said? So let's make a few good moments happen. You can tell me how you got to be a Rockette."

Roxy swallowed the tears that clawed at the back of her throat. She gulped down air like a woman dragged out of a riptide. She squeezed her eyes shut, as if that would shut out all the faces, the memories, the words, but it did no good. She opened her eyes.

And there was Steve. Twenty-four inches away from her. Far enough away to not threaten her. Close enough to catch her if she collapsed.

But could she trust—

"I decided to become a Rockette after I ran away to New York," she said. She didn't know if she could trust him, but her heart cried out to her to try. "And I ran away to New York because of a fucking old Nazarene elder with a wife he browbeat into submission and a penchant for underage girls."

"Girls like you, Roxy?"

She nodded.

"Maybe I don't need to hear that story after all."

"It's not all bad, Steve. It started out bad, but it forced me to break out of my narrow little life and go to New York. It wasn't all rainbows and roses there either, but there were good times too." Roxy sucked in one more breath. "You know why I like to garden? Because while you may start out up to your elbows in shit, with enough time and work and patience you can make something beautiful grow out of it."

126

"I never learned to garden, but I've had more than enough shit."

Distraction. Steve was right about that, at least. She needed distraction. A minute to get her racing heart down to a more normal speed. Anything would do.

Anything to drown out the screaming as she shoved old memories back into their cages.

She nodded at the photos on his wall, the only decorations in the room. "Tell me about those."

Her knees still shook, but she could run if she had to.

But she didn't have to. She was safe, wasn't she? Steve was not that twisted monster from the past. Nothing was holding her here. The door was right there. But all the ghosts reached out, doing their damnedest to claw her back into the shadows with them. She'd thought she'd outrun them eons ago.

Maybe she was wrong.

For now, while she figured it out, all she had to do was listen to Steve. His voice was nice—a deep, rolling bass.

She drew in a shuddering breath and let that voice envelop her.

Chapter 15

Steve's Date with Death: T-Minus 23:33:41 and Counting

STEVE PASSED BY the photos every day but rarely gave them a thought. He'd only hung them up because he'd wanted to get rid of the box they were in when he moved in. But if talking about them was what it took to help Roxy calm down, then damn it, that was what he'd do.

"The one on the left is the only one I have of my family. That's me and Natalie in front, and Daddy, and Mama's holding my baby brother, Royce."

"You have a brother?"

Steve shook his head. "Royce died when he was three. Measles. No vaccines back then. Not a lot of good medical care either."

"They look like nice folks."

Roxy's voice still shook, but Steve had to give her credit for trying. Still, best not to crowd her.

"They were. Good churchgoing folks from good churchgoing families. You know the kind. Great big church-lady hats and foot-stomping gospel music and big family cookouts for any little occasion. We didn't have a lot, but both of them worked to make sure we had enough to eat and clean clothes, even if they were hand-me-downs."

He nodded at the picture. "Mama did whatever work she

could from home so she could take care of us kids. She sold Avon and Tupperware to other ladies who didn't have any more than we did, but they all helped each other out. They'd buy a lipstick or a little container of bubble bath for the kids. They wouldn't spend money on themselves much, but Mama could always convince them it was okay to spend a little if it was for their kids."

Steve nodded at the picture. "Mama also was a seamstress. She made those dresses she and Natalie are wearing, and my shirt. She not only made clothes from scratch but did mending and custom tailoring for the wealthier white ladies on the other side of town. Me and Nat would sit in the car and do our homework and eat a pimento cheese and pickle sandwich while Mama was inside some fancy house, making a few dollars hemming a lady's satin ball gown for a Daughters of the Confederacy fundraising gala or some such."

"Yeah, I know what that's like," Roxy said. "My mom was a widow with two kids. For a while she cashiered at the local corner grocery store. She wore hand-me-down dresses from her sister." Roxy drew in a deep breath and smiled. "A hand-me-down dress got her into trouble one time with the good folks in the Nazarene church, but she got back at them."

Steve cocked his head. Considering her earlier mention of the Nazarene preacher, maybe this wasn't a good path for Roxy's memories to take. But she plunged on with her story.

"Back in those days, folks could run a tab at the store and were supposed to pay up on payday. It was the only grocery in town. It was also the kind of little hole-in-the-wall place where men sat on the front porch and gossiped and all the ladies in the town would stand and gossip in the aisles. So Mom pretty much kept up on whatever was going on in town. And because she was just the poor widow lady behind the counter, nobody ever paid much mind to what they said in front of her."

Roxy's smile grew marginally bigger. Steve had to admire the woman's grit. He'd seen guys go berserk when the adrenaline hit, but Roxy was handling it like a trained special forces soldier.

"We weren't Nazarenes," Roxy said, "but it was the closest church within walking distance. Some Sundays we'd drive up to Columbus and go to church with her sisters, but most times we'd go to the Nazarene church. My aunt had much more flamboyant taste than Mom, so there were times the Sunday dress she'd handed down to Mom was flashier than the upright, uptight Nazarenes could tolerate."

"And that got her into trouble?"

Roxy rubbed her hands. "Oh, you bet. One Sunday she was wearing this dress with bright red flowers all over it. Now in this church, it was not uncommon for the minister to call out specific parishioners who had somehow strayed or caused offense. He'd call them out from the pulpit and make them stand up, and he'd berate and shame them in front of the all the other fine folks of the congregation, expecting an out loud confession and contrition, while all the others were cowering in their seats feeling both righteous and grateful their own sins hadn't gotten called out."

"Whoo boy," Steve said. "He did that to your mama?"

"He tried. He called her out because of her inappropriate dress. And lipstick. Now, my mom was a good Christian, as peaceful and honest and sinless as God ever made a woman. But that day she just lost it. She stood up and started calling out all the good righteous people who had run up a tab at the grocery store and hadn't paid it off in months. She called out every parishioner who'd sent their kids to buy cigarettes or beer for them, because good Nazarenes don't smoke or drink. She called out the ones who went drinking and dancing in Columbus on the weekends—forbidden activities—and pointed out those who were cheating on their spouses."

"Did she know—"

"I hadn't told her, but who knows what she knew? All I know is we never went back. And a whole lot of tabs got paid at the grocery store on Monday morning. And two months later I ran off to New York."

Steve forced a smile to match Roxy's, but in his heart he still wanted to hunt down that motherfucking minister and rip off his dick and shove it down his throat.

But Roxy's color looked better, less pale, although she continued to wring her hands as if they were cold. He wanted to take her hands, to rub them between his own big ones until she felt warm and safe, but it was probably better not to touch her right now.

Probably better not to touch her ever again. He liked this feisty, brave woman, but she wasn't going to change his plans.

He was still going to die before sundown tomorrow.

"Mom also quit her job at the store. Got a job doing accounting at a government defense plant. Life got a little better for her then. She even sent me money in New York. She dated some, but I don't think she ever really got over Dad dying, especially so young."

"Not having a dad is tough on kids," Steve said, seizing on the topic. Anything to help Roxy, though Steve had no real idea why he should care. Still, while he was alive, maybe he could do one last good deed. Might buy him a point or two on St. Peter's tally sheet.

"I was lucky my daddy was around through all my growing up years," Steve said. "During the week he worked at a dry cleaner. Inhaling all those fumes all day is probably what killed him in the end, but back then, it never occurred to him to file for workers' comp or anything. On weekends he worked as a waiter in the restaurant in one of the big hotels, catering to white folks. He could carry their steaks to their tables but wasn't allowed to sit anywhere except in the back room reserved for colored folks. He had to use the bathroom down on the corner at the gas station."

Roxy perched on the arm of Steve's sofa, like a wary bird that might take flight at any second.

Keep talking. Keep her distracted. But damn, he hadn't planned on dredging up all those old memories today. All the people he missed. Just a few more hours, though, and if he could squeak past St. Pete at the pearly gates, maybe he'd get to see them again.

"Dad was in the army too," Steve said. "World War II. The army was still segregated. When he came home, he was supposed to get the same GI benefits as the white guys. You know, money for college and a GI loan for a house."

Steve flexed his hands to keep them from forming into fists. Wouldn't do to scare Roxy, and his old anger had nothing to do with her.

"The guys approving that stuff were most always white," he said. "And they turned down all those promised benefits for Black men. Men who'd served just like they did. Flat denied them their rights. So white men went to college and got good jobs. They built whole tracts of houses for returning white GIs and set up nice little neighborhoods and they got all middle class and raised their kids with the advantages that good jobs and nice houses bring. They redlined whole neighborhoods so folks like Daddy couldn't buy there. Colleges and trade schools were segregated or just plain refused to admit Black folks, so he couldn't get job training. It made Daddy mad, but there wasn't nothin' he could do about it. Mama said it didn't matter; they'd work and save up. And that's what they did. They bought themselves a little house. It wasn't anything fancy, but it was ours. They wanted to be able to leave something to their kids. Natalie and her husband lived in that house and helped take care of Mama and Daddy when they stopped being able to tend to themselves."

"Do you still have that house in Mississippi?"

Steve shook his head. "I never wanted to go back to that town. Nat sold it not long before she died, when she knew she'd never be going back either. She split the money with me. It wasn't a lot, but it was the legacy our parents wanted us to have. I used my share for a couple of investments that are so far underwater they may as well be in the Mariana Trench. I've left this house to my lousy nephew, who'll probably sell it and blow the cash on a couple of RPG-7 rocket launchers and a used tank.

So much for all my parents' hard work."

"Was it any easier for you to get your GI benefits? Did you use them?"

Steve shrugged. "Some. I used it for a couple of college courses I needed to get on at the DEA. Curtis insisted I try for a GI loan on this house. Got it too, no questions asked. Then Curtis turned around and paid off the whole thing—cash. He'd just wanted to prove that even though the world is still shit in a lot of ways for us folk, times are changing too. Not fast, but some."

Steve sucked in a deep breath, then moved cautiously to perch on the arm of his recliner. He didn't want to get too comfortable in case she got it into her head to go racing off again and he had to stop her.

"No point in being mad about that crap after all these years," he said. "Daddy wasn't happy about me going in the army, but it was like I was called to it. And I was young and stupid and stubborn."

"Apparently still are. Stubborn, I mean."

"And stupid?"

Roxy shrugged. "Haven't decided yet."

Steve turned back to the picture. "I hope he would have changed his mind if he'd seen how I turned out. I've done some bad shit, but I tried to do good now and then too."

"I'll bet he would have been bustin' his buttons with pride."

"I'll never know. He died while I was in Vietnam."

"I'm sorry to hear that. It's never easy, though not so bad for me, I guess. Mine died when I was two," Roxy said. "It made Mom sad that I have no memory of him. Weirdly, it was probably fumes that killed him too. When he and Mom met, he was a driver for a bread delivery truck."

Roxy unfroze a little but still didn't sit back on the sofa. "Babushka, his mother, didn't like the idea of her boy driving around in the dark mornings all alone delivering bread, so she insisted on going along with him. She's the one who spotted my mom and picked her out and demanded Dad ask her out. When us kids came along, delivery driving didn't pay as much, so he got a job at a factory spray painting numbers on crates. Nobody thought to provide masks or protective gear back then. He had a stroke and died when he was thirty-two. Mom got a small payout from the company and social security for us kids until we turned eighteen. That's how she was able to go to school and get the accounting job."

"Your grandmother sounds like a controlling woman."

Roxy rolled her eyes. "You don't know the half of it. She went along on Mom and Dad's honeymoon, insisting they spend it driving cross-country to California to visit her relatives."

Steve raised his eyebrows and gave a low whistle.

"I know, right?" Roxy pointed to the other pictures. "And those?"

Steve nodded to one. "That's Natalie and her son, Curtis. My harebrained crackpot nephew."

"You really love him, don't you?"

Steve nodded. "Yeah, he's an asshole, but I love him. That's the job of uncles. To love the kids and keep them from turning out like we did. Unfortunately, Curtis is more like my old army buddy, Glen Wilson: always ready to make a fast buck and not too choosy about who's paying. But yeah, that picture was taken in Sorrento. Curtis lives there in a compound with a couple of pals and wives and kids. It's complicated. But Natalie went to live with them all. I took that picture the first time I visited, before we knew she was sick. I saw her again after that, but she wouldn't allow any pictures."

He pointed to a low cabinet and the only real source of color in the gray room. "That box over there came from Sorrento. It's what they call intarsia. Inlaid wood."

The box was big—ten inches by eighteen inches—bright blue, and inlaid with an intricate muted pattern of cream and yellow flowers. It sat in the center of eight ceramic cups and matching dessert plates, all painted with vivid lemons.

"Natalie gave me those on that last visit. She loved those colors. Said she wanted me to have a little sunshine in my life."

This wasn't going to do either him or Roxy any good, talking about sad memories. Roxy was up and pacing again. Although she'd bitten off all her lipstick, her shoulders were more relaxed. She rubbed her hand over the polished wood of the box but didn't try to open it. She glanced past the cute pictures of Curtis's kids, straight to the one he had no idea why he'd hung up. It wasn't a happy picture.

Or maybe it was. One goofy, carefree moment in a world full of blood and shit.

"Vietnam," he said, responding to her unasked question. "It stunk all the time there. Not the good green scent of your garden. The jungle stink of decay. So humid you inhaled more water than oxygen. That pic was taken on a street in Saigon. It stunk too. Motorbike fumes mixed with rotting vegetables in the market. Raw sewage and vomit from the guys who'd spent their twenty-four-hour leave getting as blind drunk as possible."

Roxy leaned in for a closer look. "I can pick you out," she said.

A way-too-young Steve Stephens stared into the camera lens with his perpetual old-man's dead-serious expression.

"Who are the others?"

Steve moved beside Roxy. Not too close; he didn't want to scare her into bolting. Or punching him again. Or running her switchblade through him. He rubbed the spot on his chest. Now wouldn't that just be God's last little joke, for him to have a nice, simple suicide planned and then end up murdered in his own doorway by some crazy white woman?

He pointed to the photo.

"Chip Porter," Steve said. "The one holding his arms up like he scored a touchdown. Died in a car accident in 2002. Orin Gallo, the one with his hands in his fatigue pockets, repairs pickup trucks in Montana or Wyoming or some damned place."

"The one staring off into space?"

Steve shook his head. "Jack 'Chopper' Reynolds. Stoned out of his gourd on opium. Fucking miracle he never got any of us killed, but when we needed evac, the son of a bitch could

Pat Edwards

land a chopper on a mosquito's dick. Last I heard he was a veterinarian or something down here in Florida. Knowing Jack, he's probably getting paid a thousand dollars a pop to trim the toenails on a teacup poodle and slip a quickie dick to the poodle's owner."

"And the last guy?"

Glen Wilson bearing a crooked, toothy grin—smoking a cigar and flipping his middle finger at the whore operating Steve's old rangefinder camera. *Goddamned Glen Wilson.*

"His name's Glen Wilson. He's in the news now and then. Maybe you heard of him?"

Roxy wrinkled her brow. "Something about Alaska? Some scandal?"

"Yeah, that's him. Elected to Congress, then some shit went down. Hushed up somehow. I don't know how he got that to happen, but he always seems to manage it. Slicker than snot on a doorknob. I was his sergeant in Vietnam. You remember that old TV show, Sergeant Bilko? Guy always had a scam or grift going? That was Wilson. I was a supply sergeant. He was always trying to get around me with one of his schemes. Later on we crossed paths a few times when I was with the DEA. Stubborn, wrongheaded, ringmaster of his own circus, and asshole-in-chief. That's Glen Wilson."

More honestly, Steve kept track of Glen as he traveled. He was a complicated mystery, one Steve had never been able to solve. Maybe he hadn't really wanted to. How could a former drug dealer win a congressional race in Alaska? How could he recover from having it ripped from under his feet like a Turkish rug? How could one man survive when he'd made such powerful enemies? What was the nature of Glen's engine? What sustained that bizarre agent of chaos? Really. What would the madman—the wretched, insane jester in God's court—Glen Wilson do?

"Any idea what he's up to today?"

Steve shook his head. "Whatever it is, it's probably teetering on the fine line of being legal, is batshit insane, will probably get somebody killed, and will make him a shit-ton of money."

Steve sighed. "We have a complicated relationship. Sometimes he'd do me a favor. Give me a tip. Sometimes I'd do the same for him. But he's never to be trusted. I always try to keep that ledger balanced. Unfortunately, he gave me guidance that helped me get Curtis out of a jam a few years ago. It's like being pinned to a table under one of those swinging axe things, waiting to see when Glen's gonna call that favor due. At least Murphy got away from him, last I heard."

Roxy raised her eyebrows. "Wife? Lover? Kidnapee?"

Steve shuddered. "Thank God she's never been that stupid. None of the above. Glen keeps an entourage around him, folks devoted to him for whatever reason. It's not just the money he makes for them. Maybe they like the buzz. No, Margaret Murphy is a retired cop who used to work for Glen. I taught her a lot of what she knows. We were colleagues in a way. The only sane one in Wilson's orbit, which is probably why she doesn't work for him anymore. Last time I asked, she was head of security for an international rock star and living with the love of her life. Murphy's good people. We stay in touch. Maybe once a week or every couple of weeks, we connect just to catch up."

When Steve was dead, would anyone think to let Murphy know? Maybe he'd need to spend a couple of minutes in the morning adding to the list of people to be called once they found his body. Curtis wasn't the kind to take care of details like that. And nobody would even know to call Roxy.

Not that he wanted her to know. He'd known her what, two days? He had no claim on her. Didn't want to.

Steve turned away from the wall of photos. Roxy's shoulders had dropped from their defensive stance and her eyes had lost that wild look, but her breathing still sounded too fast and shallow for his liking. That adrenaline would be fading fast.

Steve hadn't planned on having pizza for his last supper.

And yet here he was. He offered Roxy his arm.

After a moment's hesitation, she placed her hand in the

crook of his elbow and pasted a smile on her face. "Walk me home, and if you play your cards right, I'll tell you the story of the man who fell out of the sky."

Yeah, Steve would walk her home, listen to her story, and get the hell out of there. Gain a few more points in the plus column of God's book of deeds without adding to the negative column by taking advantage of a vulnerable woman. This close to the finish line, he couldn't afford to fuck up the score more than it already was.

Chapter 16

Sexy Firefighters Calendar Word of the Day:
Dissilient: [dih-sil-ee-uhnt] **Adjective.** *bursting apart; bursting open.*

ROXY HAD STARTED stripping off her dress before the front door was closed. She'd hadn't really gotten close enough to get the scent of Old Spice on her, but the memory of the cologne filled her nostrils. Steve stood outside the bathroom door and demanded that she hand the dress over. She'd hoped he would burn it, but when she'd stepped out of the shower, she'd heard the chug of her washing machine. She couldn't remember if the dress was dry clean only. It didn't matter.

Her second—no, third—shower of the day had helped. As had the nap she'd taken immediately after. Steve had offered to close the door and let her rest, but she hadn't wanted to be alone with her memories. He'd curled around her back like a big comforting blanket, not doing anything but holding her. She'd woken up once with his hand wrapped around a tit, but that was okay with her; it was more like someone cuddling a favorite toy than a sexual advance, and she'd immediately fallen back asleep.

She'd woken the second time to a dark, empty room and the scent of garlic and pizza. She wandered into the kitchen to find Steve with a beer in front of him, engrossed in another episode of *The Guiding Light*.

He blushed sheepishly, muttered something about stupid addictions, and poured her a glass of merlot. He must have rifled

Pat Edwards

through her pantry while she'd slept. Merlot was not her favorite, but she kept a bottle there for those who did like it. Right now the only thing that mattered was that the wine was wet and probably better than the shot or three of bourbon she'd thought about chugging.

They sat across from each other at Roxy's kitchen table. She wore a set of 1940s-style lounge pajamas she'd found in one of the vintage shops over on the beach.

Lunch had been too many hours ago, and she'd awakened utterly ravenous. She looked over the array of food, opting to start with a slice of the cheesy garlic bread. She waved at all the food on the table and overflowing onto the counter. "Planning to feed a platoon? Are we expecting company?"

"I wasn't sure what you liked on your pizza, so I got a couple different kinds. You can always call that Iggy kid to come over and polish off the leftovers."

"So," Roxy said. "If I recall, I promised to tell you about the time the dude fell out of the sky and almost landed in my neighbor's lap." Roxy sucked down a healthy draft of the wine, poured another, and settled back in her chair.

Steve grabbed a slice of pizza and took a big bite. It was good to see him eating. Good to have company. Good to have Steve sitting there with her, filling up her kitchen with his warmth with his simple presence.

Yeah, she had it bad. But all those heated, complicated feelings could go on tomorrow's worry list. For now, there was only food and wine and avoiding the present issue of falling for a guy she had no business falling for by escaping into a funny story of someone else falling from the past.

She sent up a quick prayer that her fall would be less painful than that man's had been.

"This story begins," she said, "with a push from a local developer who bought up the vacant land around Darby Glen. The whole village of Darby Glen had been started in the nineteen twenties as a campground for folks looking to escape from Columbus in the summer. Each lot was no bigger than a

140

small camper. Folks would buy a tiny little lot and pitch a tent on it for a weekend or a week. Maybe park their fishing boat on it, since there was a wide creek—like a small river—right there. But the lots were ridiculously cheap and pretty soon folks were buying a couple at a time and putting up little houses on them. Fishing shacks and stuff at first, but later on, real houses. That's what my grandmother did, when Mom and Dad got married. She bought seven of those lots and gave my parents the money to build a little four-room house on them. Two bedrooms, a kitchen, and a front room."

"No bathroom?"

"Not at first, though later on they walled-in the back porch and added a tiny bathroom. But it used well water, not city water. Babushka lived in terror of the well running dry. So we flushed the toilets with buckets of water. And there was no water heater, so even though we had a bathtub, water was heated on the oil stove in the middle of the front room, also our version of central heating."

"Damn," Steve said. "I grew up dirt poor, but at least we could flush toilets and take baths."

"Lucky you. Anyway, you remember how controlling Babushka was? Well, one of those two bedrooms was for her. I guess she never considered my parents would actually have s-e-x and add a couple of kids. And see, the deal was, she gave the house to Dad on the condition that he always take care of her. Then he suddenly died."

"Oooh boy." Steve whistled.

"Mom inherited the house, but she kept the promise Dad made. Plus, Babushka made a great built-in babysitter, even if she mostly spoke a hybrid Russian-Polish and damn near no English. Mom gave one room to us kids, and we used it until I got old enough to finish up the attic and make it our room. Babushka had the other, and Mom slept on the sofa."

"So, the man from the sky?" Steve dabbed pizza grease off his lips and hands, wadded up his napkin, then leaned his elbows on the table.

141

"Right. Well, it wasn't long before a big-city developer came sniffing around. He bought the vacant land on the other side of the creek and tried to buy up our houses. He wanted to make the area more posh, more upscale. Rename it Sussex Shire or Cambridge Meadows or something. But the good folks of Darby Glen wouldn't budge. So there he was, stuck with nothing but a bunch of wide-open fields but not enough room to put in his fancy development. So he got the bright idea to rent all that open, worthless ground out to flying clubs on weekends, as a place for folks to practice skydiving."

"Oh no. This isn't going to end well, is it?"

Roxy smiled and reached for another piece of pizza, taking her time arranging it on her plate. She liked the way Steve leaned in. Yeah, sure, he spent a fair amount of time ogling her boobs shifting under the sky-blue silk of the pajamas, but wasn't that why she'd chosen the outfit?

But he also seemed to be actually listening. It was nice to have someone new to tell her stories to.

"Let me back up a minute and tell you about Mervin, since he plays a starring role in this."

"Mervin? He the guy that presumably fell out of the plane?"

"Well, it *would* be like him to go skydiving and forget his parachute, but I don't think anyone in their right mind would allow him near anything that could actually leave the ground. Anyway, Mervin Lovingshiemer and his wife, Barbara Jean, lived across the street from us and three doors down."

"I was eight years old when this happened, and of course folks tried to keep the kids from getting all the details, but one of Mervin's boys was in my class, so I heard the whole story from him, and my best friend Meg saw it all too. 'Course, it being summer and a Saturday afternoon, and everybody's doors and windows all open, you couldn't have missed seeing and hearing all the commotion anyway."

Roxy laughed. "Well, Mervin Lovingshiemer wasn't the brightest tool in the box and an accident with a crib made him 4F for the military—"

"How they hell does somebody hurt themselves with a crib? And how did it make him 4F?" Steve asked.

"You're old enough to remember those days, Steve. When we were kids, there weren't all these safety rules and requirements to pretty much keep your kid in Bubble Wrap. The Consumer Product Safety people were doing their best, I suppose, but kids' pj's were made of flammable material, metal roller skates came flying off your shoes and damn near sliced your Achilles tendon to ribbons, and it's astounding how many babies actually survived cribs jammed with blankets and bumpers and pillows and enormous stuffed teddy bears. In Mervin's case, nobody at the product safety place had gotten around to mentioning that the sides of a crib shouldn't go crashing down like a guillotine."

"Wait. Are you telling me he had his head cut off?"

"Well, of course not, idiot. He wasn't like that chicken my grandma killed when I was about three or so."

Steve raised his eyebrows in that questioning way.

"We kept chickens for a while. Babushka decided she wanted chicken and dumplings for Sunday supper. I was just a toddler, and all I knew was that she was going out to see the chickens and I liked them, even though the rooster chased me up a fence pole every chance he got and there I'd be, sitting on top of that pole hollering and screaming until somebody came out with a broom and chased him off."

She still didn't like being around the stupid things with their pointy beaks and flapping wings and big scary spurs. She lifted her pizza and took a bite, taking her time chewing and swallowing before she continued. Greasy, cheesy goodness was exactly what she needed right now.

And maybe another glass of wine. Or bourbon.

"So there I am, toddling along behind Babushka," Roxy said, "all happy and la la la and thinking I'm going to get to pet the chickens. Babushka went out to the coop and grabbed one, along with her axe, and put it on the stump we used for a chopping block, and lopped its head off. Needless to say, I was shocked. Even worse, that saying about running around like a chicken with its head cut off? It's true. That headless chicken jumped off that stump and started running around, right toward me. I took off screaming like a banshee and raced around the house, and swear to God, Steve, that chicken raced right after me like it could see where I was! Imagine it. I'm three years old, a fucking bloody headless chicken is chasing me, and every time I pass my grandmother, she's standing there with a chicken head in one hand and a bloody axe in the other and laughing her fool head off!"

It still made her indignant to think about it. "I tell you now, I had nightmares about headless chickens for years afterward and it was years before I could eat it again."

Steve's laughter was billowing out in great, gusty whoops. "Roxy, you make a man laugh so hard, I'm about to piss myself." He stood up.

"Pause," he said, pressing his finger on the table as if it were a TV remote. He disappeared down the hall, the toilet flushed, water ran, and he reappeared in the kitchen, grabbing another beer before settling back again at the table.

"Play," he said, pressing the table again.

"So, back to Mervin," Roxy said. "One morning, when he was about a year old, Mervin's dad was busy getting ready for work and his mom was trying to dress and feed five other kids, and as far as they could tell, Mervin decided to get out of the crib by himself. I heard his mama tell the story a million times. She was in the kitchen and she heard *BOOM*! *CRASH*! and then a lot of screaming. The side of the crib had crashed down," she said. "Mervin kept his head, but lost a hand."

Steve's nose wrinkled in disgust. "My buddy Glen Wilson, that guy I told you about, is missing a few fingers, but at least he still has most of the hand."

"How'd he lose them?" Roxy asked. Without waiting for an answer, she said, "More than one boy in my high school lost a finger in woodshop. Shoulda known better than to hire a teacher who was missing a thumb and index finger on one hand and a pinkie on the other, but when your district is as poor as ours was, you take what you can get."

"For all I know, Glen's wife lopped them off when he tried to feel her up. Damned if I know, Roxy. I swear, you're more easily distracted than my uncle Jimmy who got hit in the head during WW I and came home drooling. This Mervin guy with the missing hand?"

"Didn't slow Mervin down any," she said, shrugging. "Well, no more than his IQ would have done anyway. Nice guy, but I'm pretty sure marrying cousins was a long-standing tradition in the Lovingshiemer family, if you know what I mean."

Steve nodded but didn't say anything.

"It didn't help that Mervin was the baby of the family. Folks always said his daddy had used up all his best sperm on the first five kids. Whatever sperm made Mervin was the best one left, and it was probably old and dusty and a little bit broken. And his mama was pretty much past her best baby-making years too."

"You're saying he was what they call *challenged*."

"I'm saying that even if anybody had bothered to notice Mervin was snacking on the lead paint chips peeling off their walls and tried to stop him, it wouldn't have made one iota of difference to that boy's IQ. Anyway, Mervin got work as the janitor at our elementary school. He was burning trash out in the burn barrel one day, back in the days when you could do that, and thought maybe a little splash of gasoline might help move things along faster."

She paused for another bite of pizza and another sip of wine, watching Steve watching her.

"The explosion didn't cause much damage," Roxy said, "other than to take out part of the teachers' lounge and half of Mervin's hair and leave one of his ears looking like—what do you call it when a boxer's ears get all curled up?"

"Cauliflower ears," Steve said. "When they get hit too much." Steve scratched his own ear and put another piece of pizza on his plate, one loaded with pepperoni and sausage and onions and banana peppers.

Roxy was going to have to make sure the man had an antacid before bed. He'd been sick last night, and she was pretty sure that that slice of heartburn-on-a-crust wasn't going to make him feel much better tonight.

"Yeah, that's right. Well, Mervin had one ear that looked like that, and the principal was real careful after that to keep the gasoline under lock and key in the storage shed so Mervin didn't get any other bright ideas or couldn't carry them out if he got them."

"So we've established this Mervin is one sandwich short of a picnic. Not the sharpest tool in the box. Not the brightest bulb—"

"Yeah, well, he had a few disadvantages, but he meant well. After all, he'd managed to convince Barbara Jean to marry him and they had a couple of kids, even though Barbara Jean wore the pants in that family. Rumor had it her daddy bought that property for them and loaned them money to build the house and promised to get Mervin a job just so Mervin would take Barbara Jean off his hands. But Mervin tried. He really did. Keep that in mind when I tell you the rest."

Steve leaned back in his chair and crossed his arms over his chest.

"Picture it," Roxy said. "It's Saturday. Summer. Kids out riding bikes up and down the road or running through lawn sprinklers. Women doing chores, and men in the gardens or hanging over fences sharing beers and catching up on baseball scores and gossip. And pretty darn often small planes flying overhead with folks jumping out of them and everyone turning to watch, holding their breaths until the parachutes opened and they landed in the big open field on the other side of the crick. *Creek.*"

Roxy hated when the old hillbilly slang of her childhood slipped through.

"Don't tell me. Let me guess. Somebody candlesticked?"

Now it was Roxy's turn to look puzzled.

"That's what I've heard it called," Steve said. "Instead of opening into a big beautiful canopy, the chute gets tangled up and stays straight as a candlestick."

"Yep, that's it," Roxy said. "With a man's life burning out at the end of it."

"Must have been hideous."

"Well, I didn't see it. I was inside doing my Saturday chores after a morning of watching TV. But I heard the screaming and the stories. This guy came straight down out of the sky, but the wind must have caught him. Instead of the open field, he headed for the houses. Specifically, Mervin's house. With Mervin sitting right there on his plastic lawn chair in his yard, with his binoculars and his beer, enjoying a cigarette because Barbara Jean wouldn't let him light matches in the house."

Roxy leaned forward. "They said the guy missed the road by inches and landed in the ditch in front of Mervin's house, almost in Mervin's lap. My best friend Meg lived next door and saw it happen and loved to scare the crap out of us with the story at slumber parties."

Roxy shimmied her shoulders, remembering the long-forgotten mix of thrills and horror. "The parachutist, of course, was a goner," she said, "a pile of mush and guts that had splattered, Meg said, like the time we dropped a watermelon from the window of the church choir loft onto the parking lot. Meg said that for a minute Mervin just sat there while folks came running. Then they all stood there, debating what to do while they waited for the ambulance to get there, not that they'd be in any hurry, seeing as how there was no chance he'd survived. One of the guys poked him with a broom to make sure, and a couple of them thought maybe they ought to rake some of the uh...*stuff* up to make it easier for the squad, but this was Mervin's yard and he took charge."

"Oh God."

"Exactly. He decided nobody should touch anything in case the cops had any questions, but he didn't want to let this poor man lay there roasting like hamburger in the sun, seeing as a neighbor had heard on the scanner that there'd been a pileup up on the highway and it might be a while before an ambulance or the cops could get there. So Mervin decided the only decent thing to do would be to cover up the body so the kids would stop crying and to keep old Mr. Dixon's coonhounds from running off with any evidence or important body parts."

Steve's expression was a cross between glee and being appalled. Most people had the same reaction whenever she told stories about Mervin and it delighted her that she'd been able to lighten the mood.

"Someone pointed out that right there a few feet away there was a whole row of nice white sheets hanging out to dry in the sun. Mervin hadn't taken two steps toward them when Barbara Jean came tearing out of the house with a cleaver in her fist and threatening to remove Mervin's other hand if he so much as thought of touching the sheets she'd spent the whole damned morning washing and running through the hand wringer. Turned out she'd been in the middle of chopping up meat to grill later for supper, but Barbara Jean was not a woman to be taken lightly even on a good day. So Mervin looked around his yard and came up with the best plan he could."

"Again, oh God. I shudder to think—"

"A screen door."

"A fucking what?"

"Screen door. He'd leaned it up against the house, and Barbara Jean had been bugging him for a week to get it patched up and rehung, but he'd been busy. So the door was just sitting there. And Mervin went and got it and threw it over the body."

Steve's mouth could not have hung open any further. He sucked in a long breath, but before he exploded in laughter, Roxy continued.

"Nice wooden-frame one too. Of course, it sort of teetered there in the ditch, not covering much, but all the menfolk decided it would do and went and got beers and lawn chairs and guarded the body and the screen door, and a lot of the women found reason to wander over for a gander too, and it kind of turned into a picnic except us kids were all sent over to the schoolyard to play on the swing sets and jungle gym, and we were just glad to get out of our chores."

Steve's shout of laughter could probably be heard three doors away. She had the feeling that he hadn't done that in a long time, just letting go, and that laughing wholeheartedly was something he desperately needed.

Roxy wrapped one long red curl around her finger then let it spring lose. "Of course," she said, "Mervin had gotten some of the, um...*overspray* on himself, and Barbara Jean had just mopped all the floors and wasn't about to let him in the house with all that... effluvia all over him. So she made him strip down right outside there and throw his clothes in the burn barrel because she said she wasn't going to touch them either. She spent the next two months bitching to anybody who'd listen that she'd just 'bought them jeans brand-new at the Sears Roebuck the month before' and that his T-shirt was one of his good ones with no holes and a new John Deere cap wouldn't be easy to come by, until finally the nice ladies at the Baptist church took up a collection and bought him new clothes at Sears and got the local feed and grain store to donate a new John Deere cap just to shut her up."

Steve's face was a decidedly plum color, and for a moment Roxy worried about him not being able to catch his breath from laughing so hard, but she plunged on.

She leaned toward him and dropped her voice into a serious tone to say, "That wasn't the worst of it, Steve. Once he'd stripped down to his tighty-whities, Barbara Jean insisted he finish the job and throw those shorts in the burn barrel and hose off in the side yard. She threw him out a towel and a new bar of Zest soap and told him to burn the towel too when he was done. And that's about the time I came out of my house on my way to the schoolyard with the rest of the kids."

Another sip of wine emptied her glass. "You ever seen one of those cartoons of a naked Donald Trump with big old man boobs and a giant gut that isn't quite big enough to cover his little mushroom of a dick? Now imagine that blinding white except for the farmer's tan on his head and arms."

Roxy shook her head. "For years after, folks would talk about that day at parties; they'd have rather seen another body in the ditch than the sight of a stark naked Mervin Lovingshiemer taking a hose-bath in the yard on a Saturday afternoon. Some folks said that for years the scent of Zest soap made them retch more than their memory of the odor of that body sizzling in the sun while they waited for the ambulance."

Steve's hooting and shouts of laughter went on a good five minutes. Every time he tried to say something, he'd give her a look and start in laughing all over again.

It did Roxy's heart good to see the big man laughing. Maybe this relationship had possibilities after all. If that was what she really wanted.

Her heart had decided long before her brain did. She'd always sucked at resisting temptation.

Chapter 17
Steve's Date with Death: T-Minus 16:27:39 and Counting

STEVE GLANCED AT the clock on Roxy's wall. Earlier than he thought, but the day had been a long one. And except for the last couple of hours with Roxy, not a good one. Even with her near meltdown and her attempt to puncture his hide with a switchblade.

Maybe he wouldn't even wait until sunset tomorrow. No reason to put off the inevitable any longer. Everybody died. Rather than prolong the agony, the smart ones picked their own time. And Mama hadn't raised no stupid boy.

Thank God tomorrow was going to be a short day.

And his last one.

Still...it didn't have to be. Maybe if he—

No. The doctor had tried to be gentle this afternoon. Matter-of-fact. No pussyfooting around. But all his fancy, kind words hadn't changed what Steve already suspected. He could string Roxy along, drag this out for a couple of months, but the future was going to get ugly real soon, and Roxy seemed like a nice woman. She'd already had enough shit in her life.

All the reasons he'd hesitated last time were gone. Curtis didn't need him anymore. Natalie was dead. He'd clipped every string tethering him to the past and to this life. He'd fucked up six ways to Sunday, and maybe he'd saved a life or two along the way, but he was done with it all. The world would barely notice Steve Stephens was no longer taking up space. This time he was going to follow through on his carefully made plans.

And on his way out, he'd save one more life. Roxy's. He'd save her from any unrealistic expectations and from getting her life all tangled up in his before it was too late.

Maybe it already was too late, but hey, that was on her. He hadn't invited the redheaded typhoon into his life.

But he was glad to have her there. Glad to have known that on his last night alive, he'd helped her through a rough patch.

Glad he hadn't had to spend it alone.

"Penny for your thoughts, Steve."

"Not worth even that much." He pushed back from the table, a little too forcefully.

Roxy stood as well. "How about a walk around the yard? You can smell all the flowers in my midnight garden."

"That sounds like something dirty."

Roxy laughed. Yeah, he was glad he'd gotten to share a laugh with her, and a bed, even for one night. There were worse ways a man could have spent his final days. "So you going to show me what you got going on in that overgrown toolshed out there?"

The smile on Roxy's face faltered a moment. "Nothing there for anyone but me. Storage. Old stuff. Nothing to see."

Steve didn't know why, but her words hit him wrong. He hated secrets. Hated people who lied. All his years around the scum of the earth had honed his radar. And just like that, the mellow floating feeling of the last few hours evaporated like sweat in the Sahara.

Roxy was lying to him.

He had a pretty good idea why.

"Look, Roxy. I'm not the kind of asshole to call in his cop buddies on a little old lady doing what you're doing, but somebody's going to come along who's not so nice. The kind of thing you're into back there attracts sharks. The kind that won't care so much that you're a nice lady. The kind who probably have a favorite dumping site all picked out in the Everglades. I'd hate to think of that Iggy kid missing out on his world tour just because they never find your body."

If Steve didn't know better, he'd have thought Roxy's gape-mouthed stare was genuine puzzlement. Then he remembered she'd spent years on the stage, hiding her real emotions behind a crap-ton of makeup and fast footwork.

That's all this was too. Window dressing. Or maybe she actually thought he was just another one of those big dumb animals she cared so much about. Some poor lonely fool in need of rescue.

He didn't need rescuing. Not by her. Not by anybody. Not ever in the past and even less so now.

He was old and dying, but he wasn't demented. How dare she play the innocent with him? He wasn't exiting this world being bamboozled by some broad.

From out of nowhere, his blood boiled. All the locks on all the cages holding all the black memories shattered at the same moment, unleashing a tidal wave of rage. Every shadow, every nightmare crawled out of its dark corner and leapt at once, adding to the river of pain and fury gushing through his veins along with his rotten, poisoned, dying blood.

This woman. This beautiful, kind, treacherous woman. How dare she? And God *damn* it, why did she have to tap dance into his life at the last possible fucking second? And then lie to him?

God was an out and out motherfucker.

It wasn't fair. It wasn't fucking fair, goddamnit!

Before she could utter a word, he plowed ahead. "How stupid do you think I am that I wouldn't notice what exactly it is you have growing in your oh-so-innocent garden, Roxy?" He smacked the table, causing the dishes to rattle.

Roxy jumped back. Good. He meant to scare her. Better him than some cartel member out of Miami pissed that she was cutting into his profits.

Or maybe she was working with them already. Looking at

the size of that building out back—

"Steve, have you lost your ever-loving mind? Are you having a brain seizure or something? Can I get your pills? I'm a really fast runner. You just tell me what you need and where to find them and I can be at your house and back before—"

"What, you don't have a private stash of something here? Or do you just stick with dealing weed?"

"Dealing..." Roxy's shoulders relaxed a millimeter or two, but she kept her chair between her and him. "I wondered if you'd spot that."

"I was a fucking DEA agent, Roxy. What the hell did you think? Hell, these days kids in diapers recognize that shit. Yes, I saw those fucking pot plants towering over your precious ferns and fronds. A hell of a lot more of them than could remotely be classified as being for personal use. And you've got that big fucking shed back there. A grow house for the good stuff? A drying shed? Got some illegals stashed in there packaging it up for you? Are you into trafficking too?"

Steve had lost his mind. One part of him stood outside himself staring at the epitome of the large violent Black man. The other part of him, the eighty-year-old part of his body that was rotting away inside him, killing him, was nothing but a frail old man powerless to stop the tidal wave of grief and rage and fear and regret the doctor had unleashed that afternoon.

Roxy had grown preternaturally quiet in the face of his fury. "Yes, Sergeant Stephens, that is the devil's lettuce you see growing among my ferns and fronds. And no, Mr. DEA agent, that isn't a grow house. And no, I'm not a dealer." She shrugged. "I suppose you could call me a supplier, but I don't sell it."

"You're not going to try to tell me you smoke all that yourself."

"I don't smoke it at all. I turn the pot into brownies and cookies. It's for a group that call themselves my garden club. And yes, I do use it myself."

"So you're admitting you're a drug addict?"

"No more than you are."

Steve's heart raced as he clenched his fist on the back of the kitchen chair. "I have never in my life done any damned drugs. I hate drugs," he said through gritted teeth. "I hate the people who use them and sell them and——"

That was a lie. He'd used drugs once. Years and years ago, coerced by a Russian with a death wish. The Russian had gotten his wish. The stain had never left Steve's soul.

"You are liar, Steve Stephens."

How did she know? Was this maddening redhead a witch? His fingernails dug into his palms, but some part of him had gone beyond feeling any pain. For a second, he longed for his KA-BAR, longed for the sweet sensation of it slicing through his skin, just so he could feel the pain, feel something physical instead of the tsunami of emotion that threatened to swamp him, drown him right there in Roxy's too bright, too fucking cheery kitchen.

"You use drugs every day," Roxy said. "I saw them when I got in your medicine cabinet. I even handed them right to you. Drugs for your heart. Drugs for your blood pressure. Drugs for cholesterol and God only knows what else. Drugs all day every day, Steve." She pointed toward the table. "Hell, what is that beer sitting right there if not just another drug?"

"It's not the same thing. Those are——"

"Those are cooked up in a lab God knows where by God knows who. Just because they have paper shufflers who filed all the right forms and lobbyists who paid off all the right people doesn't make them any less drug dealers. Pot used to be legal in this country. Do you know why it's not?"

"Every Black child knows why," Steve said. "White folks going to Black jazz clubs where pot was a popular drug. Couldn't have all those nice white kids taking all those evil drugs and mixing with those lowdown, nasty——"

"Right. And there are those of us trying to change that. To decriminalize it. To get wrongly incarcerated folks out of jail and scrub unjust prison records. But the change isn't happening fast enough."

Sweat had broken out on Roxy's forehead. Her cheeks were bright pink splotches, her knuckles white where she clutched the back of the chair.

Good. He hoped she was scared. And angry. It would make it easier on both of them.

"It's legal here in Florida," he said. Why the hell was he still talking?

"It's legal for medical use only, and it's a damned miracle they even managed to get that passed. The governor right now is trying to lower the amount of actual useful stuff in legal marijuana products. And the list of those who can qualify to get it is ridiculously narrow. Dispensaries are few to nonexistent in a lot of areas. The hoops and the red tape people have to go through is pure government nonsense, designed deliberately to make a useful, legal drug impossible to use. And the cost. Steve, do you have any idea how much it costs to get your hands on the legal stuff?"

"Maybe that's for a damned good reason." He'd lost control of his mouth. Why the fuck wasn't he walking out the door?

Roxy, that was why. Roxy and her damned chattering, catching him like a fly in her silken web. Goddamned Roxy and—

"The members of my group—a lot of them your neighbors—don't have that kind of money," she said.

She wasn't going to stop talking. Wasn't going to let him escape.

"Or time or transportation or the ability to jump through hoops like trained circus animals. Or maybe what ails them isn't on this list of *approved* conditions. Conditions approved by a bunch of asshole legislators instead of actual doctors. But that doesn't mean they don't have a need."

"Who, Roxy? Who are these vaunted members of your so-called garden club?" Maybe he could make one last quick call to Tommy or Paul Tinker. One last bust on his way out.

"Once a narc, always a narc, right, Steve? Still fooling yourself that you and you alone can save the world?"

Oh, this woman didn't need a sword in her hand. Her words cut more deeply than her katana ever would. And could she fucking read minds?

"I'll tell you who they are." Roxy rushed on, neither noticing nor caring about the gaping, gushing wound she'd slashed open in his soul. "A couple of them are cancer patients. Chemo is a motherfucker, Steve. Poison the patient in order to save them. Who cares if the patient ends up bald and sick, their teeth loose, the inside of their mouth filled with sores and raw skin, unable to eat even if they weren't throwing up and too weak to swallow? Well, pot helps with the nausea. Helps them keep down the food they need to help nourish the body that the cancer is trying to kill. Yeah, pot's legal for them, but again, it's damned expensive and insurance doesn't cover it. So yeah, I give them a pretty little box of brownies, and it helps them."

"They can still get it legally. You don't have to be their friendly neighborhood dealer." Steve's words bounced off Roxy as if she wore Kevlar under the skimpy silk clinging to that trim body.

A body she was never going to let him near again.

Which shouldn't have mattered one bit, considering the state his own body was going to be in a few hours from now.

"You know who makes up most of the friends who come to visit me and have a few cookies and a laugh?"

Steve didn't care anymore. He needed to get out of this sunny yellow kitchen. Away from the maddening woman who'd made him care way too fast and way too much. But her words held him firmly lassoed to the chair he gripped.

"Soldiers, Steve. You know a thing or two about those guys, don't you?"

"Roxy, don't you dare—"

"You know the ones. Like those guys in that picture on your wall. A lot of them did drugs in those places and came home and never touched another one. A lot more of them came

157

home and lost themselves to drugs way worse than pot. And a lot of them never touched a drug at all while they were over there. It doesn't matter if it was a jungle or a sand pile or a barren mountain deep in the backcountry of some godforsaken place the government doesn't even recognize. They went over there and they did their job. But when they got home, they had pieces missing."

He had to get out of there. Her words had gone from sword to scalpel, and he hadn't had enough beer to anesthetize the places she was slicing open.

Turn. Walk out the door. Down the sidewalk to his house. Easy. Get out now. *NOW!*

"Maybe it was a leg they left behind. An arm or an eye or half their body. But the worst are the ones who came home with wounds that didn't bleed. With screaming nightmares that terrify their wives and husbands and kiddies. Or they're so touchy that a piece of burned toast will turn them into a raging hulk. Or they have memories so sensitive that a slammed screen door will send them diving for cover and the closest weapon. A weapon that way too many of them turn on themselves every fucking day." Roxy's breath hitched, and she swiped her hand across her eyes, but nothing slowed the thundering cataract of her words.

His breath heaved in his chest as if he'd run miles and yet he hadn't moved an inch. Run! Run! Run! But his body wouldn't listen to his screaming brain. The unleashed demons, the howling shadows, and the voice of one sad, angry woman held his feet nailed to the floor.

He needed to apologize, admit maybe he'd overreacted to the pot in Roxy's garden, and leave. Go home and line up his pills and his booze and the note for the cop who'd find his body.

Because he fucking *knew* about those nightmares. Because parts of him had been missing for a long goddamned time.

But Roxy wasn't finished. He didn't need his KA-BAR; Roxy's words were doing the same fine job, slicing him to bloody ribbons.

"There are more, Steve. The ones who come home with souls so numb they cut themselves just to feel something. *Anything.* And so they come here. Some come alone. Most come to meet with friends. Cancer patients on Sunday afternoons. The ones who've survived rape and abuse and trauma, and the PTSD that goes along with that, come once or twice a month to sit together in the garden and listen to the birds and share in a place that's safe and green and open."

Roxy was on her feet, her whole body vibrating. The low hiss of her words flayed him more than if she'd shouted them at him.

"The soldiers, Steve? They like to come over a couple of times a month and play poker and have a beer and a couple of brownies. Sometimes they talk. Most times it's just the unspoken knowledge that the men and women sitting around the table out on the lanai all have the same nightmares and that every one of them is still surviving and they can be a lifeline for each other, a raft in a shit storm for each of them to hang on to."

"Is that why you use pot, Roxy? Because of what happened when you were a kid? That guy with the Old Spice?"

Roxy stalked across the kitchen, grabbed a napkin from the basket on the counter, and blew her nose. She kept her back to him, her shoulders rigid. After a long moment, she turned to him, her belligerent little chin thrust out, eyes blazing.

"Yeah, Steve, I'm a survivor. Of a lot more than you'll ever know. These days I use pot for the pain. Physical pain. Do you have any idea what years of dancing does to a person's body, the sheer grinding destruction of hips and knees and ankles and feet and shoulders and spine? My rheumatologist prescribed a million pills, but none of them did a damned bit of good. I sure as hell wasn't going to be some addict strung out on Percocet or Hydrocodone or Oxy, so yeah, I smoke a doobie now and then or have a brownie."

Not a single word she'd said had eased the fury in his gut. She didn't know what she was talking about. How dare she think she understood a damned thing? Had she sat by her sister's bed while the cancer ate her away?

Had she crawled through the sucking mud and dragged a buddy's maggot-filled body to a chopper so his family could have something to wrap in the almighty flag and bury? Had she scraped a kid off the pavement when some junkie thought a drug-fueled joyride was a good idea?

She had no fucking clue.

The breath Steve sucked in did little to ease the aching tightness in his chest. He pursed his lips and blew it out, long and forcefully. "Roxy, I was right. This—whatever seems to have started between us—this is going nowhere."

"You're right, Steve. You don't need anybody, do you? Big, tough, go-it-alone macho hombre." The volume of her voice rose as she strode back to him, her blue eyes glittering with both tears and fury. "You don't need anybody, and you sure as hell aren't going to let anybody need you. How long have you lived on this street, Steve, and how many of your neighbors do you know?"

"Plenty of people have needed me. I did what I had to do. What I was told to do. But every single one of those broken, needy people took a part of me. Sometimes you get to a point you got nothin' left to give. So yeah, when I moved in here, I wasn't in the mood to let a whole new batch of people start sucking the life out of me."

"They didn't want to suck the life out of you, Steve. They wanted to welcome you. I personally know at least three women who knocked on your door and offered casseroles or cookies or—"

"Bunch of damned busybodies wanting something to gossip about over their margaritas at the club. Or looking for a new man to take them out and wine and dine and fuck them. Someone to buy them stuff. Someone to reassure them they weren't old dried-up husks. That they could still get a man. Well, that wasn't going to be me."

Color drained from Roxy's pink cheeks, leaving her suddenly ghastly pale.

Hell, he hadn't meant her.

Then again, maybe he did. But his casual cruelty didn't stop the onslaught of her words.

"And what about the men, Steve? Some of those women who knocked on your door have husbands. Those men invited you over to the club or for poker nights. They invited you to the VFW. Do you think they wanted to fuck you as well?"

"There's more than one way to fuck somebody. Probably just wanted to sell me insurance or Amway. I don't golf. I never worked in the usual backstabbing, ladder-climbing corporate environments—what would I have in common with any of those guys? And why would I be interested in hearing yet more war stories?"

And why the fuck was he still talking? Goddamn it! He didn't have to stand there and listen to this.

But he couldn't move.

"We all caught on pretty fast, Steve. For a while we called you Garbo because you so obviously wanted to be alone. You were the neighborhood ghost. Your garbage cans appeared and disappeared on the curb, your newspaper disappeared from your driveway, your car went up and down the street, but nobody saw you and you never returned anybody's wave. Just Garbo the Grouch, squirreled away in his tidy little yellow house living his tidy little gray life. You rebuffed all of us and every overture to become friends. None of us were trying to suck the life out of you, Steve. We were just being neighborly."

"Is that what you call crawling in bed with me last night, being neighborly?"

He'd crossed a line. He knew it.

He didn't fucking care.

Maybe he should. But there wasn't a single cell in his body that still had room to care for anything or anybody other than his own immediate pain and grief.

He'd expected Roxy to explode in fury. Her reaction was a thousand times worse. Instead of answering with fire, warm, vibrant, beautiful, fiery Roxy turned into the Ice Queen.

"When you got sick at the club and clearly needed help? It was the *neighborly* thing to do to help you get home."

Every word dripped with icicles, and every icicle stabbed him straight in the heart.

"When you needed someone to help you with your pills?" she said. "That was the *neighborly* thing to do. Offering you a meal when I saw the sorry state of your refrigerator? Just being *neighborly*, Steve. But if you think I casually *crawled into bed with you* to just be *neighborly,* then you have a sickness no doctor can ever cure, because as far as I know, there's no pill to cure *being a fucking asshole.*"

Steve opened his mouth, but Roxy's torrent of words rushed on, drowning him, sweeping him over the boulders in her river of words, scraping him raw.

"The absolute arrogance! How dare you, Robert Stephens! I liked you. Maybe it could have been something more—I wanted to find out. I didn't fuck you because I wanted anything from you. Not any more than anybody else. Don't you ever get lonely? Hungry for the touch of another human being? Haven't you ever felt instantly attracted to someone? But oh, no, in just two short days I've learned the truth. The almighty Robert 'Steve' Stephens is incapable of feeling hunger or attraction or love. I don't know why you're acting all butt-hurt, Steve. I'm the one who should be feeling used here. Tricked."

Steve had felt remorse before in his life. It wasn't an alien emotion, but it was damned unwelcome right now. So it turned out the last human act in his life would be to infuriate a woman.

Not the first time.

But it would be the last.

Roxy leaned back against the counter and crossed her arms over her chest. "So fine, Steve. You go your way, and we'll just forget about this."

He spun on his heel.

"Everyone hurts, Steve. There's no shame in reaching out for something—someone—to help ease the pain now and then." Her words floated past him as he slammed open the door and stalked out into the night.

Fuck her.

And for good measure, fuck God for bringing her into his life just at the moment his life was ending.

Chapter 18

Steve's Date with Death: T-Minus 15:04:07 and Counting

FUCK HER, FUCK her, *FUCK HER*!

Steve stomped down the sidewalk, his thoughts churning. Roxy's words played over and over again, a record stuck in a groove: *The ones who come home with souls so numb they cut themselves just to feel something. Anything.*

She had no way of knowing. Or maybe she did. The scars had faded over time but still slithered like pale silver worms over his skin. They'd been doing that slithering for more than ten years.

Since the last time he'd planned to kill himself.

The insidious thoughts had begun with the cutting. His retirement from the DEA had been coming up, thirty-seven days away, but the cutting had begun the year before. His footsteps pounded the pavement as old memories crawled out of the crevices in his brain and boiled to the surface.

It was a good thing long sleeves were standard in the office. The bulk of the bandage was barely visible under the fabric. Folks associated cutting with bulimic, angst-ridden teenage girls. No one thought a depressed, nearly retired, Black law enforcement officer would do that.

They would be wrong about that.

The cutting started by accident. He'd been honing the

ultra-keen carbon-steel edge of his KA-BAR when the blade slipped. The resulting cut wasn't deep—just a little crease in the dark skin on the inside of his arm. The knife was so sharp that the wound didn't hurt. Blood oozed nearly black under the harsh fluorescent lighting of his apartment.

It had struck him that there he was at the trailing end of his useful life, and everything smelled like bullshit except the harsh reality of sobering pain and the blood seeping from his arm. He knew he was depressed. He'd needed professional help, but he thought he could handle it.

Pills? No way. He was no pathetic hausfrau-hypochondriac; he was a field-toughened law enforcement professional.

Besides, the hypocrisy was too ironic. He'd spent fourteen years tracking and prosecuting drug dealers. Now he'd throw himself into their world of mind-altering pharmaceuticals? Xanax, Paxil, Zoloft, Celexa, Elavil and old-school Prozac? How was that different from using cocaine, heroin, marijuana, roofies, uppers and downers?

Ten years later, how was that any different from what Roxy was doing, giving people a way to escape the pain? He'd been in those shoes, been one of the broken ones who'd left more than body parts in godforsaken hellholes.

Now he had nothing left to give. Not his heart or mind or soul had a millimeter of room left to care for anything or anyone but the paroxysms of resentment and misery consuming him.

Roxy, at least in her own way, was trying to help.

His steady march slowed, his body too old to keep pace with his churning brain.

He half turned back to the light on her porch, to the rainbows and flamingos and gnomes in her yard.

No.

Damn her. And damn God. And fuck no.

He'd just stand there until he caught his breath. Then he'd go home and lay out everything he needed to make his own permanent escape.

Escape the pain. Escape the memories and the anguish and

the rage and the goddamned un-fucking-fairness of love ambushing him, of finding the smallest possible crevice to sneak its way into his dead, adamantine heart just as the final seconds ticked away on his life.

He bent over, his hands on his knees. Breath sawed in and out of his lungs, but none of it seemed to reach his brain or did a damned thing to slow his thumping heart.

Yeah, he'd made the right decision. Walk away from her. Get her out of his life by any means possible. Then go out tomorrow exactly the way he'd planned. Maybe before he even had breakfast. Why waste another whole day when everything was ready? In Sorrento, Italy, it was probably already tomorrow. Curtis was probably already awake, remembering that two years ago today Natalie had died.

Curtis *would* remember, wouldn't he? Hell, for all Steve knew, Curtis was drunk on his ass in some place even Google couldn't find, ready to marry yet another wife. Or out risking his life for the almighty moola, trying to solve problems that could never be solved for people who didn't give one hair on a rat's scrawny ass about Curtis. Or his kids.

Or that Steve missed his damned nephew. Missed his sister.

Missed Mama and Daddy and Auntie Althea and good potato salad and drinking brown liquor out of the trunk of his uncle's car at the cookout.

Missed not knowing exactly how many tomorrows were actually left to him.

None. That's how many tomorrows Steve had.

Zero.

His choice. His way.

Steve straightened and gulped another breath.

Please don't talk about me when I'm gone.

A fragment of a song, dredged up from the bottom of time's river, called to him across the chasm of the years.

The words floated on the air, wrapping around him as seductively as a woman wrapped a silken scarf around her lover, leading him to pleasure.

Another breath. Deeper, stretching burning muscles over aching bones, filling lungs, defying his longing for death.

There was nobody left to talk about him when he was gone. Nobody but Curtis, who probably wouldn't care. Probably didn't even remember that it was the anniversary of his mama's death.

Roxy would remember him. Roxy would say something nice about him at his funeral, even after all the bile he'd heaped on her head tonight. And damn it, she'd be the kind to take it on and plan the funeral since he hadn't bothered to. She'd forgive him, because that's the kind of woman she was. She'd blame his death on his unwillingness to deal with his illness.

Oh God.

What if she blamed herself? Blamed it on their argument? Blamed it on some failing on her part, her inability to help him instead of his own resolute determination to die?

Roxy wasn't pretending problems didn't exist. She wasn't lying to herself or anyone else.

She wasn't inviting death in on a silver platter.

You're born, life sucks, and then you die. But Roxy, at least, was doing her shuffle-ball best to make it suck a little less.

He had to tell her. Let her know it wasn't her fault. That his suicide had nothing to do with her.

No. Damn it. He jammed his fists in his pockets. His life had spun wildly out of control, and the time and place of his death was the only choice left to him. Other people had to make their own choices. And if Roxy chose to believe his suicide was her fault, then that was on her.

No. It was on him.

His fault. His own, selfish, stupid fault.

Steve stood on the sidewalk in the dark place between other people's porch lights. Other people's lives. All around him in the steamy night, creatures creaked and croaked and buzzed, fucking and feeding and breeding and dying, unaware and uncaring of his stygian thoughts. Just living their lives, taking no interest in his.

Did God even notice or care about the sorrows of one old lone Black man when the whole world was on fire?

Steve inhaled deeply through his nose, the sweet scent of gardenia awakening a sleeping memory, a dream from so long ago it hardly seemed to have been real.

Until Roxy, there had been nobody at all to take an interest in his life.

Maybe because he'd long ago lost interest in his own life.

A dog barked in the distance.

And out of the night the music came again. He knew without a question where it came from.

Billie Holiday—Lady Day—called to him again.

She'd saved his life once before. Looked like she was going to try save it again tonight.

And this time she was using Roxy to do it.

He turned toward her house.

Stared at it for a long time.

In that direction was light and life and a woman he'd hurt for no damned good reason. A woman he was just about to hurt even more, to inflict a wound so deep it might never heal.

Steve turned back toward his own house.

In that direction lay peace. An end to all the grief. No waiting around until pain squeezed every last breath from him. No agonizing wait for his body and his brain to rot, drooling and pissing and praying while God took his own fucking time before finally releasing the busted-up lump of flesh that used to be Steve Stephens to go on to whatever came next. In that direction lay death on his own terms and at the time of his own choosing.

Goddamnedmotherfuckinggoddamnedsonofabitch!

Why, God? Why are you fucking with me? Why can't you just let me fucking go?

Steve stared up at the starry night sky. Natalie…

Neither the stars nor Natalie answered him.

But Billie Holiday did. What her voice lacked in power she made up for with texture, with sinuous emotion that wound its way through the night, over the chirping night creatures, and enveloped him. Swamped him.

God's own angel sending him a message. Just like she'd done so long ago.

Maybe God was listening after all. Maybe there was something left for one old, sick, tired Black man to do before he died.

He took his hands out of his pockets. Unclenched his fists. Shook his head. There was no more resisting the music's call than there was for a drowning man to resist the ocean's waves washing over him.

All he had to do was surrender and let the waters carry him.

All he had to do was stop fighting.

He took a step.

Stopped.

Took another.

He raised his eyes to heaven. One last look at the glittering firmament, beseeching God for the right answer.

But even without a response from God, Steve had already made his choice.

Chapter 19

Steve's Date with Death: T-Minus 15:04:07 and Holding

HE DIDN'T BOTHER approaching Roxy's closed front door. The music came from behind the house. From that shuttered-up building at the bottom of her garden. The one she guarded so fiercely.

Steve opened her gate, the well-oiled hinges making not a sound. As he trudged through the garden, following the stone path, each step felt a mile long, but with every step he became lighter. The music drew him onward.

He'd heard people say that when they died they walked toward the light. For him, that light came from a building at the bottom of a moonlit garden. Tonight the doors were flung wide open, spilling their secrets and music into the night.

Tap shoes stomped and pounded out fury and heartache and rage against a polished wooden floor in time to Billie Holiday's soulful, bitter voice.

Makes no difference how I carry on
Please don't talk about me when I'm gone

Here was the heart and soul of Roxy Fields. All the answers she'd so glibly danced around when he'd questioned her.

The absence of photos in her house was countered by the plethora of photos here.

And in the middle, the real-life Rockette, eyes closed,

stomping and twirling, feet flying faster than Steve had ever imagined a human being's could.

He'd watched the TV specials with the Rockettes.

It was absolutely nothing like watching one in real life. He stepped closer.

She'd changed from the silky blue pajamas into black tap shorts and matching sports bra. But over that she wore a loose white men's shirt. One flashing with sequins and rhinestones. Little shards of glass that caught the brilliance of the overhead spotlights, turning them into diamonds that seared his eyes and sliced into his heart and flayed his soul.

What she was doing was in no way related to the precision, percussive dancing of the Rockettes. This was all Roxy.

The flying arms, the spinning body, the staccato flurry of her feet, her entire being consumed with her emotions, pouring everything inside her out into the world in a tsunami of passion and fire and fury that rushed faster and faster toward Steve.

Engulfing him.

Consuming him.

The maelstrom created by her feet continued unabated, one song into the next without pause. The mirror along one long wall doubled the storm, Roxy dancing as if she were trying to outpace the glittering shadow-self in the mirror.

The tempest drowned him.

It cleansed him.

Steve sank into the overstuffed armchair that sat in a corner of her studio.

This was the secret of the locked building.

It held Roxy's true essence. The one she showed no one. Her whole life was on display on the walls, photo after photo, from little Polaroids to a full-size poster of a grinning woman in full makeup and glittering white costume, arms over her head, feet perfectly posed in shining white tap shoes. The tight-fitting cap on her head covered every inch of hair, but there was no doubt in Steve's mind.

Here was Roxy. His Rockette.

He slid his eyes away from the poster to the woman who dipped and turned and punched the hardwood with heels and toes as if grinding her demons to dust and dispatching them back to the underworld.

The woman in the poster was beautiful. Young and vibrant, her whole life ahead of her.

The life Steve had lived had sucked the essence from him. The life Roxy had lived had only added to her essence. The woman on the dance floor was a thousand times more beautiful than the girl on the poster *because* of her life, not in spite of it.

He wanted to ask her about the people in the photos. So many of them were candid shots, groups of young people laughing and hugging, chugging beer at long-ago parties, or carefully posed shots in front of New York's most famous tourist spots. Other later ones looked like Atlantic City or Las Vegas.

Yet more photos, spinning into the shadows in a long line, kept Roxy's life and loves and friendships forever alive on the walls.

Christmas trees and turkey dinners. Cruise ships. Much, much older images mingled with the rest. One of a pair of girls, one dark, one fair, the small one with skinned knees in a sunsuit offering a goofy, gap-toothed smile to the photographer. Roxy and her sister. Steve would bet on it. Another photo showed a pair of women and two little girls, all of them dressed in their Sunday finest, the little ones holding Easter baskets. Roxy must have gotten her height from her mother. The old woman next to her wore the dour expression he'd seen more than once in Russian women.

A fat, toothless baby grinned from one old black-and-white studio portrait, petticoats peeking out from under a frilly dress, a ribbon holding a sprout of fine, blond baby hair on top of her head. Next to it, Roxy—back when she was still Rita Jablonski from Darby Glen, Ohio—wore red jeans and a T-shirt over a barely blossoming chest as she blew out candles on a cake that read "Happy Sweet 16."

In another, a little Rita, maybe six or seven years old, wore a black leotard and tights, colorful harlequin ruffles around her neck and wrists, a matching conical hat on her head, and beribboned and gleaming patent leather tap shoes. Lipstick red circles had been painted on her nose and cheeks. A childhood recital probably. A foreshadowing of the wooden soldier costume she'd wear not so many years later.

Not all of them pictured Roxy. Friends from Roxy's life gathered here as well. A very large, very black Marilyn Monroe must be her drag queen friend Jubilation, who'd made Roxy biscuits. Steve had no names for the others, not for the two young men posing arm in arm, one wearing a chef's toque. Not for the actors and dancers on barren stages captured during rehearsals for shows that had succeeded or failed long ago but who were all a part of Roxy's past. And therefore a part of her present as well.

All of them there, gracing the walls of Roxy's studio, her silent, loving audience.

But tonight Roxy did not dance for them.

She danced for herself.

And for one stupid, lonely, broken old Black man.

In one image she stood next to a tall gawky pockmarked boy, their arms wrapped around each other as they posed in front of a white clapboard house. The boy's suit hung awkwardly on him, but his green tie matched the satin of her formal-length gown, contrasting with the corsage on her wrist. Both of them smiled at the camera with tolerance, knowing that they must wait and pose and let the family make memories, even as they quivered with impatience to race off to the dance and the night and whatever adventure awaited them.

Steve had left for boot camp a week after his high school prom. Somewhere out there in some long-forgotten or lost box was a similar photo of him and his date. Leila had worn gold, a dress made for her by his mother. Leila had written to him the first few weeks of basic training before sending the inevitable Dear John letter. The boy she'd ended up marrying had been a second-stringer on the football team, a year behind him in school. He'd been a Marine and lost a foot in Chu Lai and ended up taking Leila to Detroit and getting a job on an assembly line.

Pretty Leila, with her warm bronze skin and deep brown eyes and generous lips and hips.

The music slowed. The tempo changed. Billie Holiday called out to him again.

Love me or leave me or let me be lonely

Steve wanted to close his eyes, to melt into the past before everything got so complicated. So ugly. But he didn't want to miss one single second of Roxy dancing.

He didn't want to miss one single second of Roxy. *Period.*

Dancing, cooking, laughing, arguing with him. Generous, giving, brimming-with-life Roxy.

She'd been right. He'd never needed anybody before.

And now she was wrong.

He needed her.

Not just to keep himself from dying alone. But because whatever tiny sliver of life he had left in him should be spent right down to the nub. If he was going out, he was going to do it knowing he hadn't wasted a single second of the time he'd been allotted.

God, why did love have to walk in the door just as he was walking out?

Without warning, Roxy spun toward him, eyes wide, her mouth a grim, expressionless line. She pulled something from her pocket and pointed it at him.

Steve almost laughed. This was indeed the perfect ending.

"Go ahead and shoot, Roxy. I'm already a dead man walking."

Chapter 20

Sexy Firefighters Calendar Word of the Day:
Kairos: [kahy-raws] or [kahy-rohs]. **Noun.** Translated as "the right time" from Ancient Greek, kairos variously refers to an "opportune presentation," 1. a propitious moment for decision or action.

ROXY POINTED THE remote at the sound system that took up half the wall behind Steve.

The silence was as much an onslaught to the senses as the music had been.

"Why are you here, Steve? I thought you said—"

"I said a lot of stupid shit, Rox."

"And?"

She wasn't going to give an inch. Not a single millimeter. She wasn't the kind to love easily. To let just anyone into her heart. Why the hell should she let this big asshole moose of a man in? This prick. This grouchy curmudgeon. This—

"I was wrong."

Damn it.

She was a sucker for honesty. For a man not too proud to apologize.

She stood for a long moment, waiting for her heart to stop pounding. Her chest heaved after her wild dancing. She walked to the barre that bisected the mirror, her heels clicking loudly in the silence after her personal storm. She kept her back to Steve as she peeled off her soaking wet shirt and draped it over the barre, grabbing up the soft, dry towel she'd hung there earlier. She rubbed away the sweat that streamed down her body, that chilled her in spite of the humid night. She pulled her hair up on top her head, fanning the back of her neck, then draped the now damp towel around her neck before turning to Steve.

Her thoughts whirled as wildly as her feet had moments before. Her emotions battled their own maelstrom. She needed time for the riot in her brain to settle and slow, just as her heart and breath slowed.

Why had he come back? And was she going to let him stay? She was too old to play games, too old for any more stupid risks.

Had had her heart broken too many times. God, she was tired.

A fragment of memory slipped into her mind, sharp as a switchblade.

She'd assigned herself the task of packing up Jubilation's possessions after his death. She'd been sitting on the floor of his closet, surrounded by Florsheim shoes and stilettos, business suits and feather boas, sobbing until she was dry and retching. A line from Psalm 69 had popped into her head: *I am weary of my crying.* That voice, the one that came when least expected, had sounded in her ear that night, as if sitting there on the closet floor with her. *Then let yourself be happy.*

The voice had given her permission to stop beating herself up about not doing enough. Permission to go out among the living again. To dance. Permission to find joy.

And she'd tried. God knew she'd tried.

But the dead had always been her companions. Jubil. Joey. Lisa Michelle. Tally. And she'd tried to pay them back, to live a long and joyous life for those whose lives had been cut too short. And she kept right on trying to fix all the broken places in all the people she found.

And now there was Steve.

Wouldn't it be better for both of them if she just accepted his apology and booted his ass back out the door?

She'd watched him in the mirror while she dried off. He

hadn't taken his eyes off her. Eyes full of contrition.

He'd come a supplicant, hands twisted together in his lap, his body tense, poised to leap to his feet and walk out of her life if that was what she demanded.

Tap, tap, tap, the sound of her shoes on hardwood, a sound that had been integral to her life. She slid the shoes off and climbed up on the fat cushioned arm of the chair where Steve sat.

They sat like that for long minutes.

Steve finally laid his head in her lap. His big body shook.

Roxy didn't hesitate. She laid her hand on his grizzled head, rubbing gently, then moved it down to his shoulders.

"The doc says three or four months. Six on the outside."

The words slammed into Roxy, upending the hard-won calm of a moment before. Hadn't she already stood witness to enough death sentences? Lights danced at the edge of her vision, but everything else grew dark.

She'd watched a television special on black holes once. Time sucked in and in and in, into a void so deep and unknown, nothing could escape. The void sucked Roxy in too. Into dark and nothingness—

Kintsugi.

That damned voice again. Sometimes she really regretted taking that pottery class. *I've failed at this too many times already.*

The old, familiar sense of futility swamped her. Why fight a battle when you know from the onset that it can't be won?

"How do you know what can be won if you stop trying to win?"

There was no stopping the tears coursing down her face.

"He has brought all his sharp edges to you," the voice said. *"He fears hurting you with them, but he has no place else to put them without using them against himself. Kintsugi, Roxy."*

She shook her head. *This one is too much broken.*

"Not yet," said the voice.

She bent her head to rest on Steve's. Pulled herself back

177

from the event horizon of the void. "What do doctors know? Can I ask—"

"Cancer. What else? Pancreatic. Some folks last a while. Most don't."

"Are there drugs? Treatments?"

"The usual. I don't plan on doing any of that. A person's dying and they fill them full of poison to try to kill the beast that's killing them and all it does is prolong the dying. It doesn't do a damned thing for the living part of it. And I plan to live as much as I can until the angels call me home."

Roxy couldn't let him know he'd just torn her beating heart out of her chest, thrown it across the room, and smashed it on the floor. She was shocked that there wasn't any actual blood splatter on the walls.

"Are you sure it's gonna be angels, Steve?"

He chuckled and sniffed and sat up. Took off his glasses and pulled a huge white handkerchief from his pocket and blew his nose. "Sorry about that. I hope I didn't get snot all over your lap."

"I've had worse things in my lap."

Good. She'd made him smile. A watery, grim smile, but it was a start.

"We can fight this, Steve. Together—"

"I'm tired of fighting, Roxy. I fought in Vietnam and it made no difference. The Middle East. The streets of West Palm Beach and the halls of Washington, DC. Back alleys and drug dens all over the world. And it didn't make one goddamn bit of difference. The oligarchs and power brokers have just exchanged jungles for sand dunes. I fought to get drug dealers off the streets, but now the Sacklers and their ilk have made a killing off turning good kids and nice middle-class mommies into opioid junkies and every bit of it's legal. There's just no goddamned point anymore. I'm just so fucking tired of fighting."

His sucked in a long breath and shook his head as he half sobbed. "So fucking tired period."

Yeah, me too, but Roxy didn't say the words out loud.

She slid off the arm of the chair and onto his lap. She leaned her head against his chest and wrapped her arms around him. They were both hot and sweaty and sticky, but it didn't matter. One day, far too soon, she wouldn't be able to hold him like this. But for tonight she could, and she had no intention of letting a single second slip away.

"I was going to end it all, Roxy. Tomorrow. Go out my own damned way. I almost did it once before. It was such a great plan too. I was going to go out like Marilyn Monroe."

"You were going to dig up a Kennedy to murder you?"

Steve snorted and shook his head. "It was suicide, woman. And I was going to do the same thing." He closed his eyes. "Accidental overdose, alcohol, and barbiturates. A fifth-gallon bottle of Bacardi 151 rum. Seventy-five point five percent pure alcohol. Four Dramamine tablets in a line on my table, chewable, and orange-flavored to reduce nausea. Wouldn't want to botch the job by throwing it all up."

Roxy hummed softly under breath. The pills she'd spotted in his medicine cabinet the day she'd helped him home. This is what he'd planned to do with them.

"The final course was going to be Nembutal," Steve continued. "Oral pentobarbital. Twenty-four capsules washed down with fresh orange juice."

"You didn't have any orange juice in your refrigerator when I was there."

"I was going to go shopping," Steve said. "And then you went and bought some for me anyway. Saved me the trip."

"And you'd have let me feel guilty for buying the orange juice that killed you?"

"It wouldn't have been the juice, Roxy." He patted her shoulder and pulled her tighter against him. "Now where was I? Oh yeah...a Cuban cigar—illegally imported, a real one, not the ones they sell the tourists in Miami. I know a pilot who brings them in regularly."

"A cigar? Really? Smoking will kill you."

"So will cancer, Roxy."

"Cancer is an asshole, Steve. It doesn't discriminate and it doesn't play favorites and it doesn't give a damn what plans you have made or whether or not you're ready. When Tally died—"

Roxy's words stuck in her throat like a crosswise chicken bone. She sucked in a breath and swallowed hard. "Tally was older than me, and we'd never been that close. Our relationship was mostly Christmas cards and maybe a call on birthdays." She glanced up at the pictures on the wall, then snuggled back against Steve's chest. "Our lives were so different. She married a local boy, Duke Fisby, and had a couple of kids. Then she got religion. As in going to church constantly and wanting to homeschool the kids and go to religious retreats and stuff. Duke was a good old boy who liked to drink and smoke and play cards. Tally joined the Nazarene church."

"The same one with that guy who...who..."

"Who raped me. You can say it, Steve. Yeah, that one."

Steve whistled low and long. He pulled her closer. Steve's tight hug didn't feel like a trap. It felt like a homecoming.

One she was going to lose soon.

Wouldn't it be better, safer, if she ran now? If she just told him she was sorry and sent over a few meals without getting too close?

But it was already too late for that too.

"Yeah, well, so we lost touch even more after that," Roxy said.

Words poured through Roxy. Words that were meaningless in the moment, but words she needed anyway. Anything to give herself distance from Steve's awful announcement and time to get her breath under control.

"Then one of her kids called me," Roxy said. "Tally had cancer. She was refusing treatments because she'd been washed in the blood of Jesus and he was going to save her. They wanted me to come home—back to Ohio—to see if I could talk sense into her."

"Who's to say what's sensible? Faith might be every bit as healing as chemicals. Miracles happen."

Roxy sat up and gazed into Steve's eyes. Yes, she'd been right when she'd thought earlier that they hadn't looked right. The whites were distinctly jaundiced. And there was something else there. The beginnings of trust? A longing for reassurance? He looked the same way a child looks when he wants to be told everything is going to be all right even as the tornado bears down and rips their house apart.

Steve needed this distraction as much as she did. So Roxy did what she did best. She kept talking.

"Yes, I believe in miracles too, Steve. But I was selfish. And scared. I didn't want to face that church elder, who was spending a lot of time with her. I didn't want to accidentally blurt out the truth in front of Tally. She had faith in him. And faith was just about all she had left. And well, I'd told a whopper of a lie to the elder, years before, and I didn't want to fuck that up too."

Steve raised an eyebrow. "The man raped you, Roxy. And you were afraid of lying to him? How bad of a lie could you have come up with?"

Roxy wriggled out of his arms and paced the floor. One of the two people who knew the truth lived in a convent under a vow of silence. The other was Graciela, who would go to her grave keeping Roxy's secret.

"There was a baby, Steve."

She paced the other direction, needing to avoid his eyes as she rushed through this next part. "She came too soon. Way too soon and parts of her just missing or not working. I guess church elders with pencil-sized dicks don't make very good babies. But I loved her anyway. And I wanted him to pay for everything he did."

"Blackmail?"

"Not exactly. I waited and told him she'd been born just fine but that I was going to need money to take care of her. To keep her in New York. Or I was going to have to move back to Darby Glen and hope like heck it didn't slip out who the baby daddy was."

"That's called blackmail, Roxy. And I'm proud of you. How'd that work out for you?"

"That's how I got the money to move into the Barbizon. It paid for a lot of dance lessons and groceries and went to help some friends in a time when friends like that weren't getting much help from anybody else. The son of a bitch did his Christian duty whether he knew it or not."

"He never caught on? Never demanded pictures?"

Roxy shook her head. "He didn't fucking care. And neither did I. I just kept cashing those checks. Tally got religion and joined his church. And I was dancing at Radio City. And then her kid called and said Tally was dying and—"

All those years ago and the memories still carried barbs that stabbed her heart. She'd failed Tally, failed her own flesh and blood when she'd needed her most. Since then, she'd sat by too many bedsides of dying men. She'd run from New York. Run from all the dying. Now here it was again. She'd run from death, and death had let her think she'd gotten away.

But now it had found her again.

She clenched her fists and paced. Could she do it again? Watch someone she'd come to care about—maybe love—die?

Steve held out his hand, stopping Roxy's pacing. "Come back here. If I'm gonna die, it would be nice to do it with a woman in my lap."

Roxy resumed her former position, laying her ear against his chest, listening to the slow and steady thump of his heart. "It was Christmas time," she said. "The only time of the year the Rockettes dance. Folks never think about that. It's not a full-time gig. It's only a few months out of the year, but for those few months, our schedule was insane. And we were going to march in the Macy's parade. I called Tally. Told her I'd be home after the new year. That we'd visit and have a good talk then."

"She didn't make it that long, did she." Steve stated it as a fact. As if he knew.

Roxy tensed, but now it was Steve's turn to rub her shoulder, to run his hand up and down her back, soothing her.

"Duke was the one who called. And he was enraged. Called me all kinds of ugly names. Said that the whole town had watched me in that parade. Said that Tally had to have her boobs cut off because of the cancer and there I was on national television wearing a bathing suit no decent woman would wear in public, with my tits hanging out and kicking up my legs to show the whole world my cootch, and he was pretty sure my sister had not died from cancer but from the pure shame of seeing what I'd become."

Steve's hand tightened on her arm. "This Duke fella still around somewhere?"

"Steve, honest to God, you don't have to put a hit out on every man who's pissed me off. You'd be at it every day from now until the end and still not get them all."

"Guess I'd be at the top of that list."

Roxy sat up and stretched. "Yeah, you probably would be. Anyway, somebody got to the church elder and dealt with him not long after. Probably the father of some other little girl, which was only justice, but it cut off the money he was sending. But yeah, Tally died before I got home. Death has its own schedule to and comes calling in its own good time."

Roxy drew up her knees and curled up tighter on Steve's lap. Yeah, this right here. This felt like home. "I'm scared, Steve. I'm not afraid to admit that. I've held the hands of too many dying friends, and I'm scared I won't be strong enough to do it again. That I'll fuck it up somehow."

Steve moved beneath her, as if he was preparing to stand. "I shouldn't have put this burden on you. I'm sorry. Sorry for the loss of your little girl, and your sister, and your friends. I should have just kept right on walking tonight. Shouldn't have come back here and dumped this on you. I'm so, so sorry."

Roxy clung tighter and wouldn't let him move. "And I'm mad and sad and want to go find God right this minute and throw rocks at him and dig a deep hole in my garden and bury myself in it so I don't have to do this, and at the same time I want to go make you a huge pot of chicken soup and feed you ice cream. And some bourbon."

She stared off into space and bit her lips to stop the torrent of words and emotions from pouring out. "Maybe I should feed myself some chicken soup and ice cream and bourbon."

She turned to Steve and grabbed his dusky cheeks between her pale hands. "Am I going to be able to trust you to wait for death to come calling on its own schedule, or are you still planning to take matters into your own hands?"

"I'm scared too. And mad and sad and a whole bunch of other feelings I don't even have words for right now. But I've never been afraid of dying alone, Roxy. You don't have to stick around for what's coming."

Roxy hated every second of this. Hated the knowledge there was so little she could do and that none of it would matter in the end.

But she loved Steve more.

"Big tough guy. Being persistent and stubborn? Yeah, sometimes that works for you. For a while. But all day every day of your whole life? That shit can fuck you up, Steve."

She made sure Steve was looking at her before she said, "My philosophy is that life is like the Indy 500 and each of us is in the race whether we like it or not. Yeah, we can run that race alone and limp or crawl or dash across the finish line; everybody gets there sooner or later. But it's a whole lot easier if you've got a pit crew, people who will be there to help you along the way. When you're low on fuel? That pit crew will fill you back up. When your check engine light comes on and you're pretty sure your world's about to about to blow up? Yeah, a pit crew may not be able to fix everything, but they'll be there and they'll try their damnedest to find a way to help."

"So you want to be my pit crew?"

Roxy didn't hesitate. "Yeah, I guess I'm signing up for that." And fuck God and that damned voice in her head for making her go through this again.

Steve stood, keeping Roxy hugged close. "Since it looks like I'm not going to be dying tomorrow, I have something to ask you. An old buddy of mine from the patrol invited me to a cookout next Saturday. Tommy Jackson. He's good people. Seems his daughter got a top grade on her master's thesis and they're having a barbecue to celebrate. He told me I could bring a plus-one if I wanted."

"Are you asking me to be that plus-one?

"Well, I don't know; it's kind of risky. You've probably never been to a cookout like this."

"Why?"

"Because Tommy's a brother. Black. Like me. And barbecues with Black folks ain't nothing like white folks' barbecues. It's gonna take me all week to get you ready for it. Know how to do the Cupid Shuffle?"

Roxy smiled up at him. "I've been taking choreography all my life. I think I'll catch on."

Cupid Shuffle, Funky Chicken, electric boogaloo, or shuffle ball change—the dance or style didn't matter. All that mattered was that she'd be dancing with Steve until the music finally stopped.

Chapter 21

Steve's Date with Death: T-Minus 15:04:07 and Holding

ROXY HUGGED HIM tighter as he nuzzled her ear.

"That music you were playing when I came in."

"Billie Holiday?"

"Yeah. Lady Day. That woman changed my life."

Roxy leaned back in his arms. "You gonna tell me about it? Or are you planning to keep the story all buttoned up inside?"

"I'm done keeping secrets, Roxy. If I don't tell my stories now, they'll never get told." He hugged her hard. Letting go of her for even a moment was going to be impossible. But they both needed to breathe. "If you can find me something to drink, I'll tell you about it."

Roxy walked to the opposite end of the studio, flitting in and out of the spotlights. As she walked, she pointed her remote at them, changing the colors to pink, blue, and amber, her own personal rainbow.

Steve wished she still had her tap shoes on. That she'd dance for him again.

The sound of a refrigerator door opening and closing came out of the darkness, followed by the grinding chug of an ice maker. Roxy returned carrying a small tray with two bottles of beer, a pitcher of ice water, and glasses. At a large desk strewn with papers and charts, Roxy used her elbow to make room and set her tray in the cleared space.

She poured water for herself, chugging it down quickly, then filled it and held the ice-filled glass against her forehead, then in the deep vee of her sports bra.

Steve reached for a beer, then changed his mind. If he was going to live, like Roxy wanted him to, he was going to need to check on the effects booze had on his meds.

He was going to live. Not long, but he was going to see sunset tomorrow. And there was going to be another one the day after that.

The thought poleaxed him. He'd been so focused for so long on his death, but now that space in his brain, the one so taken up with planning his death, was empty, the desire for death sucked out, leaving a void.

Was the rest of his life going to be like a tsunami? The sea rushing out, exposing everything that had lain hidden beneath it, tempting the curious and foolish to come poking around, only to come rushing back, swooping away everything with a deadly force?

What was he going to think about every day now that death had been delayed?

Delayed. Not canceled. It was still going to happen. And he suddenly wasn't ready.

His knees grew weak. The light faded in and out.

Roxy caught him.

Roxy.

Would she always be there to catch him? She'd said she would.

She guided him to chair. Not the plush maroon one he'd just vacated but a sturdy leather office chair next to the desk. "Welcome to my real office," she said. "The chair has wheels, in case you need a hand getting around. If you faint, I don't think I can drag a man your size back to the house, and Iggy isn't around to help me move any bodies tonight."

Steve shook his head, the world coming back into focus. "I'm not in need of a wheelchair yet."

"Just thought I'd get in some practice now, in case I need it later," Roxy said. She silently pointed to the options on her tray, and Steve pointed to the water.

He gulped down a full glass, easing the dryness that clawed at his throat.

Roxy perched on a hard-backed chair next to the desk, flicked on a gooseneck halogen light, and leaned on her elbows, the light encircling her head like a halo. Like a spotlight.

Steve closed his eyes, conjuring the image of a long-ago spotlight. But the woman in that light didn't have red curls. Hers were glossy black.

Steve swallowed more water, slower this time, and let the river of time carry him into the past. Into the seminal moment that had changed everything. He worked to untangle the threads, to find the place where the story truly began.

"It had been a long, hot summer in Picketsville, Mississippi," he said. "Hell, they all are. This was 1956. The whole world felt like it was balancing on a knife's edge with a lit powder keg underneath. That poor kid, Emmett Till, had been lynched the summer before, not all that far from me. Our good ol' boy governor Jim Colman had his own private version of the KGB making sure no uppity negro or nigger-lovin' white folks were gonna do anything to upset his nicely segregated Jim Crow state. I was seventeen years old."

Steve clenched his water glass, letting the ice cool the heat in his hand. "And at seventeen, in a dusty town with nothing to do and no opportunities and hormones raging, you could almost feel disaster coming, like the way clouds pile up on a summer's day, getting higher and blacker, weighing down on folks but offerin' no relief until your skin feels too small and tight and your feelings too big and you know when it all finally breaks lose, things are gonna happen and things are gonna change and nothing will ever go back to the way it was before."

Steve sipped his water. "Elvis was on the television, scandalizing the nice white folks with all that hip-shakin', but for me, there was only one singer who mattered. All that summer me and my friends had been listening to Billie Holiday. My buddy—Ray John—his daddy owned a bar and they had a record player, and we'd go there and drink Coca-Cola and sometimes shoot pool when the older guys would let us, and listen to Count Basie and Frank Sinatra, Artie Shaw and Satchmo. And Billie. Over and over again it was Billie Holiday. The woman they nicknamed Lady Day."

He took another sip.

"Then one day Ray John came in all excited. Lady Day was going to do a concert. Carnegie Hall in New York City. And Ray John said we were going to go see it. It may as well have been on the moon, and I for sure thought Ray had taken up doing some of those drugs that so many of the older guys did. I mean, I didn't blame them. Not then. Not much to do in Picketsville but drink and get high." Steve shook his head, as if he still didn't believe it after all these years. "But no, Ray John had a cousin. Someone on his mama's side, I think." Steve waved his hand, pushing that detail away.

"Anyway, this cousin, Bobby, lived in New York. Him and Ray John had been close when they were little, and after Bobby's family moved, they stayed in touch, even though Bobby was ten years older. Anyway, Bobby worked as a janitor at Carnegie Hall. And if we could get our scrawny asses to New York in November, there was a chance Bobby could find us a way to see the concert."

Steve leaned his elbow on the desk, his hand in his chin, to this day awed by the unpolluted optimism and dauntless naiveté of his seventeen-year-old self. "We'd both been doing odd jobs that summer, but mostly we worked at not working. But the promise of seeing Lady Day in concert? Yeah, that lit a fire under us. Suddenly there wasn't anything we wouldn't do. Pop got me part-time work at the dry cleaner. We cut enough grass to cover twenty football fields, all with one of those little push mowers, not the kind that ran on gas. We ran errands. Gave up movies and sodas, and made do with the old *Playboy* magazines we had. Our mamas fretted and worried, and looking back, they had every right to. They had the right to be downright terrified."

Roxy cocked her head, but didn't interrupt the flow of his words.

"Traveling anywhere, for any person of color in the 1950s, was a fraught journey. You ever heard of *The Negro Travelers' Green Book* or sundown towns? Traveling while Black could get you killed. It's still not great today, but hotels and gas stations and restaurants, for the most part, have to let you use them. Although there are still some places…"

Steve took off his glasses, laid them on the desk, and massaged the bridge of his nose. Yeah, things were better today. But that wasn't saying much.

"Did you have a car?"

"Ray John's daddy had one and considered driving us to New York, and his mama wanted to visit with her family. In the end, his parents decided to ride along with us on the bus. I won't bore you with the details of that trip. Riding the bus for a Black family wasn't that much easier than driving would have been. Segregation for buses was in flux right about then. We were allowed to ride with white folks, but bus station waiting rooms and restrooms and all were tricky and dangerous to negotiate. But we got there, and stayed with Ray John's family in Harlem. His mama and daddy had no plans to go see Billie and thought we were damned fools who were going to get ourselves killed and get Bobby fired from his job, but nothing short of an apocalypse was going to stop us."

Steve closed his eyes again, lost in the memory. "The event was sold out. We stood on the sidewalk and watched all these fancy people in their fancy clothes getting out of their fancy cars. Me and Ray John had dressed up too. Bobby knew a way to sneak us backstage. He told us exactly where to stand so we would be out of the way of everybody rushing around, how to stay small and unnoticed. Hell, we'd spent most of our lives practicing how to do that. And then, there she was. On stage. Standing there talking and singing and only a few yards away from us. Billie Holiday. Lady Day in the flesh. So goddamned magic and beautiful, I could not even believe she was real."

Steve sighed. "Mama always was a churchgoer and believed in her heart that heaven was real. I always had my doubts. Still do. But hiding there in the dark that night, with my collar itching and my suit too big and sweat running down my armpits, I got the closest glimpse of heaven I may ever have. She was just coming to the end of a set, and I needed to piss in the worst way. So I left Ray John there and went looking for a bathroom colored folks could use, because you know they were still separate back then. Maybe not at the Carnegie. I don't know. I just knew I didn't want to get in trouble for no reason that night. And because I had to pee, that changed the whole trajectory of my life. It changed everything."

Roxy made a humming sound, indicating she was listening, but she said nothing.

"I found the bathroom, way down a hall in a place I sure as hell wasn't supposed to be. I finished up, washed up, and was trying to figure out how to get back to my hidey-hole where Ray John was. Then suddenly there's a crowd of people coming down the hall, right toward me. And I had no place to hide. And there in the middle of all those folks was Lady Day herself, Miss Billie Holiday. Looking like one of God's own angels, wearing a dress that was white and sparkly, with a wilted white gardenia in her hair going brown around the edges."

Steve sniffed the air. Maybe it was Roxy's garden. Maybe it was only in his memory. But he'd have sworn in that moment he could still smell the gardenia from that night.

"Gardenias were her signature flower," he said, "and perfect for her. They're big and showy—glorious—but fragile as hell. And short-lived, just like Billie. She was exhilarated when I saw her, but starting to crumple from the work it had taken to stand on the stage and give the performance of her life. Like Jesus in the garden, she'd given everything she had and like she knew she didn't have long, but she'd done it anyway for all those folks in the audience and all those little colored kids coming up who were gonna need her grace and voice and

191

inspiration in the fights that were ahead. Civil rights battles and war and Black Panthers and Black Lives Matter—that was all in the future. But Billie sang like she knew it was comin' and we were gonna need all the strength she could give us."

Steve shook his head. "You know, I don't know how saints insist God loves them when they're the ones he tortures the most. Billie Holiday was no saint, but she did good, and that's more important. She was her own, unique self, and she influenced so many who came after her. But she was surely a tortured soul. I saw a lot of whited sepulchers stand up and preach in church. Men who professed holy virtue from the pulpit but were wicked in their souls, corrupt as a Chicago politician. Lady Day was the opposite. The drugs corrupted her, threatened to steal her voice, but God had surely touched that lady's soul. He'd given her a gift she just had to share, even if doing it killed her."

"There I was," Steve said, "standing in my church clothes, because going to see Lady Day was like going to church and bein' in the presence of God and one of his finest angels. But that night, after the show, you could see that this angel was gettin' tired of living. That she'd given all her heart and body and soul to something too big for her to carry much longer. And then she saw me—all six feet of me—pressed up against the wall, trying my damnedest to be small and unnoticeable. And then she smiled and reached out and she touched my cheek."

Steve's hand went to his cheek. As long as he lived, no matter what woman he'd lain with, no matter the punches or kisses life had thrown him, he had never forgotten the profound moment of Billie Holiday's hand on his cheek.

"When she touched me that night, it was like I'd been blessed directly by God. Nothing I ever felt in church, no laying on of hands or tossing back grape juice and crackers ever felt the way it did when Billie Holiday touched my cheek and graced all of us with that weary—exhausted—smile. But then she spoke, just to me, like a secret message God had asked her to pass on. 'Do good things with your life,' she said. That was all. But it was enough. I understood in a way I could not explain to you even today. We all knew, even then, what the drugs had done to her. And that's the moment, right then and there in the presence of that battered, tired angel, that I decided to commit my whole life to stopping the sons of bitches who did that to her and to too many others like her. I would stop the bastards who poisoned angels like Lady Day."

He shook his head as if waking from a dream. "The world didn't offer a lot of opportunities for a kid like me. You have to understand what it was like for Black folks in the fifties. Even if we moved out of the South to the factory jobs in the North, there was still segregation. Redlining. It kept us locked up in certain neighborhoods. We were freer than in the South but still not free. So I dreamed the biggest dream I knew how to dream. I decided I was going to finish school with the best grades I could manage and then join the army. It would be my ticket out of Picketsville, Mississippi. My ticket to the whole rest of the world. I knew there wasn't a chance of me getting to be a cop back then, but in my head, the army was the answer. I could fight bad guys, even if they weren't the bad guys who were growing and making and selling the poison to Lady Day. All that would come later. But her words that night, they guided every damned step of my life. Not much chance of a kid from Picketsville being able to do something big and important, but I'd start with enlisting the second I could."

Steve paused to gulp more water, then mopped his dripping forehead with his already damp handkerchief. A meager breeze trickled though the open studio doors, providing a measure of relief, but somewhere in his memory he was coated in the sweat and dust and raw hunger of being seventeen and trapped in a fly-speck town.

"In the army", he said, "it didn't matter so much that I was a poor Black kid from Mississippi. The law said it wasn't so anymore, but the truth was there was still segregation. But my army pay was the same as any white boy's pay. My job was the same. Point gun. Shoot. And if I could do it better? Then they couldn't stop me from getting a promotion, even though they tried."

He shook his head, the memory still rankling after all these years. "The military gave lip service to being equal and fair and shit, but the truth is, there were bigots and racists, just like back home. Commanders with Confederate flags hung over their bunks. White sergeants from Alabama or Louisiana always assigning the most dangerous shit jobs to Black men and thinking nothin' of calling a grown-ass man *boy*. Some of the brothers got deep into the resistance—defying regs, wearing Afros, protesting the war. More power to 'em. But I kept my head down and my nose clean. I had a mission and I was goin' places. And Lady Day had pointed the way for me. Three years later I was stationed in California when I got word she died. Too young. Way too young."

Roxy swiveled in her chair and pointed her remote at the spotlights overhead, extinguishing all but one of them.

"You see that light, Steve? Only the great ones can survive under those lights." Roxy stood and walked to the spotlight. On the way, she grabbed her sweat-soaked shirt and pulled it on. Under that light the bedazzled white shirt caught the light and cast rainbows out into the shadows. She dipped and turned and did a gentle soft shoe. No music played. Her bare feet made only the slightest noise on the wood. She cast off the shirt again and left it lying in the light, still sparkling but empty.

Lifeless.

She stepped out of the light and returned to Steve, sinking into her chair.

"I've known every kind of performer. For some, the only time they are alive is when they are under those lights. And oh, how warm and bright and inviting they are. But they're hot. And they can burn you. Blind you. When you're on a stage, most of the time you can't see beyond those lights. All you can do is perform and perform and give and give and hope like hell that somebody is out there watching and that there's applause at the end. Because that's the only thing that makes some people feel whole. Without the audience, without the applause, they're like that shirt. Empty."

"Some performers," Roxy said, "are the opposite. They're terrified of the lights, throw up with nerves before every performance, and suffer almost debilitating impostor syndrome. They throw themselves into the light to prove they can. I found that for the most part, the ones who crave the light are not nearly as talented as those who are afraid of it.

"And then there's the last kind. They don't give a rat's ass if anyone is listening or watching or boos or applauds. They have something to say, with their voice or their feet or their music or their script or libretto, and if they don't get it out, it's going to kill them. It comes from the raw places inside, the tormented, hurt places, and the places of abiding faith and profound love. I think Billie was that last kind. It was gonna kill her, but she was going to say her piece anyway. So she used drugs to help ease the hurt and just kept on hurting herself. She couldn't *not* hurt. And for those people, Steve, the ones with real gifts to give to the world, we can all be grateful. But we can't save them. No matter how hard we love somebody, no matter how we pray or wish, we can't save them."

Roxy clasped Steve's big hands between her own.

"Auditions can be brutal. You go out there and give it your whole heart, and they reject you. Hope and rejection, hope and rejection; it's a cycle that can eat a sensitive soul alive. All those hopeful people, they come to New York all starry-eyed. They were the star of their school play back in Peoria or Beaumont. They sang the lead every year in the high school Christmas show. Maybe they did a TV commercial as a dancing cockroach for the local pest control company. And their friends and teachers and parents said 'You've got a great future. You're going to be famous!' And they went to New York or Hollywood and suddenly they're a teeny-tiny minnow in an ocean of other minnows and the sharks are ready to gobble them up and spit out their bones. I got a lot of rejections and worked a lot of scummy jobs before I became a Rockette. I loved every second of my journey and would never trade a moment of it or regret a thing about it, but I got lucky. Just one of the lucky ones who got to live out a dream for a little while before discovering I'd rather follow a different dream and got to go do that instead. But for others, the pressure is surreal. The great ones, the really, truly talented ones that do make it? Every time they perform, they give away a little piece of themselves. They have to. That's why people perceive them as being great, because they walk away from a show with a little piece of that performer tucked away in their pocket. Some performers manage to find ways to renew themselves, to protect themselves. But too many don't. They just keep giving until they have nothing left of themselves. And they try to fill that big empty nothing with drugs and booze and sex and the spotlight."

Roxy looked at the photos on the wall. They were in shadow, but Steve had the feeling she didn't need the light to see them. The images—the lives behind the images—lived in her memory.

"I got lucky," she said again, this time very softly. "Not everyone did. I had a friend like that in my New York days. One of those insanely talented ones. He'd grown up in the Bronx and gone to Julliard. He played the violin mostly, but really, anything with strings, he could make it sing. A real virtuoso, but he couldn't get a break. And that was the only thing that mattered to him. Being there," she said, pointing to the spotlight. "He played in the subway tunnels for pocket change. He went to every audition. He practiced until his fingers bled. He got amazing reviews when he played in small venues, but callbacks to larger orchestras never quite worked out. He stood out too much, too good for his own good. And so, one night, he smashed every instrument he owned and flung himself off a roof."

Roxy wiped away the tears that straggled down her cheeks and into the fine lines and crevices of her face, the tears tracing the contours of a long life. Steve reached out a finger to capture a tear that she missed. Then he couldn't help tracing the same path, wondering what else she'd experienced in her life. Whatever it was—the good and the bad and the spectacular and the devastating—had made her the woman she was today. And now he'd get a chance to know her.

She leaned into his finger and smiled sweetly before shifting position.

"Look at all the really great actors who've killed themselves with booze and pills," she said. "All they left behind was broken hearts and unfulfilled possibilities." She shook her head, staring into the distance, into that shining shirt on an empty floor. And then she pointed the remote again, and the spotlight winked out.

"I tried to live up the unfulfilled possibilities of Lady Day," Steve said. "I don't know if it was enough."

"It was enough, Steve. You will never know the lives that were changed, made better, because you got bad people off the streets. So the drugs never got to some kid and they never died and their families never grieved. Children were born that might not have been. Young men who might have gone to jail are now old men with a 401K and grandchildren drawing crayon birthday cards for them. People survived because you did, Steve. Lady Day didn't make it, but she changed the world for a lot of people because she changed the world for one tall skinny kid from Picketsville, Mississippi."

"You make me sound like a...I don't know. Some kind of hero. I'm no hero."

"Heroes have it hard. All those expectations, from themselves and others. I'd hate being a hero." She traced a finger down his cheek. "But yeah, you kind of are. You're a man who did his best. That's all any of us can do."

"Thank you, Roxy." Then he sighed. "It never gets any easier, though, does it?"

"It helps if you have someone you can lean on. Share the burden with. Very, very few Rockettes ever dance solo. We work together. We twine and turn and do our own steps, but everyone in the audience is always waiting for that one moment. That moment when we all come together and form one long unbroken line, a line that goes back decades, really, and we kick up our heels—precisely to eye level—and dance together. It's always better when you have someone to dance with, Steve."

Roxy stood, walked to the sound system behind him, and fiddled with the record player. A moment later, deeply familiar trumpet, drums, and piano filled the darkened studio.

Roxy stood in front of Steve, her arms outstretched in invitation.

Lady sings the blues

Steve drew in a long breath. God alone knew how many more of those were allotted to him. But for now, tonight, while he still had a few more breaths left to him, he'd take advantage of the gift an unpredictable God had offered. He swiped his hand across his face, wiping away the tears he hoped Roxy hadn't seen.

Hell. What did it matter if she did? He stood and matched Roxy's stance, then shuffled his feet in the slow, awkward waltz his mother had taught him all those years ago. The radio playing, the linoleum under their feet cracked and curling at the edges, the scent of honeysuckle drifting through the open window, and the chirrup of locusts and crickets and frogs was drowned out by the music and the laughter in the kitchen. Daddy dancing with Natalie and Mama with him. And then they'd turn to each other and smile and dance together.

Steve pulled Roxy close, just as Daddy had done with Mama. Pulled her close and shuffled alongside her, gently rocking to the music.

I ain't gonna just sit around and cry

"I don't know what you see in an old fool like me, Roxy, but whatever it is, I'm glad of it."

Roxy smiled up at him, pulled him closer, and kept dancing.

Chapter 22

Steve's Date with Death: T-Plus 6 days 15:04:07 and Holding

"I'M GOING TO flush my stockpile of pills," Steve said the following morning after another of Roxy's enormous breakfasts. She must have decided that since he was dying anyway, sausage gravy and biscuits with hash browns and fried eggs wasn't going to kill him any faster than the cancer already was. "You want to watch me to make sure I do?"

"You can keep them or take them to one of those safe places for destruction, but don't flush them. The water supply in Florida is already hosed up beyond belief, and the fish don't need any more drugs in their systems. It's your choice, Steve."

His choice. His choice to live. Or to die. Roxy had made it clear last night what she wanted his choice to be, but hadn't pushed him into any corners. Hadn't forced her choice on him.

Except she did, in her own Roxy way.

He bagged up the pills and stashed them in the back of the closet in his empty guest room. But the room didn't stay empty for long.

Two days later a small U-Haul backed up in his driveway and unloaded furniture into the guest room under Roxy's direction. Within two hours he was the owner of a twin bed, a dresser, a nightstand and a lamp, and linens with matching curtains.

"Sometimes you snore, Steve," Roxy said as she hung one of her Dean Lauderdale paintings on the wall nearest the bed. "Sounds like an avalanche of boulders thundering down a canyon. This is just some stuff I had in storage, and this way I can get some sleep on nights I choose to stay over here."

Steve knew the truth, though. Roxy had left a pamphlet for one of those visiting hospice nursing care agencies on the kitchen counter one morning. The newly furnished guest room would be a nice haven for one of them.

Steve moved his pills back to his own room and stashed them under his mattress. In spite of what he'd told Roxy, he'd take them all before he let some Nurse Ratched wipe his ass and mop up his drool.

"You watch too much television," Roxy said when he expressed his thoughts to her. "We had a hospice worker for Mom, and those folks are doing God's own work. Angels, every one of them."

Yeah, angels of death. He stashed the pamphlet with the pills, and Roxy never mentioned it again.

The rest of the week flashed by in a blur. The barbecue was tomorrow, and the thought of being around all those people churned Steve's stomach almost as much as the thought of being a helpless, bedridden lump of flesh left to the not-so-tender mercies of some stranger.

Roxy wouldn't let anything bad happen to him, would she? Maybe he should start being a little nicer to her.

Nice was never something that had come easy to him, though, and eighty was a tough age to be learning something new.

"I've changed my mind," Steve said for at least the fifth time that week. "I'm not going to the barbecue." He flopped down on his bedroom chair and gave an exasperated growl.

"Steve, it's a simple get together with old friends."

Roxy hadn't listened the first four times he'd changed his mind either.

"With people who like you and want to see you. If anybody

should be nervous, it should be me. You have me half-terrified of saying or doing the wrong thing and violating some sacred taboo."

"Aw, Rox, they'll love you no matter what. You have a knack for making friends and fitting in." Steve dismissed her concerns and changed his mind yet again. Maybe it wouldn't be so bad to see Tommy and Paul and some of his old buddies.

No, it would suck. What did an old geezer like him have in common with guys still out on the streets? And half the stuff he'd done at the DEA still couldn't be talked about. And until Roxy, his day-to-day life had revolved around staring out the window and watching ancient reruns on TV. He didn't have anything to talk about.

No, he wasn't going.

"I don't want them to know I'm sick," he said. "I don't want people fussing or making sad faces at me or whispering in corners about me."

"The only thing they're going to be whispering about is how a big ugly brute like you ended up with such a hot date and wondering how much you paid me."

That got a laugh out of him. He'd also spent too many hours of the week fretting about what to take to Tommy Jackson's barbeque and that was still uppermost in his mind. He couldn't just stop at the grocery and pick up a roasted chicken or cold cuts.

"I gotta bring something, Roxy, or they won't invite me to take a plate home, and that's one of the best parts about being invited. And not just me. You gotta bring something too. And it can't be mac and cheese or potato salad." He gave her the side-eye. "You're not one of those white women who puts raisins in her potato salad and no spices and not enough mayo, are you?"

"Raisins are gross, no matter what they're in. I loathe wrinkly food."

"And yet just last night you ate—"

"It may have been wrinkled when I started, but it got pretty damn plump before I was finished."

Steve hooted with laughter. Things were never going to be spectacular in that department, but given the circumstances, they did okay. He wasn't sure how much longer that would last, but even just curling up next to Roxy at night was an unexpected gift. He was going to treasure every moment, no matter how few they might be.

"Danni says you should bring a bottle of Crown Royal or Hennessy. And aluminum foil. Apparently there is no such thing as too much aluminum foil."

"Tommy's Danni? How did you get in touch with her?"

It was Roxy's turn to give him the side-eye. "I've told you a dozen times to set a passcode on your phone. You were in the shower this morning and your phone was right there and Tommy texted to remind you. Danni says you've turned down every invitation to cookouts in the past and they're excited you're coming this time. They want to make sure you don't forget or just don't show up."

"I'm not big on living in the past, hanging out with guys that are still working, or reminiscing about glory days. They weren't so glorious."

Steve levered himself out of his chair, walked to his closet, and went back to what had him currently so frustrated. He shoved hangers from side to side while Roxy lounged on his bed, shaking her head at his choices. Since when did he give a fuck what he wore to a party he didn't want to go to anyway?

But he did care. He didn't want to embarrass Roxy. Wanted her to be proud to be seen with him. He sometimes woke up at night and stared at the ceiling, waiting for the churning in his gut to stop and pondering the ineffable wonder of a woman like Roxy lying next to him. Even though she snored sometimes too. But nice little kitty-cat snores. Not thundering boulders in a canyon.

"I'm not wearing one of those guayabera shirts," he said after Roxy pointed to one. "The guys would never let me live it down. And I'm not bringing Crown Royal. That's what old uncles who can't cook bring to the barbecue."

Roxy snorted. "Have you looked in the mirror lately, Steve? You *are* the old uncle."

Steve huffed and pulled another polo shirt out of the closet. This one was mint green. Roxy shook her head. Damn it. He'd fussed less about his getup for that long-ago prom. But this was Roxy. He had to look his best. To look like he deserved to have the tall, shapely redhead on his arm.

"I brought up the issue of what to bring with Danni, and she said I should bring a dessert," Roxy said. "Not sweet potato pie or, God forbid, pumpkin pie. She said there were already folks bringing peach cobbler and 7-Up cake, and only her mother is allowed to bring banana pudding, but anything else would be fine. Honestly, how many desserts do people need? I told her I have a killer baked bean recipe. She sounded a little wary about it, but nice enough. Do you think I was being too pushy?"

Steve blew her a raspberry. "Yeah, because *nobody* in the world has probably ever called Roxy Fields pushy, right?"

She stuck out her tongue at him.

"Is that an invitation, woman? Because that's a better way to spend my time than picking out a shirt. And no baked beans. For sure, some uncle already has his own secret recipe, and that will be the only one folks want. And there is absolutely no limit to the number of desserts that can be consumed at a barbecue."

Roxy rose gracefully from the bed and pushed Steve out of the way, sliding hangers back and forth far more gently than he'd been doing, pulling out one shirt after another, rejecting them or laying them on the bed for consideration.

"Danni did say the barbecue starts at noon."

Steve plopped himself on the bed and snorted. "That means we daren't show up before one thirty."

"Colored people time," Roxy said, eyeing his shirts.

Steve elbowed her. "You know about that?"

"Jubilation Duval explained it to me. She drove me batshit crazy never being on time for anything until she explained that just because the rest of the world ran on white people time, that did not mean she was ever going to do it."

"Yeah, I damned near got my head taken off and disinvited to the cookout one time because I showed up at the time they said instead of the time I was supposed to."

Roxy flopped on the bed on her belly, next to Steve, avoiding the clothes she'd laid out there, and propped her chin in her hands. "Do tell."

Steve grinned at the memory. "I had a very short break—a three-day pass—between boot camp and being sent off to advance training school in the army. So of course I made a beeline for home, where the fam was planning a barbecue to welcome home the shiny new soldier. Same like Tommy's barbecue—Auntie Althea said it was going to start at noon. Now, you have to understand; I had just spent eight miserable weeks getting my ass kicked from here to kingdom come by some of the meanest sons of bitches the army every minted. And I'd spent a lot of those first two weeks on latrine duty and KP and digging holes and filling up holes because I could not seem to master the fine army demand of getting anywhere on time. Then Master Sergeant Briggs showed up one day with a clock. And not some itty-bitty dainty thing. That sucker was two feet across if it was an inch. And it was my job to carry the damned thing with me everywhere I went. And every fifteen minutes he made me sing out the Westminster chimes and announce the time. You know those chimes?" Steve sang a few off-key notes.

Roxy laughed and covered her ears.

"All day long—running laps, during firing drills, in the mess, everywhere—I had to carry that damned clock and stand up and sing and announce the time. And it wasn't just during the day. Master Sergeant gave me a break and said I only had to do it once an hour at night."

"How many days did you last?"

"After the first night, the squad threatened to cut my throat just to shut me up. By the second night they decided to throw me a blanket party instead. You know what that is?"

Roxy shook her head.

"A couple of guys grab you and throw a blanket over your head. Then any number of others join in and beat the shit out of you. The blanket prevents a lot of bruising and soaks up any blood and prevents you from being able to identify the hitters. It's a pretty damned effective way of getting somebody's attention. They took it easy on me, but I was still a mess. So Master Sergeant made every single one of them responsible for getting me places on time. And it wasn't only me. On paper the army was a fully integrated unit, but that didn't mean all those white recruits felt the same way, and they damn sure weren't going to take a punishment because some damn Black boy from the South couldn't tell time. Especially in boot camp. There were a couple of other brothers there with me, just as bad, but they were faster learners than I was."

"That's my Steve," Roxy said. "A born rebel."

"Yeah, well, whatever. I caught on eventually. Only took two days and a solid beatdown. I learned to be on time. And when I got home from boot camp that weekend, I was still running on army time."

"Oh no."

"Oh yes. I showed up at Auntie Althea's house at twelve o'clock on the dot. She was wearing her housecoat and had her hair wrapped around those pink foam roller things women used to use. Worst of all, she didn't recognize me. I'd filled out a lot of muscle in those eight weeks and had all my hair buzzed off. She took one look at me and got it into her head the army had sent somebody to tell her I'd been killed because that's what they did in the old movies."

Steve shook his head. "She'd had it happen to friends a few years earlier. World War II and Korea weren't that far in the rearview mirror and still pretty vivid for people her age. And it wasn't too many years before we got all tangled up in Vietnam and folks had good reason to start screaming all over again the minute they saw strange men in uniforms on their doorsteps, but it wasn't like that yet."

He'd never had to work the death notification detail and

was glad of it, but as a sergeant, he'd written more than a couple of letters of condolence to families who'd forever have an empty seat at their barbecues.

"Anyway, once she got done having palpitations and screaming at me, she called my daddy to come get me, and he talked her out of disinviting me altogether. I came back ninety minutes later with a case of beer and the biggest bouquet of roses I could find, even if I spent a good chunk of my first paycheck on them, and she forgave me."

Roxy had been rolling on her back, laughing. She finally sat up, catching her breath. "God, I would have loved to have met the younger version of you."

"No, you wouldn't have. You think I'm a hard-ass now? Young Steve would have ground you up and spit you out and walked over your bones."

Now it was Roxy's turn to blow raspberries. "Not once you got a gander at these tits. You'd have followed me around like a faithful puppy with your tongue hanging out." Roxy winked at him.

It did something to his insides when she did that. Made his heart beat faster, but not like he was going to need a nitro tab again. More like the excitement he'd felt going to that barbecue so long ago right after boot camp. The feeling that he was coming home and couldn't wait and that a whole new world was right there at his fingertips and all he had to do was reach out and grab it.

He'd spent his whole life waiting to come home to Roxy. And he'd almost blown it.

He wanted to say something, to let her know how he felt, but he'd always sucked with words.

"Looks like you still have that army buzz cut today." She reached over and rubbed her hand on the quarter-inch of gray mat on the top of his head.

"Mama cried the first time she saw it, upset they'd cut off all my curls. But I like it. The thought of hair on my neck today makes me itch. I don't have time to spend at a barber shop getting a fancy fade or worry about the upkeep on some line-up or twists or something. This suits me just fine."

"Indeed it does. Especially with that nice panama hat of yours. Which gives me an idea."

Roxy snapped her fingers and leapt off the bed, disappearing into his living room. She returned a second later with his hat. She went through the shirts on the bed, holding the hat next to each before plucking one up.

"This one," she said, holding out a pale peach-and-white-striped polo with a darker orange collar and orange bands on the sleeve, an exact match to the orange band on the hat.

"Add that snappy white blazer of yours and you'll be the belle of the ball," she said.

"Now we've got that sorted," Steve said, "you suppose we've got time for something else?"

"Are you thinking about lunch?"

Steve tumbled Roxy back on the bed, atop all the clothes piled there.

Roxy gasped. "Steve—"

Steve sucked with words, but he'd always been a man of action. All he could do was hope Roxy got what he was trying to tell her.

"Just following orders from Dr. Roxy to live the hell out of every minute I've got."

Steve had always hated following orders, but this time it was pure pleasure to do so.

Chapter 23

Steve's Date with Death: T-Plus 8 days 15:04:07 and Holding

STEVE AND ROXY sat on her lanai, basking in the afterglow of the barbecue. Well, Roxy basked. Steve, even after a long nap, still nursed a hangover.

Roxy found a streaming station that played the same music that had filled the afternoon. Prince. Whitney. At the moment Luther Vandross currently crooned sexily from her sound system.

"Bringing home empty pans and full plates is the sign of an excellent party and that folks enjoyed having you there," Steve said. He picked listlessly at the salad in front of him. Roxy had decreed that after a full afternoon of stuffing their faces with meat and carbs and sugar, the plates full of ribs and greens and macaroni now in the refrigerator would have to wait for tomorrow's supper.

"I had the best time, Steve. Your friends are nice and they were so glad to see you."

Steve grunted and took a long gulp of the sweet tea Roxy had allowed him to have with the salad. "What were those brownies you brought to the party? You didn't put any of your magical ingredients in them, did you? I heard a bunch of them cackling over school brownies or something."

"No pot in those brownies; I'm not an asshole. They were

what a lot of folks call lunch lady brownies: peanut butter brownies with milk chocolate frosting. Maybe they didn't serve them in Mississippi schools, but when I was a kid, before school lunches got all healthy and nutritious, the highlight of school lunches was on Friday, when they served pizza made on hamburger buns and those peanut butter brownies. Tommy's sisters and cousins had a great time introducing the younger ones to those brownies."

Steve put a leaf of lettuce in his mouth and choked it down. "I don't suppose—"

"I made an extra batch. Eat all your salad and maybe I'll let you have one."

"Did you also make an extra batch of those lemon things? I did manage to snag two of those."

Roxy dipped her fork in the dressing she'd served on the side, then speared a cucumber slice. "Lemon cream cheese bars. No extras of those, but I'll make more next week. You're in charge of going out and grabbing more lemons from the yard."

Steve snorted. "Didn't I just fill up two whole grocery bags of them this morning?"

"You did. And Danni loved them and asked me to make the lemonade with them. All you had to do was fill up the bags, Steve. I had to squeeze every single one of them. I had no idea people could go through so much lemonade."

"Yeah, well, the cousins liked mixing it with what I brought."

Roxy nodded. "I thought some of those glasses of lemonade being carried around had a suspiciously brown tint. I told you Crown Royal was the right choice. As was the cooler of beer."

"Yeah, well, you're the one who thought of taking that other gift for Danni."

"Limoncello. It's not like I have a scarcity of it. One bottle for Danni and one for Tommy's grandma, the family matriarch. She seemed like a perfectly harmless little old lady until I saw her at the dominoes table. My God, that woman has a mouth on her."

"I warned you to stay away from there. Folks at a barbecue can get petty as fuck and throw shade like the Empire State Building on a sunny day. You didn't get roped into being anybody's partner at Spades, did you?"

Roxy shook her head. "I had more than my fill of any kind of cards when I was a blackjack dealer in Las Vegas." She shrugged at Steve's questioning look. "It paid better than waitressing, and there was a table and a pit boss between me and the drunk, grabby customers. And besides, you warned me not to play Spades, not even if you begged me."

"Well, you should have kept an eye on me and not let me play either. My old pal from the patrol, Paul Tinker, got me in a game. We did all right, but I'm not sure Tommy's daughter's boyfriend is going to have anything nice to say to me for a while."

"She can do better," Roxy said. "I liked Emmy. Tommy and Danni were busting their buttons with pride over her. Danni told me all about why they named her what they did."

"Emmy?"

"It's actually Emerson. Emerson Imani Jackson."

Steve rubbed his temples. When had folks stopped giving kids sensible names like Bob and Jenny and Lena? "Emerson? Damned peculiar name for a girl. At least it's not one of those 'sh' names. Shaniqua or Keishani. Like that."

"That's what Danni said. While she appreciates her mother's creativity in naming her Dannisha, there are those in the world—you, for instance—who are not fond of really beautiful African American names. That's why she goes by Danni. Well, to her pediatric patients she's Dr. Danni. She said that in spite of what folks say, there's still a lot of bigotry out there. She said it's already tough enough for a Black woman without someone taking one look at her résumé and immediately throwing it into file 13 based on her name alone."

"Same happens to white women, I guess. How many Fortune 500 CEOs are gonna be named Tiffany or Brandi or Brittany?"

"Or Roxy. Anyway, she said Tommy wanted to give her a name that honored her culture and heritage, and Danni wanted to give her a name that would open doors that might otherwise be closed. So they named her Emerson Imani—Emerson to give her wings and Imani to remind her of her roots." Roxy popped a cherry tomato into her mouth, glanced at Steve's plate, and raised her eyebrows as he listlessly poked at his salad.

Tough luck. He wasn't hungry. Especially for some damned rabbit food.

"Emmy's sensible," Roxy said, "and pretty as a model, and whip-smart from what I could tell. And it was a pleasure to talk to another woman as tall as me."

Steve managed a small laugh before the hangover stabbed him right behind the eyes again. "Yeah, Danni's side of the family are all pretty height-challenged."

"Half of them looked little enough to have fallen off a charm bracelet."

That did make Steve laugh, to his regret.

Roxy refilled his iced tea. "Hydrate. It's the best cure for a hangover. And back to bed again to sleep it off."

They'd come home while the party was still in full swing, pleading the excuse of old people not liking to drive after dark. Roxy had driven, muttering something about him looking fatigued after an afternoon enjoying adulterated lemonade. She'd given him aspirin and a glass of water, then poured him into bed to sleep off the worst of it.

"So, when did you learn to do the Cupid Shuffle?" Steve asked.

Roxy *tsked*. "Today. It's not like it's hard. The words are right there in the song. You should have tried it."

Steve shook his head. "Somewhere in the book of barbecue rules is one that says 'thou shalt not dance if thou has two left feet.' Right after the one that says 'not all brothers are born with rhythm.' You did good with that wobble one too."

"Yeah, well, I'm a dancer, Steve. Picking up choreography is what I do. You know how being able to fire a gun is kind of a basic requirement for being a cop? Picking up choreography is like that for me. A lot of auditions, they'd show you the steps once and then you'd have to try out. A really great dancer who can't pick up the steps fast enough will almost always get beat out by a good-enough dancer who gets the choreography the first time."

"I'll bet you were both a great dancer *and* a fast learner."

"Not great, but good enough to be a Rockette, which kind of does put me in an exclusive class. Right height, right leg length, right body type. Right skills. It took me three years of trying out to make it, but yeah, I did okay. Just like you did with the Electric Slide."

Steve grunted and pushed away the soggy remains of his salad. "Yeah, well, that one's been around since Moses was a little boy. Hell, even white folks do the Electric Slide at weddings."

Roxy chuckled, then gathered up their empty bowls. She returned a few minutes later with two plates of peanut butter brownies, forks, an ice bucket, a pitcher of water, and a dark brown bottle. "Hair of the dog," she said. "I didn't have any Crown, so Jack will have to do." She dropped ice cubes in the glass, added the whiskey, then splashed in water. "Three, two, one," she said. "Three cubes of ice, two fingers of Jack Daniels, one splash of water. It's called Sinatra-style Jack. It's how he always drank it. If it was good enough for the Chairman of the Board, it's good enough for me."

Steve sniffed the glass, then sipped appreciatively. "I liked the Rat Pack. They ragged on Sammy Davis a lot, but they treated him with respect and made sure he got respected by others. I'll always have a soft spot for Frank for being a stand-up guy that way."

Roxy sighed dreamily. "Oh my God, I loved Sammy. I mean, yes, most folks think of him singing, but that man was flat-out magic in a pair of tap shoes. One of my idols. I saw him once in Las Vegas. It was all I could do to keep from screaming like some teenaged Beatles fan."

"Sammy was like me. He liked his women tall, blond, and white."

"Yet here you are with a redhead."

"I'm flexible that way."

"I used to be a blonde when I was a kid. Then I got older and turned into common-as-mud dishwater blond."

"Ditchwater."

"What?"

"You said dishwater. I grew up hearing it as ditchwater."

"Either way, it was ugly. When I got to New York, first thing I did was get a bottle of peroxide and bleach it."

"Huh. How'd that work out for you?"

"Burned the fuck outta my scalp, dried my hair to straw— what didn't just break right off—and turned it orange."

"So what did you do about it?"

"Cut it into one of those pixie cuts, bought a cheap wig, and saved my money until I could get it fixed. Then I had it dyed red. Figured it would make me stand out. Be memorable, you know?"

Steve nodded.

"Turns out the Rockettes wear so many wigs and hats, it doesn't matter. They want you to look alike, not stand out. And they only allow one hairstyle—a French twist. My hair had grown out plenty by the time I got in."

He tentatively stretched out a hand and stroked her hair. "Feels real good now," he said.

She shimmied her shoulders and leaned closer to his hand. "And it's all mine. Except the color. I owe that to my beloved Mr. David." Roxy sipped her drink. "I think Tommy's daughter appreciated the checks we gave her."

"Master's degrees aren't cheap. Every little bit helps."

"I saw you off in a corner talking to her," Roxy said. "What was going on?"

Steve shrugged. "I asked if I could read her thesis, so she put it in a Google doc for me. It's mostly way over my nappy old head, but I understood the summary. It had some long fancy bullshit title like those things do, but it essentially had to do with her specialty, security and intelligence. Do you know she went to a university in England for it? Anyway, she had some pretty innovative ideas about stochastic terrorism and how to identify those who are likely to be radicalized and become lone-wolf terrorists. So I sent off the doc to some folks I still stay in touch with in D.C."

Roxy sat back in her chair. "So that's what all the screaming was about."

"Woman, there was so much screaming going on this afternoon, I'm not sure which part you're talking about."

"The part where Emmy stepped away to take a phone call and then ran out of the house screaming about having just gotten off the phone with somebody at the FBI and she has an interview next Thursday and then Danni started crying and said Emmy had promised her she wouldn't go into any kind of job that required a gun and then Ms. Lavinia, Tommy's grandma, started cheering and yelling *PEW PEW* and doing that finger-gun thing— although honestly, that may have been the limoncello talking— and then Emmy's sister started screeching something about what was she going to wear, and then their brothers said they were going to escort her to Washington because it's full of politicians and shysters and a nice girl like her could not go to that wicked city alone." Roxy paused for a breath, winked, then plunged on. "And then there was a lot of crying and hugging and toasting and that's when Uncle Tony shouted that the ribs were ready and then there was a stampede and after that I sort of lost track. I did manage to stay out of the way until the crowd thinned and I could find you so we could get some food."

Steve stretched and patted his belly. Somehow during Roxy's speech, an entire brownie and all of his drink had disappeared.

Roxy stood and hauled him out of his chair and to her bedroom. She kissed him on the cheek. He made a half-hearted grab for her and missed, mostly due to her only having two fingers of whiskey over the course of the day compared to his two fistfuls. The thought made him chuckle, but apparently made no sense to Roxy when he tried to explain it to her.

"Go to sleep, Big Guy. I'll be in after I clean up."

Steve was just drifting off when a new sound came through the open window: Frankie Beverly and Maze and the sound of tap shoes making a pleasant clatter on hardwood. The music would stop and start, repeating a section several times.

Roxy out in her studio, probably in those sexy shorts and dancing bra. Doing her own choreography. Always curious, always alive, always trying something new. He'd never have to worry about being disinvited to the cookout with her as his date.

He might be dying, but he was going out with a funny, talented redhead at his six. Damn, he was glad he'd stuck around for this. Paul Tinker had invited them to his Labor Day cookout. A couple of months away, but Steve could already taste the steaks and the sweet ripe ears of corn, could almost feel the juice from a plump rosy watermelon dribbling down his chin. For the first time in a long time he had something to look forward to other than dying. He could stay alive at least that long. Maybe he'd eat more of Roxy's rabbit food. Cut back on the beer. What the hell did doctors know anyway? It was all a crapshoot, and he'd won against longer odds than this in the past. And now he had Roxy on his side too.

Maybe God wasn't a complete and total dick after all.

Chapter 24

Sexy Firefighters Calendar Word of the Day:
Ephemeral: [ih-fem-er-uhl]. **Adjective**. *lasting for a very short time.*

THEY SETTLED INTO something of a routine over the next month. Sometimes they spent the night at Steve's house, but more often at Roxy's just because she liked cooking dinner in her own kitchen, which usually left them too full and happy and tipsy to think about anything other than tumbling into bed together.

More often than not that didn't mean sex, but Roxy found it comforting just to wake up next to Steve. She'd worried about him looking fatigued at the barbecue and stuffed him with grilled fish and veggies when she could or pork chops and mac and cheese when he wouldn't eat anything else. He asked for salads sometimes, but more often than not left them wilting on his plate.

He didn't sleep well and groused at Roxy because of her insistence on getting up with him at night if he was gone for more than a few minutes. The worst were the nights she sat next to him on the bathroom floor, mopping his face after he'd been throwing up, waiting for him to be empty enough and exhausted enough to crawl back into bed. She fed him Dramamine until he'd finally gotten a prescription for something stronger.

Even when nights were spent at her place, a lot of afternoons were spent at Steve's house, especially if he'd had a doctor's appointment that morning. He liked coming home and taking a nap in his own bed. He hadn't wanted to get Roxy involved in those appointments.

"I don't need anybody to come hold my hand and give me a lollipop afterwards if I behave."

"A lollipop might be exactly what you need. I make special cherry ones for the members of my garden club. Helps with nausea."

But Steve had blown a gasket at the idea. In one of those three o'clock in the morning, curled-on-the-bathroom-floor episodes, he'd told her a dark tale of once being forced to consume opium at gunpoint on a godforsaken mission that had ended with a dead Russian in an alley. One of the very few times in his life he'd ever surrendered control, he said, and he'd hated every second of it. The whole experience still haunted him.

Roxy stepped carefully, always making sure Steve understood that he had complete control over his choices and actions. She wanted to push him to do more, to try the treatments the doctors offered, but with his days dwindling, he'd seized firmly to the control he'd felt cheated of his whole life.

That need for control sometimes showed up when she least expected it. One argument ignited when she'd done a load of laundry for him.

"You didn't need to do that, Roxy. In fact, I'd rather you didn't."

"No worries. I folded everything just the way you like it. You just sit there and enjoy your show, and I'll put it away. I'm thinking of making chicken and rice casserole for dinner."

"Damn it, Roxy, you're not my maid, and I'm not helpless."

His vehemence startled her. "I never said you were. I had to do a load anyway and threw your stuff in with mine. And we both have to eat. No need to send your blood pressure skyrocketing over it. Just settle back, and I'll bring you some iced tea in a minute.

"Roxy, I appreciate what you're trying to do, but I'm done following orders. Done doing what everybody else thinks I should do."

"I'm not trying to tell you what to do, Steve. I'm just—"

"Just worrying. Just taking care of me. Just doing what you always do. Show you someone with a little boo-boo, and you go into instant nurse mode. You missed your calling, Rox. Have you ever let anybody just take care of themselves? Or get themselves out of a jam? Maybe sometimes you just need to let people figure things out on their own. I don't need a nurse, Roxy. I just need…" He'd stared into space for a long moment.

For once in her life, Roxy resisted the urge to jump in. So many people had helped her in the past, she always felt the need to pay it back. But maybe he was right. What Steve needed was to figure it out on his own.

"A friend, I guess," he said at last. "I've never had too many of those. And I'm trying to figure out what friends do and how to be one too. Did it ever occur to you that maybe somebody might like to help *you* now and then? That maybe *you* should sit down for five minutes and let somebody do something nice for you? Maybe bring *you* a glass of iced tea?"

She plopped into a chair and left the laundry basket at her feet.

"Thank you, Steve. A glass of tea would be lovely." She'd never let him know what it cost her to sit and watch while he struggled out of his chair and clattered around in the kitchen before returning with her tea.

Why did she have to fall so hard for someone so damn stubborn?

"*Kintsugi, Roxy.*"

I don't know what the fuck more you want from me. Just shut up.

And so the voice fell silent for a while.

Roxy gave up on the idea of feeding Steve her marijuana edibles, even though she knew they might help. She could have baked some pot into the cookies he loved so much—the ones with both chocolate chips and toffee bits—but she wouldn't do that to him. Steve didn't have much left he could control. She wouldn't take that last bit from him.

Which had led to more arguments over medical appointments.

"There's nothing they can do," Steve said, "so why do they insist they still need to see me so often and keep wanting to send me to this specialist and that specialist and for dozens of different tests and hundreds of vials of blood and each and every one of them keeps asking me the same damned questions over and over again even though all the answers are right there on their fucking computers, the exact same every time? The Mexican cartels and the Russian Bratva have got nothing on a bunch of doctors forcing you into their damned boutique specialties and clinics."

Steve eventually relented enough to let Roxy drive him to his appointments, but made her sit in the waiting room. He was more taciturn than ever after each one, enduring the drive home in silence.

Roxy, on the other hand, did the only thing she know how to do. She chattered on those drives, relaying all the gossip from the country club or the latest insanity from her fencing pupils. A lot of times she simply turned on the radio and sang along.

"I can see all your talent is in your feet," Steve said one morning.

"That's why I was never picked for a singing role, not even to be in the chorus, except for one off-off-Broadway gig that ran all of one night." She turned up the radio and sang louder.

Steve put lawyers in the same category as doctors, classifying both as denizens of their own subspecies of some demonic consortium.

"You need a will, Steve. Medical directive. Durable power of attorney."

"You have all that stuff?"

"I told you I did, remember? My money's going to Iggy and Dolly Parton's charity and the elephants. If I turn into a rutabaga, Graciela and Iggy get the honor of pulling the plug. I thought about having an attorney as executor. Honestly, it's a job that should go to your worst enemy. Mom made me executor of her will because she didn't like my sister Tally's husband and even though there wasn't much to her estate, the fights with Tally's children were epic. And then Mom's cousin, who wasn't even in the will, got her knickers in a twist about it all. There's still at least one relative I'll never speak to again. So pick out somebody you hate and make them executor."

Steve rubbed his chin. "Can I pick only one? Because motherfucking Glen Wilson might be at the top of that list. There's a couple of guys doing twenty to life somewhere that I still hate a damned lot. Maybe—"

"Maybe in your case you should stick to hiring a lawyer."

"Nope, I don't have much and nobody to fight over it. Just the house, and I'll probably give that to Curtis in case he ever develops some sense and wants to come back to the States." Steve shook his head. "No, I want somebody I can trust."

"What about that ex-cop you talk to all the time? Murphy?"

"Murphy already has her hands full. And she doesn't know I'm not feeling the best, and I want it to stay that way. Same goes for the Wednesday poker guys."

If one really good result had come from the barbecue at Tommy Jackson's house, it had been Steve's reluctant reentry into social life.

Roxy still made time for her bridge club and ballet classes and fencing classes. Steve had taken to joining some of his former police and highway patrol buddies for raucous Wednesday night poker games, held alternately between police captain Paul Tinker's house and Steve's, given that they were both bachelors without wives who'd be screaming about the smell of empty beer cans and the full ashtrays and lingering cigar smoke.

Roxy sent over trays of snacks, but she spent those evenings swathed in Korean face masks and olive oil hair wraps while bingeing on old movie musicals and reruns of *CSI: Las Vegas* without having to listen to Steve bitch about how they got all the police procedures dead wrong and would never get a conviction with that kind of work.

So she watched her shows on Wednesdays in peace and quiet, enjoying the fantasy of instantly solved crimes and perfect justice.

Steve walked in for dinner one evening and slapped an envelope on the table. "The key to a lockbox at the bank is in there. And some papers for you to sign to give you access. You need to get those back in the next couple of days. If anything happens to me—"

When, not if. They both knew that.

"You told me to pick somebody I hate, but I need somebody I trust. Maybe somebody I love."

Roxy eyed the envelope as if it were a black widow spider. She studied Steve's face for a long moment, reading in his eyes the words he couldn't say, then reached for the envelope. "I'd be honored. Love you too, Steve."

Chapter 25

Steve's Date with Death: T-Plus 37 days 15:04:07 and Holding

STEVE'S PHONE RANG just after breakfast. He didn't recognize the number, but the phone didn't note *scam likely*, so he answered. The minute he heard the voice on the other end, he concluded the message should have read "biggest scammer on the planet."

"Sarge, this is your old pal Glen Wilson calling."

"I'm old, I'm retired, and you're not my pal. What do you want?" Nothing Glen Wilson ever wanted ever led to anything good.

"It's great to talk to you too, Sarge. Are you still lurking around Miami?"

"Yeah, West Palm. I'm dating a redheaded former Rockette. Roxy. She has legs that go from sunset to sunset and where they meet at midnight, I'm telling you, it's heaven on earth. We're happy. You should leave us alone. What do you want?" Steve was pretty sure Glen hadn't heard a word he said. The guy was all output and no input. Always had been. And he never, ever called just to chat and catch up. Glen Wilson always had an agenda.

"Grab a pen and write down this name. Sylvia Goddard. Do you have it?"

"Yes, I have it, but why would I want it? Goddard doesn't

ring any bells. What's up?"

"Are you on Facebook? I can message you her address."

"No, I'm not on Facebook. I don't even know what it is and I don't want to know."

Roxy loved social media and happily argued with strangers, chatted with distant friends, and insisted on showing him cute or funny videos of cats knocking down Christmas trees or puppies curled up with babies. He had no interest in talking to anybody, much less faceless strangers.

Glen rattled off Sylvia's street address and repeated it until Steve had it written down.

"I suggest you call one of your cronies and ask them take a look-see," Glen said. "Just scope her out, okay? Uh, I suppose I should tell you…this woman could be hazardous to your health, okay? I told you."

Yeah, like he didn't already have a dozen other things already going on in his body that were hazardous to his health.

"I'm not doing anything until you tell me what this is about."

By the time he finished speaking, Glen had disconnected.

Steve tried calling Glen's number back, but it rang with no answer. Not even voice mail. Steve's next call was to his old friend Margaret Murphy. If anybody knew what Wilson was up to, Murphy might. But her phone went to voice mail. He left a message.

Steve and Glen had traded favors for years. Steve racked his brain trying to remember who was in debt to whom at the moment. And then he remembered: Glen had helped him out with Curtis a couple of years ago. Not much, but it could technically be called a favor. Which put Steve in Glen's debt column at the moment.

"Goddamn you, Glen Wilson," Steve muttered as he shoved his phone back into his pocket.

Roxy looked up from her *People* magazine and peered at him over her reading glasses.

"Old friend?" she said.

"Not exactly," Steve replied.

After an hour of trying to get interested in *Duck Dynasty* reruns on TV, Steve heaved himself up.

"Where are you going?" Roxy said.

"Out," he said. "Lunch."

"Want company?"

Roxy didn't exactly look hurt at the lack of invitation, more puzzled than anything else. They weren't attached at the hip—except when they wanted to be—and she wasn't the clingy type, but they'd been spending most of their waking hours—and most of their sleeping ones as well—with each other.

"Not this time," Steve said. "Just need some fresh air. Maybe I'll call Paul or Tommy and see if they're free."

Roxy untangled herself from her chair, gave him a kiss on the cheek, and patted his ass. "I've got some things to do at my place anyway. We can order Chinese takeout whenever you get back."

One more thing he liked about her. She was a complex woman but uncomplicated. No interrogation, no whining. How had he gotten so lucky? He changed course and gave her a more intense kiss than she'd given him.

Then she pinched his ass as he walked away.

Because he was comfortable in them, Steve drove a retired police car, a battered black and white four-door Ford Crown Victoria. He carried an old-school street atlas in the glove box, so it didn't take him long to find the place. Sitting behind the wheel, he studied the address. South Ocean Boulevard. It was a high-end Palm Beach neighborhood with gated ocean-front estates—home to conservative pundits, politicians, investment company perverts, retired cartel bosses, and other moneyed citizens. The address wasn't on the ocean side.

He'd give the place a quick look-see and consider his debt to Wilson paid in full. What could it hurt?

Knowing Glen Wilson, even the simple act of looking could hurt a lot. Or the woman could just be an ex-girlfriend who had a beef with him. Steve could have called one of his buddies on the force, but he didn't want to end up being the butt of jokes at the poker games from now until the end of his days. Even if there weren't a lot of those days left.

And how could he explain Glen Wilson to any of them anyway?

No, better to keep it simple. Cruise over, knock at the door, take a look, and then call Glen and tell him to lose his number forever.

The house was set back from the wide street—all that was visible through coconut palms and tree ferns was a long, curved driveway and the rear of a tricked-out, lemon-yellow Porsche. It was a nice piece of property, but neglected—the yard was a tangled mess of kudzu and crabgrass. A callbox stood next to a tall iron gate. Steve pressed the button, but there was no indication it did anything.

He got out of the car and gave the place a once-over—it looked deserted. The gate was sprung, and it creaked on its hinges when he pushed it open.

"Hello?" he said.

The place had that creepy, abandoned feel to it. If this were a movie, violins would be playing that tense, nerve-jangling stuff and folks in the theater would be screaming "Run, sucker, *run!*"

Steve checked the Smith & Wesson police special tucked into his shoulder holster. He was old, but not stupid; he never went anywhere without a weapon in reach. Especially when following directives from Glen Wilson.

There were at least a dozen noisy grackles in a sprawling royal poinciana tree near the driveway. They chattered and scolded Steve for intruding. He followed the walkway as it wound through the jungle. The house was a squat two-story done in Spanish art deco style and covered in pearl-pink stucco and red-clay roof tiles. The front door was cracked open an inch. With his index finger, he pushed it open more.

"Hello? Is anyone home?"

The curtains were pulled tight, and the house was dark.

The air-conditioning was off or not working, and the inside air was humid and steamy. It had a rank smell, musky with the underlying scent of something cooking in the kitchen, like the morning bacon had been burnt. He poked in his head and caught movement at the corner of his eye.

He pulled back. From behind the door, strobe-lit by light streaming through the doorway, a huge butcher knife flashed.

Had he not jerked back, the blade would be embedded in his temple. *Jesus fucking Christ*! His heart all but exploded out of his chest.

He fumbled with his gun as he pulled it from under his jacket.

"I'm a law enforcement officer. Come out where I can see you."

"Okay." It was a female voice. "Sorry for scaring you. I thought you were a rapist. Not too many nig—Blacks—in this neighborhood, and they all want a taste of the white meat. I'm coming out slowly."

The door opened wide, and a woman appeared. Sunlight hit pale white skin. There was not a stitch of clothing anywhere on her. The huge knife gleamed at her side. Pretty, with blond streaks in her long hair, and maybe twenty-five years old. Her body was perfectly toned, with large bulbous breasts and a carefully maintained landing strip of pubic hair between her legs. Her stomach and legs were dabbed with something that looked like peanut butter. Feces?

Steve aimed the gun at her chest.

"I just want to talk to you. Drop the knife."

She tilted her head back and laughed. "It wants to talk, does it? That's nice. I'll bet a big old bubba like you has a cock like a nightstick and you'd like to stick it all up in me, wouldn't you? Well, bubba, this is your lucky day because I'm all yours. Pick any hole you want."

Goddamn you to hell, Glen Wilson. What the fuck did you get me into? He'd kill him. The minute he escaped this batshit-crazy bitch, he'd get in his car and hunt down motherfucking

Glen Wilson and kill him.

"Drop the knife, ma'am. There's no reason for this to get ugly. Let's chat a minute, then I'll be on my way."

She took a step forward.

He took a step back.

She took another step forward.

"Come on, Buck. Let's have a few drinks and party like it's the end of the world. I won't tell your mama. Don't be a fraidy-cat; I won't bite you much. Not unless you want me to." She brushed back a tangle of hair but never stopped staring at Steve.

Cold calculation glittered in her eyes. Something atavistic, barely human. Steve inched back another step, but she closed the gap.

Her knuckles whitened as her fist tightened around the knife. Her knees bent. Her thighs tensed.

Sixty years of training kicked in.

Decision time.

She leapt at him.

He pulled the trigger and shot her in the chest.

The impact pushed her back a step. She stood for a moment on shaky legs before falling to the ground like a sack of wet cement. The knife clattered on the concrete walkway beside her.

The grackles squawked and flew out of the tree in a noisy black cloud. Steve listened but heard nothing else. No screaming neighbors. Maybe they were all at work. Maybe they were all wrapped up tight in their nice soundproofed houses with the AC running. Maybe they were used to random gunshots on a weekday afternoon.

The wound was fatal, but he'd seen the medics do miracles. Whatever Glen Wilson had gotten him into, the creature Steve had just been forced to shoot had been deeply damaged. He'd seen addicts on PCP act the same way. He'd heard the stories about freaks on bath salts trying to eat off somebody's face. But something about the raw, calculating, cold-bloodedness of this woman didn't read as drugs to Steve.

Something else. Something dangerous.

Lethal.

Unstoppable.

Old survival instincts kicked in. His army training, cop training. He waited a few minutes to let her bleed out. It was probably an unnecessary precaution, but who knows what the crazy white bitch might say if she survived? Big Black man standing over a naked dead white woman was never a good combination. Even if he *was* an eighty-year-old former cop.

When he was sure she'd expired, he called 911 and asked to be connected to Paul Tinker. The conversation was terse, but filled his friend in on the pertinent info.

10-61— which meant *"Isolate self for message."*

10-23—*I arrived at the scene.*

10-26, SWF—*Detaining subject, expedite, single white female.*

10-79—*Notify coroner.*

Paul was the first on the scene. He might be Steve's poker buddy, but he was also a captain, and he'd worked with Steve when local police coordinated with the DEA. He pulled on latex gloves and felt the woman's neck while Steve hit the high points of what had happened. At least the easy and publicly acceptable version. Tinker didn't need to know about fucking Glen Wilson.

"Nothin'," Tinker said as he stood up and wiped his hands. "Anything not like it appears?"

"No. That's the whole story. I was looking for an old friend, got the wrong address. The woman came out like this and threatened me with the knife. She refused to drop the weapon and advanced on me, so I took her out. I didn't have a choice. You might want to make sure the coroner runs a full tox screen on her."

Paul narrowed his eyes, pulled in a breath, and pushed his hat back further on his head. There weren't going to be any awkward questions.

"Okay," Paul said, "this is how it went. I asked you to do a wellness check on a retired pal. I hadn't heard from him in a week, and I was worried. Let's use George Collins; his health isn't good and he lives nearby. Have you been inside?"

Steve shook his head.

"Okay, I'll check it out. The troops will be on-site shortly."

Paul unholstered his Glock and walked to the front door. "Police officer. Is anyone inside? I'm coming in. Hands up. Please show yourself. I just want to talk." He glanced at Steve, who held up his gun to indicate he had Paul's six. Paul disappeared though the doorway.

The EMS truck arrived. "Where's the responding officer?"

Steve lowered his gun and nodded toward the house.

The two-person crew moved briskly until they saw the body, then relaxed and slowed down. Clearly there was no need to hurry. They moved aside and chewed gum and gossiped about Dolphins football until the homicide team arrived to take pictures and gather evidence. One of the arriving techs took Steve's gun and the knife and bagged them. Another took Steve's statement.

Another officer arrived, glanced around briefly, then spoke to Steve. "Is anyone inside?"

"My old pal Paul Tinker."

"Brass," the officer said with a cynical twist to his lips. "I'm going in," he added, straightening from his slouch and checking to make sure his belt buckle was centered on the gig line.

At that instant Paul appeared in the doorway carrying a boy who looked to be no more than five or six years old, his arms wrapped around Paul's shoulders. The kid was nude, his ribs plainly showing under his skin.

"Crap," Steve said. "She had a kid?"

"No, the kid says his name is Juan-Luis. I think he matches a missing-persons report out of Broward." Paul handed the kid off to an EMS tech. "Get some pictures. We might have good news for worried parents out in Hallandale." He pointed at the officer. "In twenty minutes, this is going to be a zoo. Call in the cavalry, block off the street, and hold everyone back."

He turned to Steve. "I think I can keep you out of it; haul

ass out of here. This is going to get complex quick."

Steve scratched his head. "Give me an overview."

"She's been butchering neighborhood dogs and eating them, and it looks like, swear to God"—he made the sign of the holy cross on his chest—"she was planning to eat the kid too."

"Jeee-zuss," Steve said.

"Steve, what exactly was it that made you stop by this place?"

"It was a tip from an old...friend." Steve stumbled over the term. Friend? That wasn't the right word. Motherfucking dead man walking if Steve got within a mile of that fucking Glen Wilson.

"The timing was right," Paul said. "Another day and we'd be investigating cannibalism." Paul narrowed his eyes. "Any chance I could meet this friend of yours?"

"No," Steve said. "You really don't want to. Besides, he's not local. No need."

Paul studied Steve's face. "Okay, got it. Watch your six, brother."

Steve nodded and weaved through the EMTs and cops to get to his car.

The drive home wasn't long. Steve tried to sort out the chaos in his head, but all he could manage was a string of cuss words and vague plans to hunt down Glen Wilson and shoot him in the balls. Why the fuck hadn't that son of a bitch warned him what he was walking into? Shit like that could get a man killed.

He was tight-lipped and terse when he got home, still stuck deep inside his head, the grotesque images playing in a continuous, tortuous loop. He'd seen shit like that before, but it had been a long time, and he'd forgotten just how bad the adrenaline surge and resultant crash would be.

Roxy, bless her heart, asked no questions when he showed up at her front door. Just like when she took him to his doctor appointments. She poured him a beer and handed him a ham and cheese sandwich when he said he didn't want Chinese.

"Might want to get some peroxide on that shirt," she said.

"It's good at getting out blood stains."

He hadn't even noticed the small spot. If Paul had, he'd said nothing and never would.

Roxy had left him to his own thoughts and gone to bed alone when he'd said he just wanted to sit in the quiet on her lanai. By the time he got around to calling Glen, it was late on the West Coast and even later on the East. Steve had been a Master Sergeant in the army. He knew how to cuss.

Glen tried to derail him mid-rant. "You're repeating yourself, Sarge."

"...flea-infested, camel-fucking, human refuse..."

"I'm hanging up now."

"Wait, I'm almost done," Steve said. "You're a piss-sucking morsel of shit from a hobo's ass-crack." He paused and drew a few deep breaths, which gave Glen a chance to speak.

"What about the cooze, Steve?"

"Watch the news, creep. You won't be able to escape it."

"Steve, in full disclosure, there's one more in your area. Another woman, from Atlanta but last known sighting was Miami. She knew the woman you visited; they went through the process together. I can't emphasize enough to watch your back, brother."

Glen hung up before Steve had a chance to ask what *process* Glen was talking about.

He'd no sooner hung up than his phone rang again.

Murphy. His old pal. Someone who might know what the hell was going on.

"What the fuck is Glen Wilson up to this time?"

"Most people say hello first, Steve."

"Hello, Murphy. What the fuck is Glen Wilson up to this time? I had to kill a woman today, Murph."

"Do you need bail?"

"No, I need answers."

"Is this murder gonna make the news?"

"It already has. West Palm. Crazed cannibal."

"Elke, look up news out of Florida." She was yelling to her

longtime lover and into Steve's ear. He angled the phone away. "A cannibal killer or something."

He listened to the silence for a minute before Murphy came back on the line. "Oh God, Steve. I'm so sorry. That son of a bitch—"

"Answers, Murphy."

Murphy sighed. "I don't know everything that's going on. I'm late to whatever game it is Glen's playing this time, and from what little I'm hearing, it's going to shit fast. But I talked to his wife about it, and she explained it this way: Glen and his usual league of overeducated lunatics formed a company. Immortality, LLC. They're selling a process that supposedly rejuvenates wealthy clients. But not the actual person. They find people—usually desperate or poor or whatever—and pay them to give up their lives. They undergo intensive plastic surgery to look like a younger version of the wealthy client. Then there's intense brainwashing or some kind of treatment—I don't know the details—to completely wipe out the old personality and memories. They transfer personalities and memories from the client into this new host body."

"Shit, Murphy. Glen's done some put-him-in-a-straight-jacket-and-throw-away-the-key-bat-guano-crazy shit before, but this?" Steve swiped his hand over his face and shook his head. "It doesn't even make sense, Murph. Not even in a sci-fi movie. Or a horror movie. How—"

"Again, I don't know details. Unfortunately, it looks like the process creates complete and utter psychopaths—truly dangerous people, as you found out today. Glen knows they're dangerous. He should never have sent you there. Not without warning you."

"He knows I'd never go unarmed."

Murphy made a humming sound. She and Steve talked every week or so, but he hadn't told her about being sick. Had she figured it out on her own?

"You're retired, Steve."

"You mean I'm old."

"Didn't say that."

"Maybe I should sign up to be one of Wilson's immortal clients."

"I'd never let you. You couldn't afford it to begin with, and even if you could, I'd just end up having to put you down, like you put down that mad, broken psychopath today. Something Glen's pal Walter said sticks in my mind. 'When we make the transfer from client to donor, I don't think everything makes the transition. The resulting versions of the clients are not wholly human.' That woman you killed today, Steve? Whatever was human in her got lost in whatever process Glen's team is doing. She wasn't ever going to get better. God knows how many she might have slaughtered if you hadn't stopped her."

Murphy's words helped, but not much.

He shoved his phone into his pocket and turned to find Roxy behind him.

"Whatever you think you owed Glen Wilson, that debt's been paid. I'm not going to ask any questions, but I'm here to listen to anything you want to talk about."

He wrapped his big arms around her and pulled her head down to his shoulder.

"Sleep, Roxy. That's all I need right now. A sleep with no nightmares. A sleep without throwing up or my guts in a knot."

"I have some cookies, Steve. Just one. I'll sit right by you and make sure you don't turn into a face-eating leopard."

Her attempt at humor hit unwittingly too close to the bone, but he couldn't fault her for that. He'd told her nothing and it would stay that way. No reason to give her nightmares too.

"I'm just so goddamned tired, Roxy."

Tired of witnessing the evil people did to each other. Tired of cleaning up the heaping dunghills they left behind. Yeah, he'd saved a kid today, but the boy was going to have a long road of trauma and recovery ahead of him. So would his family. The shit just never stopped coming. He could have died today. Was still going to die soon anyway. And the shit would just keep piling up and there wasn't a damned thing he could do about it.

What was the point? What had the point *ever* been?

Roxy wasn't a mind reader, but she always seemed to know what he needed. She kept her arms wrapped tight around him, offering him her warmth and life and comfort, no questions asked. She demanded nothing of him and just kept giving.

And suddenly the gentle oblivion she offered didn't sound so bad.

Marijuana. Pot. The devil's lettuce. And sweet sleep.

He hated the thought of losing control, but wasn't everything in his life already spinning out of control anyway? For a while, just a short while, he'd let Roxy be the rock he clung to until he found a way out of the maelstrom. And why not? Roxy was offering him what he needed most. A respite.

"Yeah," Steve said. "Can I get another beer with that cookie?"

Chapter 26
Steve's Date with Death: T-Plus 39 days 15:04:07 and Holding

PAUL HAD KEPT his word and kept Steve out of all the hoopla surrounding what the hysterical news media had taken to calling the "Miami Beach Cannibal," but Roxy wasn't stupid. She watched the news and could put two and two together as well as the next person.

"If you ever want to talk, Steve…"

"This is why cops shouldn't get married. Or get involved in relationships or whatever. Because women get so nosy and just peck a man to death with questions."

"First of all, you're presuming all cops are men," Roxy said. "Second, you're lumping all women together in a misogynistic stereotype."

"Is that one of those words you learned from your firefighter calendar?"

Roxy had zipped her lip, stomped out of his house, and ignored him for a full day. It drove him crazy to hear the music drifting from her studio late at night, knowing he probably wasn't welcome there. He showed up on her doorstep twenty-four hours later with the biggest, gaudiest bouquet the florist had, his panama hat clutched in his hand.

She'd eyed him for a long moment, firmly blocking his entry.

"I'm sorry, Roxy. I fucked up."

Those were the magic words. She accepted the flowers and wrapped him in a hard hug, pulling him into the house and kicking the door shut behind him.

"I wasn't being a nosy parker, Steve. For a lot of folks, sharing a burden cuts the weight in half. But I understand—"

"You remember once I told you I never got married because of the shit work I did? That's what this feels like, Rox. It's bad enough for me to know the crap I've had to do—why would I dump that on somebody else? Somebody I care about? There's a reason the divorce rate is sky-high with cops and firefighters and soldiers. We get so full of nightmares and—"

"Shit," Roxy said. "So full of shit. Big tough people—men and women both—who think they have to protect everyone and don't have enough sense or respect to understand that maybe the person that loves them is tough too and can take on those nightmares without shattering. You know what's *really* hard, Steve? It's the not knowing. I talked with Danni Jackson over lunch yesterday while you were being such a dickwad. She says Tommy used to be the same way, never told her anything. They got close to divorcing. But she refused to give up on him. And she told me she'd kick my ass from here to Christmas if I gave up on you or let you give up on us."

Roxy paused for a breath, but not long enough for Steve to get in a word.

"You know why a woman is willing to marry a cop or a firefighter or a soldier even knowing that every goodbye kiss might be the last one ever? Because she *loves* you, you stupid dick. She loves hard and strong and fierce. And she's willing to put up with your shit because she's glad to have you in her life no matter how much—or how little—time that may be. If all we ever thought about was that we were going to die, we'd never get a second of pleasure out of living. I haven't given up on you, Steve, and I'll be damned if I'm going to let you give up on me. Or on us."

Roxy thumped him in the chest, then spun away, but not

before he'd seen the tears.

Without a word, he scooped all five feet ten inches of Roxy and her flowers into his arms and carried her to the sofa, plopping down awkwardly but not losing his grip.

She buried her face in his collarbone and made little gasping noises while she cried, but thankfully, the storm was fierce but short-lived. Roxy hiccupped into silence, not embarrassed at all to wipe her runny nose on his shirt collar. "Not a bad performance for an old man," she said.

"That remains to be seen. I may have thrown my back out, and I can't feel my legs. You might want to lay off the snacks and bourbon, Rox."

"Fuck you," she said, but she climbed off his lap. "Speaking of which, it's almost happy hour. Come keep me company, and I'll tell you about one of my favorite jobs I used to have."

If she was feeding him, maybe she wasn't so mad at him anymore. Then again, maybe he'd need to keep a close eye on her cooking to make sure she wasn't adding a heaping helping of arsenic or ground glass to his portion.

And she was willing to let bygones be bygones enough to change the subject and tell him a story.

He followed her to the kitchen, grateful she hadn't raked him over the coals and wasn't looking for a knock-down, drag-out fight. "I know you were in Las Vegas after being a Rockette. What came after that?"

Roxy dug through cupboards and rattled pots and pans. "A lot of things. I went back to Ohio for a while, but with Tally dead, it was hard to get close to her kids. I hung out there a few years. Got a job at a company that managed workers' comp claims, but dealing all day with stories of pain and injury was so sad and gruesome that I couldn't stand it."

"But you were helping people who'd been hurt."

"Not really. This company worked on the side of the employer, not the people who'd been injured. And yeah, it felt good when we'd investigate and find some asshole claiming a bad back was also the captain of his bowling league. I liked stopping the scammers. But it was the other ones who did me in."

The silence was interrupted only by the whirring of the can opener and bottles clinking on the countertop.

"There was the guy who worked for a railroad company. He'd been run over by a train. The company said the incident was his fault and refused to pay the claim. There were witnesses who said he'd tripped over something that was badly maintained and had fallen into the path of the train. His widow had been fighting the case for three years. Then there was the guy who worked for the power company. He'd grabbed the wrong wire and got both arms blown off and permanently scrambled his brain. His wife was trying to raise three little ones and pay for long-term care for him because she couldn't keep him at home. The last work I did for them was to get that wife a huge settlement, which didn't make the employer happy but made me feel great."

"Sounds like you've spent some time protecting and serving others yourself, Roxy."

"Yeah, well, I didn't make a career of it. I had my own dance studio for a while. I loved the kids, especially the little ones. Set up a scholarship program for kids who couldn't afford lessons. But sometimes a parent would get to be just too much, certain their little Johnny or Susie with the two left feet was the next Baryshnikov or Misty Copeland if only I were a better teacher. And I was doing more paperwork than teaching. So I closed it up. I was lucky to have some money set aside. It was January. You know what January is like in Ohio, Steve? It's gray. Everything—the sky and the ground and people's faces. Gray, gray, gray. And every day it was slushy, wet, and miserable and it feels like it's going to stay that way forever. So I quit. Sold the studio to a couple of my teachers who wanted to take it over. I had a little house and I put it up for sale, packed up everything I could in a U-Haul, and drove south."

"That's how you got here?"

Roxy nodded. A pan on the stove was wafting appetizing

scents through the kitchen.

"I had no plans. I just knew I couldn't stand another day of gray. So I drove south until the sun came out. It was hideous taking that trailer through the mountains in Tennessee and northern Georgia."

She turned to Steve, waving a spoon. "Here's a little-known fact. Most folks from Ohio and Michigan and points west will end up on the west coast of Florida—Tampa, Sarasota, Naples—because it's easiest just to follow I-75 south and that's where it goes. Folks from the East Coast—New York, Philly, Boston—follow I-95, which gets them to the East Coast."

"So how'd you end up in West Palm instead of the Gulf Coast?"

"I took a wrong turn. Probably in Atlanta, which is a hell hole to drive through any day of the week but especially on a Friday night at rush hour in the rain. Hell, I don't know what happened and I've never tried to figure it out. All I know is that I kept getting up every morning and driving south. Then one morning I woke up in a tiny hotel. The sun was shining and there were seagulls making a racket and it was warm. I drove around until I found a real estate office and told the first person I saw that I wanted to buy a house." She grinned at Steve. "That's how I met Graciela Diaz. She'd just listed the house down the street from hers. *This* house."

"So a wrong turn led you to me."

Roxy crossed the room and placed a kiss on his forehead. "I've taken a lot of wrong turns in my life, Steve, but this one turned out to be the best one ever."

Dinner eaten and dishes washed, Steve and Roxy settled back down at the table on Roxy's lanai. "So," Roxy said, "I promised you another story."

"Your favorite job. Not the gruesome one."

"Well, this one does have a gruesome bit to it, but overall, it was my favorite job."

Steve rubbed his hands together, then leaned his elbows on the table. "Another Roxy tale. Have I ever told you how much I love these? Almost as much as I love your—"

"Tits. Yeah, I know."

"I was going to say your taste in décor, but yeah, tits works too."

Roxy pulled a deck of cards out of a drawer hidden in the table and shuffled them absently. She never even looked at the cards as they flew in her hands in some of the fancy shuffles Steve had seen from professional poker players—a riffle-shuffle, a cascade, and a butterfly cut. Even a one-handed shuffle.

"I was a Rockette for four years, but like I told you, dancing is only part-time work. So I started my own business. I called it Obscurities."

She grabbed a beer, popped the cap, and poured it into a glass for him. Steve didn't see the point of glasses, but Roxy liked them, so he went along. Roxy's version of bar food—a bowl of mixed nuts, a heaping plate of nachos, and a plate of cookies—sat on the table beside them in spite of the fact they'd finished dinner only an hour ago. Steve didn't know if the cookies were her plain ones or her special ones. He didn't care.

She'd been right about the cookies and their special ingredient; he'd slept better than he had in years. They eased the pain crawling around in his gut and the demons crawling around in his brain. How did he get lucky enough to find a woman with such great legs who also loved baking and made a man pot brownies? Some people got skinnier as they aged, like they were literally fading back into dust. Not Steve. He was just as big-boned as ever thanks to Roxy's cooking.

Steve had wanted to play poker, but Roxy wanted to play gin, and since she'd done all the cooking, he let her choose the game. She handed the cards to him to cut and deal while she poured herself a peach daiquiri from the pitcher she'd mixed up. She studied the cards in her hand, took the face-up king of clubs, and discarded a four of hearts.

"Obscurities was what the kids today call a side gig," she said. "I was the sole proprietor and employee, secretary and accountant. My job was to find items that other people were too lazy or too desperate to look for on their own."

"You mean like a private eye or something?" Steve asked.

"No. I worked with theater people and stage managers and movie guys and photographers, finding weird little things that they needed for their work. Say a movie guy needs a set of 1953 Pyrex dinnerware with flamingo-pink rims. That's the year they came out, and they're pretty hard to get. But this guy needs six authentic place settings for the movie he's making. He calls me and I get them for him."

Steve gave a low whistle. "And how did you do that?"

"You have to remember that this was in the days before the internet was a big thing. I think eBay was still called AuctionWeb back then and not many folks knew how to use it and many didn't trust it. I preferred the personal touch. Enough cash will get you anything, but it's no good unless you have connections. And I did."

She drew, then discarded a two of diamonds.

"In one of those locked drawers in my desk is my Rolodex. A real one. Analog data that some hacker can't just pluck out of the air. Of course, most of the folks in it are probably dead now, but I could probably still find somebody with something if someone really needed it."

"And if they had enough cash," Steve said.

Roxy nodded. "Damn right."

"So what's one of the weirdest things you ever had to find?" Steve picked up the discarded diamond and put down a jack of hearts.

A smile crossed her lips and a faraway look unfocused her eyes. "Goose wings," she said.

"You mean like those Victoria's Secret angels wear with their underwear?" The thought got something stirring down below, though it was getting harder and harder these days to tell if he wanted to fuck or just needed to take a piss.

"Yeah, like that, except those ladies wear big old wire frames with feathers glued on. Hell, the feathers are probably made of plastic in China. This photographer called and wanted real wings. Something about how the sneakers he was doing an ad for could make you feel like you were flying. I brought him a dozen different kinds of costume wings, and he threw a hissy fit because they weren't *authentic* enough for him. Like a woman flipping through a magazine while waiting for her boob exam was gonna notice the wings on some ad were fake." She shook her head and tossed the queen of clubs on the discard pile.

"Anyway, he said he knew just where to get wings. *Real* ones. Some little butcher shop in the meatpacking district. This was back in the days before the neighborhood got all gentrified. All I had to do was go pay the guy and pick them up. Easy money. Now, you have to understand that at this time I was working real hard on being a vegetarian. I'd found an old copy of Upton Sinclair's *The Jungle* on the bus a few months earlier and was turned off on the whole meat thing. So the idea of going to a butcher shop was stomach churning."

"Based on that most excellent beef stew I just had, it looks like you got over it."

"Yeah, I love a good hamburger."

Hamburger, not steak. Nothing pretentious about this woman. Steve absently glanced at his cards, drew, and discarded, without really paying attention. He shifted in his chair and leaned forward. He didn't want to miss a word of Roxy's story.

"I headed off to this butcher shop," she said, "because the rent was due and I had a reputation as a finder-of-weird-things to uphold. The photographer had called ahead, so the butcher knew what I wanted. This butcher shop was actually one of those live meat markets, with chickens and pigs and shit in cages and sounding like something straight out of that book. I thought I'd throw up. It wouldn't have made the stench any worse. The butcher told me to hold on, disappeared into the back, and then

I heard the most god-awful squawking. Then silence."

Roxy drew a card, discarded a seven of hearts, and let the silence stretch out.

Steve couldn't have gotten any closer to the edge of his seat without falling off.

"The guy comes out holding up a pair of snow-white goose wings. Do you have any idea how big those things are? And they're dripping blood. *Blood.* And me a vegetarian. I almost decided then and there that no client and no amount of money was worth it."

"Almost."

Roxy grinned at him. "Yeah, almost. Rent was due, I had a dance class I needed to pay for, and auditions were thin on the ground. Didn't make me any happier that he wrapped the stumps in butcher paper and stuck them in a big garbage bag for me to carry. They weighed more than you'd think. The photographer hadn't given me any extra money for cab fare and I didn't want to ride a pokey old bus for any longer than necessary with those wings, so I headed to the subway. And started crying. By the time I got on the train, I was full-on bawling."

Something stirred in Steve. He wanted to hunt down that man from fifty years ago and go full-on berserker on his sorry ass for making Roxy cry.

"You gonna play," Roxy said, "or are you too busy plotting how to get away with murder?"

Damn, he hated it when a woman could read his mind. He absently drew and discarded.

"So there I am on the subway, sobbing my heart out, and the bag has sprung a leak. There's blood pooling at my feet and getting on my shoes. And this is the true beauty and heart of the New York subway system in those days: not a single soul even glanced sideways at me. God knows what's in the bag, it's dripping blood everywhere, and I'm a sobbing wreck, and everyone just kept minding their own damned business." She sighed. "I don't know if it's better or worse now that people want to be so helpful all the time."

"Worse," Steve said. "These days somebody'd film it, you'd go viral and be doxed, some vigilante asshole would show up with a gun, and a loudmouth talk radio jock would hound you daily."

"Conservative or liberal?"

"The conservatives would be shouting about your right to carry bloody body parts on the subway, the libs would be screaming for donations to PETA, and the conspiracy wackos would think bloody goose wings were the latest sign that JFK Jr. is in fact returning from the dead to be their messiah and would start sporting goose wings with their BH7D double shoulder rigs and field-grade cartridge belts. So what happened when you finally got the goose wings to the guy? Eternal gratitude? Groveling?"

"I demanded double the money, in cash, up front, before I'd hand over the wings."

"Wait. You held his goose wings hostage?"

"Damn right I did. When I had the cash, I opened the bag, dumped the whole bloody mess on the floor, kicked him in the nuts, and ran."

"He didn't sue you?"

"He called me the next week and wanted me to find a specific child-size silver spoon with a teddy bear on the handle."

Steve quivered in anticipation. "Did you tell him to shove it up his ass? Blackball him from your client list?"

"I found him three," she said. "He sent an assistant to pick them up. With cash. A lot of it. I felt sorry for the girl. She refused to come in. She handed over the money, took the package, and ran like she was doing a drug deal." Roxy shrugged. "A client is a client, and their crazy demands paid for the fencing lessons. I think he was afraid I'd show up with a rapier the next time."

Steve's bellow of laugher came from his heart. Damn, if he'd met this woman twenty years ago, even ten, what kind of difference would she have made in his life?

Roxy picked up the card he'd discarded and threw out a king. "Swords—another thing you used to be able to carry on the subway without anyone asking questions. Damned Saudis with their fucking airplanes."

Steve nodded and stared at his cards. How was it possible that absolutely none of them were in any way related to each other? It was Roxy. All Roxy. Damned distracting nuisance. She cooked. She had an old-school Rolodex of obscure items and oddities, a personal web of collectors and weirdos, a wall full of swords, and she wasn't afraid to kick someone in the nuts to get what was due her. What a woman. *What a hell of a woman.* Which either made this easier or harder.

He nodded. Yeah, this was the right thing to do. Before he had the chance to change his mind again or chicken out, he reached across the table and took her hand. "Roxy, if you're not busy tomorrow, I have something I want to do. But I need your help. There's some paperwork and stuff that needs to be filled out, and you need to be there. Maybe afterward we can go shopping, grab lunch somewhere."

Roxy cocked her head and furrowed her brows, but she nodded. "Sure. Sounds like a plan. There's a new pub I've been wanting to try out—the Hicken and Spleen."

Steve shook his head. "Nah, I heard that place was a dump. Steak."

"Gin," she said, throwing down her cards.

He flung his completely mismatched worthless cards on top of hers.

"What do I owe you?"

"How long does it take for those blue pills to kick in?"

She had her blouse unbuttoned and flung over his head and was halfway to the bedroom before he could make it out of the chair.

Steve pulled her discarded shirt off his head. Damn it. He hadn't quite gotten out the words *will you marry me* the way he'd been planning, but he'd try to get it right tomorrow before they got to the courthouse to get a marriage license. Then

245

Pat Edwards

they'd go pick out a ring. He wanted to get Roxy something big and flashy to suit her personality. He didn't have much money, but there'd be enough for that. Her friend Graciela dated a jeweler, didn't she? Maybe he could get a deal.

Roxy popped her naked ass out of the bedroom door and twerked it at him, then disappeared in a cloud of laughter.

Steve hauled himself out of his chair and headed to the bedroom and the soon-to-be Mrs. Stephens, even if she didn't know it yet. Of course, first he had to get her to say yes to a crotchety, curmudgeonly, dying old man.

"Are you waiting for a written invitation?" Roxy called from the bedroom.

She'd say yes. God must have decided to smile on him after all.

Chapter 27

Steve's Date with Death: T-Plus 42 days 15:04:07 and Holding

ROXY, GRACIELA, AND Danni managed to throw together a wedding in record time: a simple courthouse ceremony with Tommy Jackson and Graciela standing up with them and a small reception at the club afterward. Roxy had worn something blue and lacy.

"It's my something blue," she said. "And it's old. I found it in a vintage clothing shop."

"You already have something old, Roxy. You're marrying an eighty-year-old man."

New shoes and sapphire earrings borrowed from Graciela completed her collection of good luck charms. She'd cried when Steve had slipped the slim silver band of diamonds on her finger.

Roxy's hand in his was all the luck Steve needed. He had to admit the tightness in his throat had made it hard to get the right words out when she'd placed a matching band on his own finger.

Three days. When he'd met this mouthy, gorgeous, irritating, lovable broad, he'd been three days away from killing himself. Now he'd been her husband for three whole days, and if his bones didn't creak so much, he'd have been down on his knees nightly thanking the good Lord for flinging the woman into his life. God must have been laughing his shining ass off at all of Steve's carefully laid plans.

God could be such a dick that way. Then again, he'd brought Roxy into his life, so maybe things were looking up. Maybe he'd do a couple of those treatments his doctor kept urging him to try now that he had something to live for. Nothing could stop the cancer, but letting them drip a little poison into his veins might be worth it if the drugs bought him a few extra days as Roxy's husband.

Nothing much had changed, really, and probably wouldn't considering the time constraints they were under. Getting married didn't cancel out the cancer, didn't alter his inevitable date with death. No point in changing houses or officially moving in together or setting up joint bank accounts. Roxy had all the paperwork she'd need to take care of whatever came up. When it came up.

But for now they settled into a simple routine that let them spend as much time together as possible. The last few days had flown by, but they'd finally had time to relax today.

They accompanied their light lunch with more of *The Guiding Light*. Steve still growled about the stupid storylines, but nothing in the world would ever get him to confess how engrossing they'd become.

"Drugs for happy homemakers," he said. "Give them something to watch while they're doing the ironing and the cooking, and they won't complain so much. Keep them barefoot, pregnant, and compliant, their brains dulled to mush with soap operas."

Roxy mulled that over for a split second. "It may look like mush to you, but there are handsome men and beautiful women and complicated plots to keep track of. And murder. Lots of murder. Maybe those housewives were getting ideas."

Steve snorted. "They'd have been caught in five minutes flat. Even in the fifties, cops and coroners weren't that stupid."

"It's a dramatization, Steve. Get your anal-retentive head out of your ass."

"What does that even mean?"

"That's my point, Steve; I was speaking figuratively. Don't

be so literal, or you'll never enjoy anything in life."

He reached out his hand. She brushed it away. "I enjoy debating with you, dear."

"Shut up and pay attention, or you'll never keep up."

"What's the schedule today?"

"Today it's fencing. I'm thinking of asking Mrs. Koffman if she'd be interested in switching to Zumba or water aerobics. She's getting scary good."

"I don't know why you do all that stuff."

"Alice Cooper said it best: If you stop, you die. Now shush and try to follow along."

They watched for a few minutes. The doorbell chimed just as a commercial for an ad for a bowel-movement drug came on. Surprised, they looked at each other.

"Are you expecting anyone?" she said.

He shrugged. "Nope."

"Okay, I'll get it."

"No, stay put. I need to pee anyway."

It was a chore getting out of his recliner, but he struggled—out of breath—to his feet, stretched out the kinks, and shuffled toward the door.

"Damnable nuisance," he muttered. He reached under his bathrobe and stuffed his Smith and Wesson Police Special service weapon down the back of the pajamas he hadn't felt like changing out of yet today. Probably just some Jehovah's Witness. Though he'd be tempted, it wasn't worth the paperwork to shoot one of them. Still, this wasn't the ritzy section of West Palm. And he'd spent a lifetime as a cop. Old habits and all.

He'd quietly filled in Tommy Jackson and Paul Tinker as much as he could about the second nutjob that Glen Wilson had mentioned might be in the Miami area, but so far, with so little to go on, they'd come up empty.

Fucking Wilson himself was somewhere in the wind, not answering Steve's repeated calls. Even Murphy had gone silent.

Light from the window caught the narrow row of

diamonds in Steve's ring. Three days. Three glorious days of being Roxy's husband. He hadn't had the chance yet to tell Murphy he'd gotten married. She'd probably send him some obscenely kinky sex toy as a wedding present.

The gun felt familiar and comfortable against the small of his back. Maybe he was being a paranoid old fool. Roxy had married a dead man walking, but he had something to live for now and he planned to give her as many days as he could possibly manage. And he finally had something worth protecting. He glanced back at her.

Roxy hadn't even glanced up from the TV.

Steve hauled the door open. The woman standing there was about thirty and dressed very elegantly, white blazer over a white satin blouse. White dress pants. White flats on her feet. Her sculpted hair was pulled back in a French roll with a diamond-encrusted clasp.

"Whatever you're selling, we don't need none," Steve said.

"Steve?" she said.

He frowned. "Yes?"

"You killed my sister-in-law. Now you die."

Swinging widely, she jammed a hunting knife under his arm and into his chest.

His *oh* came out as a grunt. He fell backwards, slamming to the floor like a harpooned whale, his glasses skewing awkwardly on his face. In spite of his ample padding, the hard landing jarred every bone in his body. The umbrella stand by the front door toppled too, clattering onto the tile of the entryway.

Roxy leapt up from her chair and spun toward the door. "Steve?"

The woman fished around in her shoulder bag and pulled out a new knife. She unsheathed the glittering blade and held it up.

"Now you," she said.

Steve was bleeding out—he could feel it. He'd been a cop too long not to know the truth, not to understand exactly what had happened. She'd hit the axillary artery. His frantically pumping heart sent blood spurting through the hole she'd ripped. She'd known what she was doing. Little white corpuscles raced to fix a wound they'd never be able to repair.

His vision grew black around the edges, eternal night closing in on him.

Motherfucker! Why now?

Still, he had a little life left. A few minutes if he was lucky. If God had ever loved him. A few seconds. That was all he needed.

Goddamn it! It wasn't time to go! He had so much to live for!

His brain still worked, every cop instinct kicking in.

Roxy towered somewhere over him. Reaching for him. Roxy who didn't have those same cop instincts.

He looked to his left.

Roxy's rapier lay on the floor. She'd left it in the umbrella stand after her last class. He pulled off the protective tip and backhanded it in her direction. She'd know what to do once she got her hands on the weapon she'd spent a lifetime training with.

Not a cop's instincts, but the instincts of a born fighter who never, ever quit.

Roxy neatly snagged the sword out of the air and assumed an attack stance.

With quick left-right sweeps, she opened wounds on the intruder's cheeks, which immediately streamed blood onto her satin blouse.

The woman dropped the knife. "Fuck this," she muttered. She reached into her shoulder bag and brought out a pink Ruger 388 LCP.

Light. Compact. Powerful.

She aimed at Roxy.

Not his Roxy. Not while there was still breath in his body. Even if he was down to his very last one.

Steve sucked in air. *Make it count. Let it last. Let it be enough to save Roxy.*

Pat Edwards

With the last of his strength, he pulled his pistol from under his ass.

He aimed up.

He fired.

Six shots straight to the woman's chest.

She still stood.

Oh God!! He'd missed! And Roxy left unprotected—

The woman stared at Steve. Never blinked.

Swayed.

Her eyes rolled back as she collapsed into an inelegant heap of white satin and red blood on the front walk, dead.

252

Chapter 28

Steve's Date with Death: T-00:00:00

ROXY DROPPED TO her knees at Steve's side as she fumbled for her phone. She called 911 for an ambulance and the police, reporting a home invasion with shots fired as she searched Steve for the source of the blood that now soaked his robe.

"Officer down," Steve muttered, coughing hard. Not much longer now, but *officer down* would get the cops there faster. Get Roxy the protection he could no longer provide for her.

Roxy pulled his head onto her lap.

"Did I get her, Roxy? Are you okay, sweetheart?"

"Stop talking. The ambulance will be here in a minute."

Unless they were already parked in his driveway, it would be too late.

Such a waste. Such a fucking waste of time. Of a life. He coughed. The blood in his mouth was not a good sign. *I spent years cleaning up shit and this is how it ends?*

Steve didn't realize he'd said the words out loud until Roxy answered him.

"You didn't spend your life just cleaning up shit, Steve. You spent your life protecting good folks and keeping them from getting hit by that shit. Spent it rescuing folks from shitty stuff. You say Lady Day rescued you. You paid back her faith in you a million times over, rescuing others. She saved you at the beginning of your life so you could do good things. And you did them. You once said there wasn't anyone or anything you wanted to save anymore. But you were wrong. Some things are still worth saving. Me, Steve. You saved me."

He raised a bloody hand toward her, the light glinting off his ring again. She seized it, laid it against her cheek.

"No, Rox. You. Saved. Me." He wasn't sure she understood the words tangled up in a mouthful of blood, but he had to try. "Love you."

She pulled him closer, raining kisses and tears in equal measure onto his face.

Roxy cradled him against her pillowy breasts. Not a bad way to go, lying against a pair of nice tits.

Steve sucked in another painful breath. Maybe God wasn't such a dick after all.

"No, Steve, he's not," said Mama. "But he and I would both like to have a word with you about how often you've taken his name in vain. And about your language."

"Fuck."

"Exactly," said Mama. "You just come along with me now, baby. I've been missing you."

"Not yet, Mama. I still got things to do." Besides, he wasn't going anywhere without Roxy. He needed to stay with her. Keep her safe as long as he could, until he knew for sure someone else would be there to protect her.

"Stevie, you can't save the world." Natalie, her brown cheeks round and glowing and healthy.

For a moment two faces overlapped and then merged. One brown, one pale white, both so dearly loved. Natalie smiled that big beautiful smile of hers and stretched her hand toward him.

"Tried to save you, Nat."

"Steve? It's Roxy. Not Natalie. Steve? Stay with me, honey. The ambulance will be here any second."

He didn't have enough seconds left. The choice to come or go was no longer his. He'd finally lost all control. His choices were gone.

At least he'd made a couple of right choices at the end of

his long, fucking, useless life. He'd chosen Roxy. He'd chosen life. And he'd be damned if he was going to give either one up now.

Someone pushed their way to the front of the crowd gathering before Steve. A tall stunning woman, black as midnight. A Yoruba goddess.

"Steve," said Jubilation Duval. Steve didn't know how he knew who she was, but he did. "This is important. You tell Roxy she don't owe no one a damn thing. You tell her to stop living for others and to live her own damn life for herself. "You tell her—"

"Debt paid. Live." Steve's words were so slow, so slurred, he wasn't sure Roxy could even hear him anymore.

"Steve," said another woman. Auntie Althea. "Your timing always did suck. But there's a barbecue today. A great big one. I made potato salad, Steve. Just the way you like it. You just come along now."

"I don't think so, Auntie. I did some shit...some bad shit. I think I'm permanently disinvited to that cookout."

Another woman appeared. "Don't worry, Steve. I got your back."

"Lady Day."

"Right," said Billie Holiday. "If they let me in, they'll let in anybody. I got a special song ready for you, Steve. You wanna hear it? You just gotta come with me."

Music started playing somewhere.

Steve never heard the sirens. Roxy's tears fell on a face that no longer felt anything.

"Steve? Steve, don't go! Don't you dare fucking leave me, Steve! Hang on just a minute more. Steve? Steve!"

But Roxy's voice was far away, and Mama stood there with Daddy and Nat and even baby Royce. Auntie Althea and a host of family and friends were smiling at him.

The band was warming up, and Lady Day crooned a tune he'd never heard before.

He opened his eyes wide. Roxy's face leaned over his, her

blue eyes gleaming. He took in the blue sky and warm sunlight streaming through the door.

And he saw a dream. Something bigger than he'd ever imagined. A dream so big he hadn't known how to dream it.

No more pain. No grief. He was so young. So strong. So filled with wonder.

He reached for Lady Day's hand. Welcomed the embrace of whatever came next.

No, God was not a dick at all.

Chapter 29

Sexy Firefighters Calendar Word of the Day:
Insuperable: [in-soo-per-uh-buhl]. **Adjective.** *impossible to overcome, incapable of being surmounted, overcome, passed over, or solved.*

CAPTAIN PAUL TINKER heard the call and was first on the scene. Tommy Jackson was only minutes behind him. The minute he'd seen what was going on, he'd called his wife. Now Danni and Graciela Diaz sat on either side of Roxy, arms around her, providing a steady supply of tissues.

Graciela, being only a few doors down the street, had shown up first when she'd heard the sirens. When the cops had pushed her back, she'd gone home, only to return minutes later, a grocery bag filled with all the ingredients for asopao de gandules—her home island's version of a wonderfully aromatic chicken gumbo—in her arms and had thrown a full-blown hissy fit, demanding that Roxy be allowed to go to her own home, where she'd then dragged Roxy into the kitchen with her, insisting that the officials interview her there while the medical guys did their thing and took pictures.

Two dead bodies. Guns to be confiscated and bagged. Roxy's sword was carefully wrapped. She'd been fingerprinted, and a female cop had taken her clothes and finally let her get a shower. She'd made a minor protest, but had generally been quiet.

Stoic.

"In shock," Danni said. Her medical bag sat unopened at her feet as she quickly took Roxy's vitals and determined she'd be okay for now.

Danni had shown up with a bottle of Crown Royal, a pan of macaroni and cheese she always kept ready in her freezer, a sponge mop, and a bottle of bleach. Tommy raised an eyebrow at his wife.

"You said Steve had been shot and killed. I wasn't sure if it was Roxy who did it. I figured she might need help cleaning up evidence. Not that it wouldn't be justified..."

Roxy's hoarse, broken laugh had been a good sign, even if it had immediately been followed by a half-swallowed sob.

"Tommy, I learned long ago that when folks experience a sudden shock, half of them immediately start cooking and the other half start cleaning. Your wife is obviously the cleaning type."

Danni had attacked Roxy's bathroom with a vengeance, ensuring not a single microbe of blood would remain in her shower, then mopped every floor in the house to make sure she'd erased all traces of Roxy's path from front door to bathroom in her blood-soaked clothes. The clothes themselves had been bagged and taken away by the police. Danni would make it her personal mission to make sure they ended up in a burn barrel.

Tommy's daughter, Emmy, had shown up, wanting to see a murder investigation firsthand. "It might be a great story to tell in that second FBI interview I have next month." She now stood in the corner of Roxy's kitchen, talking quietly with Graciela's son, Iggy, who'd placed himself squarely in front of Roxy's cutlery drawer.

"I don't want her to get any sudden ideas," he said.

Graciela had put them both to work shredding pork for sandwiches and peeling the peaches Danni had brought for a cobbler.

"I don't want——" Roxy started to rise from her chair.

"You don't want help?" Graciela said. She pushed her back

to her seat. "Roxy, you've spent your whole life helping others. Please, chica, sit down for once and let somebody help you. Let us return the favor you've done for so many others."

Hadn't Steve once said almost the same thing to her?

Steve. Oh God! Steve!

"But I don't need——"

"Roxy," Danni said. "You are the strongest woman I know, and I know a lot of women. And all of us—every dang one of us—need help sometimes. I hereby give you permission to fall completely apart with the knowledge that we'll be right here beside you to catch you."

"But I owe so much to so many who already helped me——"

Danni pulled her out of her chair and marched her out through the lanai and into her garden. Graciela followed. They stood on either side of her and locked their arms around her. A sandwich of love from a pair of ferocious dragon guardians.

Roxy struggled for a second. Where had fierce, independent Roxy gone? She could do this on her own. She always had. She didn't need any coddling. There were things to be done. Stuff to be taken care of. She'd always been the one to take charge. She really, truly didn't need—

She fell to her knees, sobbing.

Her fierce, loving friends fell with her, never loosening their embrace of her.

"I couldn't save any of them," she said when the racking sobs finally dissolved into hiccups. "Not Jubil or Joey." She gulped air. "I couldn't be bothered going home when my own sister was dying."

Words bubbled up, dredging up even more memories. All the pain was tangled up in a knot with grief and disbelief and shock and... "I was too afraid, too cowardly to tell anybody what happened when I was raped. If I had, maybe I could have saved a few other little girls from what happened to me."

Anger knotted her guts. Anger and remorse and regret and bone-deep sorrow. "I couldn't even save my own baby," she whispered. "And I couldn't save Steve."

Steve's words whispered back. *Debt paid. Live.*

Graciela stroked her hair while Danni rubbed her back.

"Roxy," Danni said, "right now your house is filled to overflowing with people you've helped. People you saved. And every single one of them is here to pay you back for that. To help you like you helped them. Rejecting that is like spitting on the gift they want to give you."

"They don't owe me anything."

"You don't get to speak for them," Graciela said. "You made Steve learn how to let people in. You badgered and coerced and loved and never let up until he accepted what you were offering. Until he accepted help and friends. And yet you're locked up tighter than he ever was."

"I never coerced Steve."

Danni snorted. "Okay, we'll just say you smothered him with love until he had no choice."

"You say you live to honor the past," Graciela said, "but that isn't true."

Roxy struggled in their arms, but neither woman let go of her.

Graciela continued. "You blame yourself and you live to work off sins you never committed. You forgive everybody else all the time, but when are you going to start forgiving yourself? You keep piling new grief on top of old and you never really stop mourning. Right now you need to mourn for Steve, but you need to make room in your heart and mind to do that."

"Steve was dying."

Graciela gasped, but Danni just nodded. "I suspected something," she said.

Of course she would. Danni was a good doctor.

"Cancer," Roxy said. "He had only a few months left. We thought there'd be time. That we'd be able to say a proper goodbye. I was prepared for that. Not for this. Not—"

Horror engulfed her. Horror and fury and the kind of gut-searing grief she thought she'd put behind her.

"No one is ever prepared," Danni said. "No matter how

many parents I've told that their child isn't going to make it, they still aren't ready when it actually happens."

"Death comes on its own schedule," Graciela said. "I sent my husband off to a meeting in New York on a sunny September day. The kind of meeting he'd gone to a dozen times before." She tightened her grip on Roxy. "We can never know, chica. You just have to tell people you love them every day. Treasure every moment. Know that in time their memory will become a blessing. Know that you were important in their life too."

"But I should have—"

Should have what? What more could she have done? If she'd answered the door instead of Steve, would he still be alive? Or would she have died too?

"Not a one of us can change a single thing that's already happened," Danni said. "We can atone. Make amends. Do better. You do that every day. Maybe you should stop beating yourself up. You did enough, Roxy. You loved Steve and he loved you and God knows the world needs more of that. It was enough."

Roxy shook her head. If only—but *if only* was a childish wish. A lament for the impossible.

"Even if I could buy you a ticket to the past," Graciela said, "so you could go back and change things, I wouldn't do it. All of that, all those things that happened, the good and the bad, made you who you are. Made you the dearly loved friend we care so much about."

"Made you the woman Steve loved," Danni said. "Made you the one and only woman he ever gave his heart to. And he'd be damned pissed to find you out here in your garden watering the flowers with your tears."

Roxy managed a small laugh. Yeah, he'd be yelling for her to stop her caterwauling and find something better to do.

Danni tried to get her to go to bed, even offered a sedative, but Roxy refused. She couldn't articulate what she needed, but having people around helped. People who had leaned on her and were eager to let her lean on them.

Why was that so hard?

It had taken much longer than Roxy ever imagined before the cops and the coroners and news crews left. People kept showing up, bringing drinks and food. Friends from the country club. Steve's poker buddies. Current and former cops. Women from Roxy's classes. Some had come and gone quickly, but many of them still filled the living room and kitchen and lanai, alternating tears and shocked whispers and laughter as they shared stories of Steve.

The television was on in the living room. It was turned low, but there was no missing the breathless blonde announcing that the sister of the Miami Beach Cannibal, crazed with grief, had murdered the former cop who'd been forced to kill her depraved sister. Steve might have been eighty years old and he hadn't been with the Florida Highway Patrol for forty years, but the news covered the cops who'd turned out to line the streets and escort the body of one of their own from the coroner's office to the funeral home.

Danni had taken charge of that part.

"You're going to want to have a homegoing celebration for him. Does he have any relatives that need to be contacted?"

Roxy nodded. "I'm going to need his phone. I have no idea what he'd want for a funeral."

Roxy asked if it could be arranged a week later. "His nephew's hard to contact. I think he has a SAT phone. If I can have some time…"

Danni promised to arrange everything. "Don't you worry about a thing. We'll have him looking casket sharp and send him home in style. He's former military and former police. Both groups are going to want a part in this."

"Bagpipes are okay, but no gun salutes," Roxy said. "And I know it's not all that common among Blacks, but he wanted to be cremated."

Both Danni and Graciela wanted to stay the night with her, but she finally assured them she'd be fine alone.

Alone. She'd spent so much of her life alone.

She'd spent three days being Steve Stephen's wife.

This was a whole new kind of loneliness.

She heard Steve's voice as clearly as if he were sitting on the lanai next to her.

"Sometimes, Rox, God is a dick. And sometimes you just have to embrace the suck."

Roxy raised her glass to the night and to absent, dearly loved friends, and to the man who'd stolen and broken her heart. "Love you too, Steve."

Chapter 30

Sexy Firefighters Calendar Word of the Day:
Apopemptic: [ap-uh-pemp-tik]. **Adjective:** *pertaining to leave-taking or departing; valedictory;* **Noun:** *parting address or farewell hymn*

THE HOMEGOING CELEBRATION was everything Danni had promised Roxy it would be. Steve had looked damned fine in a shiny black suit, a new panama hat with a red band, and shoes polished to a mirror finish. The same clothes he'd worn for their wedding.

The church had been packed. Steve had more friends than he'd ever realized, and every one of them wanted to stand up and tell their story about him. Danni and Graciela kept Roxy well-supplied with tissues, and in between bouts of laughter incited by stories from his friends, she'd unashamedly let the tears cascade like a waterfall.

The repast—the feast after the funeral—had been held in Roxy's house, all of Steve's friends recognizing that she'd been someone special in his life. Food and drink and music had flowed around her, friends wrapping her in their warm embraces until one by one they'd finally returned to their own homes and their own lives, leaving Roxy at last alone and cried out.

Steve's nephew, Curtis, had even shown up, bringing the large blue and yellow intarsia box Roxy had asked for. The one Steve already owned would have a place of honor on her own mantel. The one Curtis brought would carry part of Steve's ashes to Italy, to be cast in the sea with Curtis's mother's ashes, Steve's beloved sister Natalie. Before he headed home, Curtis planned to make a quick trip to Mississippi to visit the graves of his grandparents and leave some of Steve there with them as well.

Some of Steve's ashes would reside in the red urn on the mantel, to travel one day with Roxy's own, and the remaining ashes would be scattered around the Black Star calla lily in her night garden, the flower that reminded her so much of Steve. At least a little what remained of his big, beautiful body would always be with her, along with all the memories that would one day bring joy instead of sorrow.

The house was quiet and still around Roxy. She wandered out to the lanai, listening to the night sounds. The humidity wrapped around her like a warm blanket, like Steve's own heated embrace. Creatures creaked and croaked and buzzed, fucking and feeding and breeding and dying. A neighbor a block away blasted music accompanied by the shouts and laughter of a party. All of them just living their lives, unaware and uncaring of the void in hers, of a world that no longer held Steve.

Maybe she'd get another dog. Something big and cuddly to keep her company in all the quiet nights to come.

But all that was for tomorrow. Roxy walked across her moonlit garden, brushing her hand against her newest windchimes, which emitted a sonorous bass tone, reminding her of Steve's forever silent voice. When she came to her dance studio, she threw open the doors, letting in the night. She flicked on a single spotlight in the center of the room.

She sat down at her desk, sorting through the framed photos Emmy had brought today, along with one or two snapshots she'd taken herself.

Steve sitting right there in the overstuffed chair watching Roxy dance. Another of him grinning at her from across the kitchen, a heaping plate of food in front of him.

Grief threatened to swamp her once again. Would she ever be finished crying, surfeited with tears?

"Kintsugi, Roxy."

There's nothing left to heal. He's gone. I couldn't fix anything.

"But you did, Roxy. You made him happy. He didn't die alone."

So why are you still bugging me about kintsugi?

"Because sometimes it's the healer who needs to be healed. Kintsugi, Roxy."

No words came to Roxy. No rebuttal. God, she was simply so tired.

"I tried to tell you before, but you would never listen. Are you ready to listen now?"

The voice wasn't judgmental or angry. And she was tired of fighting.

"Kintsugi is not only about returning the broken thing to beauty and usefulness. It is also a way of honoring grief. As we honor and repair the broken thing, we also recognize and honor and seek to repair the broken places in ourselves. We must learn to surrender our broken places to others, to allow them to help put things back together. Each of us is a healer, and each of us is in need of healing. Allow others to cherish you. Don't let this close your heart. And give yourself some grace, Roxy."

She picked up the last photo, one Emmy had taken at the barbecue. In it, Steve's head was thrown back in laughter, Roxy held tight in his arms as she tried to avoid his feet while teaching him to dance. She kissed the glass, then hung the picture on the wall along with the one of Steve in the chair.

Now he was there, one more in her collection of beloved friends. One more person she'd loved.

One more who'd loved her.

Now he could always be there to watch her dancing.

It only took moments to shimmy out of the rose-colored sheath she'd worn for Steve's funeral because she'd known he'd hate black. She pulled on a pair of tap shorts and her favorite white shirt bedazzled with rhinestones.

Steve's old Panama hat sat on the chair. Roxy put it on her

head.

She laced up her oldest pair of tap shoes, then pointed the remote at her stereo.

Billie Holiday's voice wrapped her in its sweet, soulful embrace. Billie knew what pain was. Billie knew what Roxy was feeling.

And I know I won't die, because I love him.

Roxy stepped into the spotlight and danced.

EPILOGUE

MARGARET MURPHY, GLEN Wilson's on-again, off-again security chief and grieving friend of Steve Stephens, sat at her desk, peering at the computer screen and scrolling through the files she'd accumulated in the last week. Hard copies of many of them sat in fat brown folders at her elbow. It paid to know everything you could about somebody who might prove useful at some point in the future.

She started with the easy ones. Steve's cop friends, who'd become Roxy's friends. Tommy and Danni Jackson and their daughter Emerson.

Emerson Jackson was young, but she was quickly becoming interesting.

A master's in security and intelligence, an upcoming interview with the FBI. Specialist in stochastic terrorism. She needed a few years in the field, some time to knock the polish off, but she was worth cultivating as an asset. Steve must have seen something in her to call in an old favor and get the girl an interview with the FBI. Murphy read her thesis and thought she saw what Steve did; she had some innovative ideas about spotting lone-wolf terrorists, the kind susceptible to stochastic terrorism. If Glen Wilson had been at the funeral, would Emmy have spotted him as a terrorist or one of the good guys?

Her financials were also worth a second look. Like most bright people her age, she'd had a few scholarships, but most of her schooling was paid for with the standard usurious college loans. A few weeks ago those loans had all been paid off with a grant from something called the Lady Day Opportunity Foundation.

Murphy's preliminary background check into Emmy Jackson also included a look into a growing number of text messages with Ignacio Diaz, son of a well-to-do Puerto Rican realtor in West Palm Beach. Maybe a romance growing there? The FBI seemed to think it worth looking into as well.

Murphy tapped another page on the screen. That would be Iggy, the son of Roxy's friend Graciela who'd been left widowed after 9/11. Graciela was comfortably well-off, with relatives scattered everywhere, including some still living in the Puerto Rican islands. Iggy was bright, ambitious, and majoring in architecture.

Which would make him great at knowing exactly where to place bombs to bring down a building.

Murphy shook her head and sipped her lukewarm coffee. She had to stop thinking that way. Not everyone in the world was crooked.

The door to her office opened and closed quietly. Elke leaned over Murphy's shoulder, her breasts snuggled against the back of Murphy's neck. Murphy casually turned and kissed the soft flesh before returning to her perusal of the photograph in her hand.

"You keep staring at that picture much longer, I'm going to get jealous," Elke said.

"You're not the jealous type," Murphy said. "Besides, she's thirty years older than me and just lost the love of her life."

Elke kissed the top of Murphy's head, refilled the coffee cup at her elbow, and slipped out as quietly as she'd come in.

Roxy Fields, being sixty five years old, had the largest file. Most of her life was an open book. She'd never hidden the fact that she'd changed her name from Rita Jablonski to Roxy Fields. She'd been a dancer, worked in Las Vegas, at one time had her own small dance studio, and had worked various odd jobs. The most interesting was her time as a file clerk for Bernie Madoff, but old Securities and Exchange Commission files indicated a quiet investigation had determined she'd been nothing more than a low-level clerk and had cleared her of anything decades ago.

Murphy chuckled. She should probably let Roxy live out her quiet life in Florida with the so-called *garden club* she ran, making pot brownies for her friends. But Murphy had hacked Roxy's phone and had run a deep background check on the woman anyway. She had the potential to be a valuable asset.

She had that old-lady deceptiveness going for her but was more fit than a lot of athletes. She'd had an Irish mother and grandparents that were Polish and Russian.

In spite of her claim that she barely remembered her grandmother's Russian, she was in the Obsidian league in Russian on Duolingo and put in at least half an hour a day on it. Likely knew Polish even better. Somewhere along the way she'd studied French. And her friend Graciela had readily volunteered that while Roxy's Spanish accent was atrocious, her ability to get the gist of spoken Spanish was pretty good.

Her financials hadn't been easy to get hold of and still weren't entirely clear. What was clear was that Roxy had a great deal more money than could be accounted for by her checkered career. But she'd made investments over the years, supremely lucky investments.

Money wasn't going to move Roxy. She'd invested early in Amazon and Apple and a couple more obscure stocks that had done shockingly well. Glen would be jealous as hell, but Roxy Fields could probably buy and sell him, especially now with the fiasco of Immortality, LLC.

Murphy finally leaned back, stretched, then leaned into the computer again.

Roxy had taken a lot of college courses over the years. She had almost enough coursework to have a master's in forensic accounting and, based on her grades, had loved botany but dropped biology, probably when she found out they'd have to dissect animals—so no bloodshed.

Fierce. That was Roxy Fields.

She'd once owned a peculiar company called Obscurities that appeared to specialize in finding obscure objects. Steve had mentioned that, laughing about her old-school analog Rolodex. Interestingly, a company with the same name still had a small presence in a quiet corner of the internet. Looked like Roxy might still have connections and still be in the business of finding the obscure and unusual for people. Maybe it wasn't just set design pieces she'd procured for them. Could it be some kind of money-laundering thing?

Again, Murphy had to stop herself. When had she gotten so suspicious and cynical? But she already knew the answer to that. It was what had made her a good cop.

A bit more digging, and the Lady Day Opportunity Foundation popped up on the screen again. Board members were listed as Graciela Diaz, Tommy Jackson, and one Roxy Fields-Stephens.

Wait, what? What had she missed?

Murphy frantically tapped keys, but the answer was already in the paper folder on the desk. A marriage license, signed and witnessed by Tommy Jackson and Graciela Diaz, three days before Steve's murder.

He'd married her.

Oh God, poor Roxy.

Murphy pinched her nose to stop the tears that had inexplicably gathered. She was glad her old friend and mentor had someone like Roxy in his life at the end.

She also wished she'd had time to go to Steve's funeral, but she'd been up to her eyeballs mopping up after Glen Wilson's latest fuckup.

Murphy tapped more keys and found a rudimentary website for the Lady Day Opportunity Foundation. It was barely more than a mission statement and a contact page.

Murphy's finger hesitated over the number on her phone, then she tapped it.

Roxy answered on the second ring. They chatted for a few moments, Murphy checking on her as she'd so often done with

Steve. She didn't mention the marriage. If Roxy wanted her to know, she'd have told her.

Then she asked the question, the reason she'd called. "Roxy, what's the Lady Day Opportunity Foundation?"

"Doing your research, Murphy? Or just being nosy?"

"Being Steve's friend," she said. "Making sure nothing's still lurking out there waiting to hurt somebody he loved."

The line was silent for a long moment before Roxy responded. "Something Steve and I set up. Something that will outlast both of us. It will do a lot of good for a lot of people. It pays for college or pays off student debt. Some of it's going to research for drug addiction and some will make rehab facilities available in poor communities. Some of it's geared toward talented young people in music and dance. Veterans, law enforcement and their families get special attention and priority."

So that explained paying off the debt for Emmy Jackson, daughter of a cop.

Roxy continued, as if she'd read Murphy's mind. "The first grant went to Emerson Jackson. Her special area of interest is terrorism. Terrorist organizations often use drug distribution networks to fund themselves. Spot the terrorist, trace the money, stop the drugs. That was Steve's real motivation. Steer young people onto the right path. Don't give them a reason to get addicted."

Roxy's breath sounded ragged for a moment, but she continued. "He left his house to the foundation, and all his savings. I added some of my own. We rented out his house last week. A nice young Afghan refugee family. The father used to be a translator for the military. I think Steve would have liked them."

Murphy laughed.

Roxy did as well. "Well, eventually he'd have liked them. He was learning."

"You were good for him, Roxy. I'm glad he found you. And are you taking care of yourself?"

There was a long pause, then, "I'm holding up."

"Roxy, think about getting some counseling. You've been through a lot. Most folks, unless they're psychopaths, aren't wired to handle witnessing murder. You have friends who are cops. Ask around and see who they recommend."

"Already on it," she said. "Steve had more friends than he knew. They've taken me in like family too."

Murphy grunted her approval. She understood what it meant to belong to the *blue family*.

They chatted a few more minutes before hanging up.

She was pretty sure she hadn't seen the last of Roxy Fields. Roxy was honest and altruistic, and Murphy hated the thought of corrupting that. She'd loved Steve and had made his last days worth living. Murphy should probably let Roxy live happily ever after for that alone. Yeah, that was what she'd do.

For now.

But it made Murphy feel good to have an ace up her sleeve that Glen Wilson didn't know about. And Glen, in typical fashion, had missed the most important truth about Roxy.

She never gave up when someone she loved had been wronged.

One of these days, the woman was going to stop grieving and wake up. And she was going to start wondering about Steve's death. Asking questions that might get complicated.

One of these days she'd start wondering about the man whose company had created the monster who murdered Steve. Start thinking about who was really accountable for Steve's death.

Murphy knew women like Roxy. She was like that herself.

Persistent. Stubborn. Fearless.

She'd come looking for answers.

Maybe for something more.

And on that fine day, when the name Glen Wilson finally surfaced in Roxy's brain, Murphy would be ready for her phone call.

Because Murphy wasn't in the mood to forgive Glen either.

Steve had made a commitment to Roxy. They'd loved each other enough to get married, even knowing Steve was dying.

Hell, we're all dying every day. They'd known their time together would be brief, but they'd made every second count and seized their moments of joy.

Murphy closed the files and shut down the computer. She needed to find Elke. Appreciate what she had been lucky enough to find for herself.

Maybe think about making a commitment.

Death might find her at any minute, but before it did, she had a hell of a lot of living to do. She'd learned that from Roxy.

THE END

ACKNOWLEDGMENTS

STEVE'S DEATH WAS always preordained. Ken Coffman, creator of the clever, Machiavellian Glen Wilson and his coterie of colorful characters, first killed off Steve in *Immortality, LLC* (Stairway Press, 2020). While Steve Stephens has been a character in a number of books set in the Glen Wilson universe, Roxy was a new character, introduced in *Immortality, LLC.*

I was surprised and intrigued when Ken invited me to write about her. As it turned out, Steve was making a lot of noise at me as I tried to write about Roxy, and *Shuffle Ball Change* turned out to be more his book than Roxy's. He wanted, as Ken mentioned to me, a better death. The events in *Shuffle Ball Change* run parallel to the events of *Immortality, LLC*, and dovetail with that book. Both are set in 2019, before the plague came to the world.

Every writer creates in solitude, but if they are lucky, no writer ever truly writes alone. My first acknowledgment and thanks go to Ken Coffman for inviting me into the batshit crazy world of Glen Wilson. My endless thanks also to my talented, patient, and brilliant editor, Beth Hill, proprietor of A Novel Edit (https://anoveledit.com/) whose insights and encouragement pushed this book to be better than I ever thought it could be. I am a terrible, whiny client, but Beth was spot-on with all her recommendations and I'm glad I listened to her.

Writers are natural magpies, which is a polite way of saying that we don't hesitate to steal the shiny bits of other people's lives and incorporate them into our stories. A number of scenes in this book came about through writerly theft, or homage as I prefer to call it. Some of Roxy's best stories of New York are based on the real-life tales told by my sister. Newly arrived from Ohio, she really did venture into Harlem in search of KFC biscuits. A vegetarian with her own real business similar to Roxy's Obscurities, she once was tasked with retrieving goose wings, and truly was having a very bad day when she shoved past a befuddled mugger on the subway on her way to a modeling cattle call.

Other stories of Roxy's youth come from my ever-loving and patient husband. Raised by his single mother—who really did lambast a congregation after being called out by the preacher for her flamboyant hand-me-down dress—and his Hungarian grandmother, he was chased through the yard by a headless chicken and witnessed a man falling from the sky, a man who really was covered up with a screen door by a well-meaning neighbor. The stories have been embellished for this novel, but not by much. Real life is usually more interesting than anything I could make up.

I am not a person of color and hesitated to write a main character who is an eighty-year-old Black man. My lived experience is nothing like his. I respect #OwnVoices and was concerned about overstepping. I am eternally grateful to all those who share their stories and their culture on blogs, in articles, and across the internet. I hope I've treated Steve with respect and dignity and that I have accurately captured some of his truth. While I have always had some understanding of the unfairness in the lives of those who are not white and cisgendered, in researching what Steve's life could be like, my eyes and heart were more widely opened to the historical pain and injustices so many have endured and still endure on a daily basis. I was also enriched as I discovered more about the culture of Black Americans, as I explored the food and beauty and music, the rich humor, and the importance of faith, family, and traditions that suffuse Black lives. If there are mistakes in my portrayal of Steve's life, I apologize. I did my best to honor a character I truly came to love.

My thanks also go, as always, to the Writin' Wombats. The Wombats were a group of aspiring writers who coalesced online and became friends in real life. We encouraged and supported each other and many Wombats went on to become published authors. I'm proud to be one.

And always, most of all, my heartfelt thanks to my beloved husband, who is my support system, sounding board, bringer of coffee and bourbon and cake, and who makes all things possible. Love you!

—Pat Edwards

LEARN MORE

TO DISCOVER MORE about Steve Stephens, his family, and adventures, I encourage you to read *The Sandcastles of Irakkistan*, Ken Coffman, (Arizona, Stairway Press, 2014) and *Immortality, LLC*, Ken Coffman (Stairway Press, 2020).

This article linked below will provide more insight into the injustice of how Black veterans were denied their GI benefits: https://www.history.com/news/gi-bill-black-wwii-veterans-benefits. On December 7, 2020, U.S. Congressman Seth Moulton (MA-06) and House Majority Whip James E. Clyburn (SC-06) introduced the Sgt. Isaac Woodard, Jr. and Sgt. Joseph H. Maddox GI Bill Repair Act of 2020 in the House of Representatives in an attempt to rectify these past injustices. Read more about it at: https://moulton.house.gov/press-releases/moulton-clyburn-introduce-legislation-to-provide-black-wwii-vets-full-gi-bill-benefits. The bill was reintroduced by them in the House on November 11, 2021 and by and Senator Reverend Raphael Warnock (D-GA) in the Senate. While the bill has been introduced, no further action has been taken as of this date and it is predicted to only have a 4% chance of passing:

https://www.govtrack.us/congress/bills/117/hr5905

When Ken and I first discussed Steve, he mentioned he'd love it if somehow Steve got to meet Billie Holiday—Lady Day. I had no idea she'd end up being such a catalyst in Steve's life and so integral to his story. It was painful and joyful to research her life and listen to her music. Snippets from the following pieces are included in the book. I encourage you to search them out and listen for yourself: *Please Don't Talk About Me When I'm Gone*, (Clare, Sidney; Palmer, Bee; and Stept Remick Music Corp, New York, 1930), *Love Me or Leave Me* (Walter Donaldson with lyrics by Gus Kahn, 1928), *Lady Sings the Blues*, (Billie Holiday, Herbie Nichols, 1928). As an "Easter egg" to Billie Holiday, Steve's date with death is paused at T-Minus 15:04:07. Ms. Holiday's birthday is 04-07-1915.

Steve mentions *The Negro Travelers' Green Book*, originated and published by African American New York City mailman Victor Hugo Green from 1936 to 1966, during the era of Jim Crow laws. Sadly, there is still a need for this advice, being carried on by The Green Book Project (https://www.thegreenbook.io/), a mobile app that helps people from marginalized groups find inclusive businesses and avoid discrimination, available in the Apple App Store and on Google Play.

The excerpt from the sexy romance novel Steve finds on Roxy's bookshelf is from *Echoes in Stone* by Kat Sheridan (Ohio, Kat Sheridan, 2013) P. 129.

Roxy mentions several charities she intends to leave her money to, and I've included here another one not mentioned but which Steve would appreciate. These are my favorite charities as well, and I encourage you to explore further and consider donating if you are so inclined:

Sheldrick Wildlife Trust
(https://www.sheldrickwildlifetrust.org/), an orphan elephant rescue and rehabilitation organization that also encompasses environmental preservation, works to eliminate poaching, and provides work and education to so many in Kenya.

World Central Kitchen
(https://wck.org/), providing emergency food relief in disaster areas worldwide, as well as culinary training to empower local emergency response teams.

Dolly Parton's Imagination Library
(https://imaginationlibrary.com/), inspiring a love of reading

by providing free books to children.

The Brooklyn Bank (https://www.thebrooklynbank.com/), a 501c3 nonprofit organization that fosters financial independence among communities of color through teaching financial literacy.

As the book opens, Steve is determined to commit suicide. As he learns, in his darkest moment of despair, he has options and there is something better coming. If you or someone you love are experiencing these dark moments, please know that you are not alone. Please, reach out:

If you are having suicidal thoughts or mental crisis, help is available. You are not alone. In the U.S. dial 988 for around-the-clock support or call the National Suicide Prevention Hotline: 1-800-273-8255 (1-800-273-TALK)

Don't want to talk? Text Hello to 741741

Veterans: If you're a Veteran in a mental health crisis and you're thinking about hurting yourself—or you know a Veteran who's considering this—get help right away.

In the U.S. dial 988 then press 1 to connect to the Veterans Help line.

Or call the National Suicide Prevention Hotline: 1-800-273-8255 (1-800-273-TALK) then press 1 to connect to support for Veterans or go to https://www.va.gov/health-care/health-needs-conditions/mental-health/suicide-prevention/

Teens and Youth: Help is available, whether you want to talk or text. To talk to someone right now: Youth Helpline, Your Life Your Voice: 1-800-448-3000 For more teen and youth resources: https://www.healthyplace.com/suicide/teen-hotlines-and-chat-get-help-now

LGBTQIA+ kids and teens: The Trevor Project: for 1-866-488-7386 or text START to 678678

www.ingramcontent.com/pod-product-compliance
Lightning Source LLC
Chambersburg PA
CBHW020416260626
47156CB00007B/2412